Alan Mahar was born in Liverpool and since studying in London has freelanced as a copy-writer, editor and teacher. His short stories have appeared in *London Magazine* and *Critical Quarterly* and his reviews in the *Literary Review*. He lives with his wife and two daughters in Moseley, Birmingham, where he founded the city's Tindal Street Fiction Group.

Flight Patterns

ALAN MAHAR

PHŒNIX

A PHOENIX PAPERBACK

First published in Great Britain by Victor Gollancz in 1999
This paperback edition published in 2000 by Phoenix,
an imprint of Orion Books Ltd,
Orion House, 5 Upper St Martin's Lane,
London WC2H 9EA

A CIP catalogue record for this book
is available from the British Library.

ISBN: 0 75381 018 2

Printed and bound in Great Britain by
The Guernsey Press Co. Ltd, Guernsey, C.I.

i.m. E.M. 1912–93

(who wasn't Mrs C)

Marva couldn't even remember if she'd altered her watch for the time difference. Most of the flight she'd had her eyes closed. Now a woman in uniform visited and asked particularly if she needed the bathroom. Marva shook her head; toilets would be closely observed too.

'Still sticking to your story?'

'I've already told you I'm only visiting. I'm not planning to stay in America.'

'You got any family?'

Marva liked the idea of that.

'Yes, I might see family. I might be lucky.'

But the woman was already relocking the door before Marva could catch her attention. The room must have been air conditioned. It wasn't hot. When a glass of Coke arrived, a sly question came with it. 'What's with the kid's puzzle?'

Marva didn't feel an answer was deserved.

She imagined she could feel with her fingers the number of pieces inside. The box was fuller than 500; the packaging lied. She might need a bigger table than this to assemble them all. Level of difficulty – only medium, the box claimed, but probably harder than medium for Marva. Whereas the expert, Mrs Connolly, had been capable of assembling three simultaneously, on three stacked hardboard sheets. And if she tired of one, or got temporarily stuck, well she just moved on to one of the others, figuring the problem might have eased itself by the time she returned to it. Mrs C, Cissie Connolly, lady of jigsaws, lady of flowers: fondly remembered.

But Marva's shoulders dropped and her arms slumped across her table, obscuring the sheets of paper the authorities had given her. A radio was playing rap songs without break; she didn't mind, she listened intermittently to the lyrics (Frustration, Confusion, No Shit No More). The appropriate radio station thoughtfully laid on by her hosts. Such attention to her comfort when this was a scarcely lit room with no windows visible; locked, then left. No rush, they'd said. Take your own sweet time, ma'am. They were interested in her luggage – baggage they called it. They were still searching all the linings, in hope of what? They allowed her some harmless miscellaneous items – the jigsaw puzzle box, and a bundle of notebooks – all handed back to her in the spirit of a game; she might incriminate herself, left to her own devices for long enough.

Door again. A burger plonked in front of her on a polystyrene plate. The man this time.

'What about the man you spoke to on the plane? How well do you know him? We're still interviewing him.'

'I don't. I told you.'

She'd been safely belted all flight. She'd had her eyes shut tight, forcing herself to sleep, so she didn't see, even by accident, the descent. Two seats across she could have peered through the washing-machine window for the sight of black, then the sight of white. But there wasn't anything to see, and where was the advantage in seeing it? So she'd flown blind. She'd forced herself to sleep, not in any comfort, but her eyes were shut tight when a meal tray was dealt across her with a nudge, food intended for the pony-tailed thirtysomething against the fuselage roughly folding over the pages of his paperback classic. She had happened to see the cover earlier, just before he returned with his splashed blue jeans from the toilet: *Youth, Heart of* something, written on top of a choppy sea. The man had mumbled something about seeing her at Waterfront 90. She had no intention of conversing, ignored him, sealed her eyes shut. Willed her attention away from other people. A couple behind her shoulder had been breathing heavy for some time, then grunting, gradually louder, under a rug, sighing high, mile-highing, more than warm in wool blanket wrapping.

But Marva was unprepared for all the questions at immigration. For being labelled Alien. She was a visitor, a person on holiday, she might have a relative in this country, who might provide a reference for her, maybe even sponsor her – she was hopeful. Her plan was only to contact this relative who had been settled here for more than twenty-five years. She had an address somewhere – Brooklyn, Manhattan, what was the difference? The official was unimpressed. Marva was tired; the flight had been long. No, she wasn't planning to work here, only visit, maybe, OK, try and seek out her real family.

'And, connected to that guy, we want to know what's the story behind a man called Gra-ham Connolly?'

When all she wanted now was to leave his life and its mystery, for good.

'I said to you I knew both of the Connollys.'

She was even tiring of Graham's mother's life, and the flower shop. All of it behind her.

'We just need clarification about a certain incident. How much do you know about this Waterfront 90 event? And a guy called Myron. We want to rule out a few factors from the equation is all.'

'I've told you already I don't know the circumstances. Look, I've only known Graham a matter of months. I worked for his mother of course. But you must know all that if you've looked through these . . .' Marva placed a hand on

Graham's notebooks on the table, a bundle of stiff-backed stationer's exercise books, elastic-banded together.

'I don't suppose they made much sense, did they? I still haven't looked properly myself yet.'

'Plenty of time. Like we keep saying.'

This was a different officer, Hispanic, that was the sort of classification they used here. The morning shift probably.

'We could get you a physician, if you need one.'

Detained for not being Caucasian, for being unwell, unused to flight, unattached, for being spoken to by the wrong person, for trying to get away from the river city where everything happened. She fingered Mrs C's jigsaw pieces again, counted them separately like worry beads.

'Are you expecting me to cobble together some kind of confession for you?'

Either bright coloured paper or porridge-grey card, face up, face down, but no match in the colours, all conflicting.

'Well I can't. When there's nothing to confess. And I'm not in possession of the whole picture.'

Marva pawed at them, pushed and fingered their cactus shapes. One hand might hope to retrieve, from face-down depths, if not pictures whole and clear in outline, then at least hints of pictures, clues when upturned, somewhere in the cardboard box's sand-like tumble and seepage.

'I haven't a clue what Graham got up to when he hid himself away in his little room. Something vaguely environmental. Something about his Birdman. Or scribbling his memoirs inside these, for all I know. I met him in the flower shop. We visited the hospital together. That's all. And you already told me about this Myron character. I heard you say that. Complete blank, believe me. But nothing's happened to Graham, has it?'

The attendant lost interest, and with a stubborn patience paced to the end of the room, unlocked and relocked the door.

Marva refused to worry more about Graham. She tried to think of the way Mrs C used to approach her puzzles when she was concentrating. So she constructed, just like Mrs C, on one side of the table a truncated snake from all the straight-edge pieces of similar colour she could lay her hands to. She was looking for corners in this box. Which – and Marva laughed to herself – would not be at all like seeing the fresh contents of the box when it still smells of shop cleanness, when the whole sheet of Cellophane has to be ripped and peeled off, and the two tongues of Sellotape holding the box shut still have to be slit, and the pile of pieces is unfingered cardboard, and all the picture colours simply face upwards.

A new jigsaw would have been an easier proposition, certainly, but one which only ever happened when Marva bought Mrs C a present of a puzzle from a toy shop: a castle or a harbour scene. Which was the nearest the girl could offer her as gratitude – for everything, for taking her on at the shop, for looking after her, for providing an occupation. Marva was the only one to buy her brand-new jigsaws. Who else was there to buy the old lady presents? Her son, Graham, had been an absence for so long. Then he shocked his mother by coming back. And everything happened from there.

Marva tried to buy Mrs Connolly presents, but the woman wasn't easy to buy for. She couldn't buy flowers, not for a florist. Flowers, for Mrs C, could only mean stock that was no longer saleable. Who needed the left-over faded stems from a chrysanth vase; why waste the pick from that day's market? Their agreement: Marva bought Mrs C jigsaws wherever she could find them, thousand-piece puzzles, from jumble sales, charity shops, not knowing how complete the polythene bag of pieces inside was going to be. Once, she had been standing in the toy department of a large store, stuck between cloned leggy dolls with all their pink accessories and the electronic hammering of exterminator laser guns. Another person might have felt strange to be on the fourth floor amongst the family people, the child spoilers, as they exchanged their mutual accusations. But Marva was capable of looking without wanting. Children were not compulsory; nor male soulmates either. Independence being more important. She paid as quickly as she could for the jigsaw, a picture she couldn't remember seeing amongst Mrs C's stacked boxes, Wisconsin in Winter.

Generally Mrs C had a preference for big ship scenes, because of the men in her life. She liked to piece together on safe dry land any kind of sailing ship, any schooner or dhow, any ocean-going yacht or small skiff, at sea or in the complexity of harbour. And simpler shapes were often harder than crowded scenes. She relished the challenge of a Cunard hull, all painted steel and portholes, or acres of old canvas flapping on a storybook galleon. A new box would be Marva's present for Mrs C's birthday, along with 4711. ('You shouldn't waste your money, child. I'm not overpaying you, am I?') And also on Mother's Day, and only half as a joke, because it was the shop's other big day, besides Valentine's and Christmas. Marva felt sorry for her, because it would be another year and no word from her son. 'What's the odds?' Marva would say and hug her. 'There's always me. You've been like a mother to me.' Mrs C would push her away, but only slowly. ('Yes, mutual. Now shut up and don't start me off.')

Mrs Connolly's jigsaw ritual started by her taking hold of the box firmly and shaking it vigorously above her head, like shaking a dice, to wish herself luck. Then she banged it down in front of her, this was the ceremony. ('Now we can start properly.') Out would come the silver cigarette case, unclasped and laid open on the table like a hymn book, silver elasticated band across the neatest row of tipped cigarettes. Mrs C's other harmless addiction. Benson & Hedges helped, she said, and before Marva happened luckily into her life, it had always been Kensitas.

Mrs C was perfectly comfortable with the frustration of an incomplete puzzle. So what, she'd say, if there were missing pieces? Whose life was any different? But for Marva this was frustrating as soon as she opened the lid. Too many corner pieces. Too many straight pieces with a different pattern. Bound to have vital missing pieces. And besides, this was not one jigsaw, but a mixture – possibly as many as three different ones. She could distinguish different shades and different grains of cardboard. Marva realized she didn't stand a chance of finishing this. The cover picture (a ship of course) was no help: the scale was all wrong, the cropping was slightly but significantly different. And what were these pictures supposed to be of when she turned them over? Flowers belonging where? Bunches of something yellow were nothing more than brush strokes and blobs of paint: yellowness. Objects, ships, aeroplanes, flower stalks lost their lines in the mélange and disappeared. She wondered whether even Mrs Connolly could sort them. Dipping her hands in the box, she turned over the pieces again, sifting them like peat and compost mixture. And threw them back down. Hopeless. She wasn't Cissie Connolly. She didn't even want to be any more. She scooped the loose pieces back into the box and shut the lid.

An attendant appeared, hearing the noise. It was the woman again. 'Are you all right? Have you got everything you need?'

She'd been here eight hours already. Her watch didn't help her gauge the time of day outside this room. Jigsaws couldn't kill the time for her. Jumpy jetlag tiredness had robbed her of all concentration. No one had explained what she was doing there. They'd found Gray's notebooks. They'd found these jigsaws of Mrs Connolly's. They hadn't found anything incriminating. How long could they detain her? They wouldn't, surely they wouldn't, send her back to Britain. She only needed this new start in this new place.

Marva had visited Graham in his room once. No better than a broom cupboard in the grandest of hotels in that Victorian city. No windows. Dark inside. Junk piled high to the ceiling. Soiled clothes in the bottom of a wardrobe. Piles of too many newspapers on the lino.

'I presume you want to know about drugs, but I never touched them. It might have been going on. I wouldn't have thought Graham got into them.'

It was possible. But Marva didn't know too much about the company he kept. The officer had already exited again and was keyholing Marva intently from outside the door, all in the name of routine surveillance. She would wait until the urine and faecal test results proved her innocence; until they decided to tell her the results had arrived and she could go. Marva walked over to a spot underneath the beak of a closed-circuit video camera perched in a ceiling corner. She stood deliberately underneath the gargoyle and addressed it.

'OK, so I knew his mother. Graham, I knew a matter of months. And yes, I was at stupid Waterfront 90. But this American guy – not at all. Nothing.'

Her voice had diminished in the time it took to make that speech. She had nothing more to say to the camera. She sat back at the table and brushed aside the jigsaw box with the few little cardboard islands she'd pieced together. She started at last to write something on her statement form:

'You won't understand. I can't say I do myself. I didn't come in at the beginning.'

1

1957

There were fewer and fewer opportunities in France for Blaise. He was well enough known there. He'd been filmed, written about in newspapers and magazines. A journalist with a limp had helped him write a short book about his feats in the air.

Claude, his manager, was the one who made the contact. Made the contact, yes; booked him, then left him to his own devices. Other performers to manage: circus people and Tour de France cyclists. Claude made the telephone call; Claude said the English owner was delighted to add Blaise's name to the roster of performers. Top of the bill. The climax of the show. No more than he had grown to expect. A businessman with a few cargo planes and a stake in a small airport, wanting publicity for his airline. Needing to boost the small airport that had been growing hopefully out of the dereliction of a wartime airfield.

Visibility had been excellent when he'd boarded the two-engine Cessna in Bordeaux. He refuelled in Brittany. It had stayed clear over the Channel. No problem over the western edge of London – its grey cloak spread almost as wide as Paris's. Then north. Everyone he'd spoken to had said it would certainly rain, the clouds would appear from nowhere, they always did. But Blaise was an optimist. He needed to be. He needed clear sky and he needed an audience. All the better if the audience had been deprived of spectacle for years, in these dreary days in this drab country.

He had been invited by this businessman, a good man by all accounts, a strong and loud man, obsessed with his own commercial dreams of aviation, proud owner of his own small fleet of airworthy transport planes. He would most certainly have spent the war in the RAF, as indeed Blaise had been allowed to himself, while training, in preparation for a famous landing. Before Liberation he'd met those men who had learnt to fly, had known like him the excitement of stomach lift and air rush, but who hadn't since then had the opportunity of practising. All grounded. Nearly all. Never such excitement again. Poor country. In France the bourgeois seemed more able to enjoy their lives, the war good and forgotten.

Everyone said it would rain, but why should it? This was summer and everyone needed a festival in the summer. A man needs an excuse to get his family sitting round a check tablecloth spread on the grass. Some excitement needed too for those who had to work on the railways and on the dockside and inside the factories and down the coal mines. What did they experience of wind and fresh air? The open-air show was a treat for those people so attached to their raincoats; they could carry them on one arm, or in a generous gesture spread them open for a weekend sweetheart. Balance two bottles of beer, break bread and cheese, make her laugh with a boast. But Blaise found that their beer was too bitter, and their cigarettes didn't taste half so sweet.

Blaise had met these men in the RAF during his parachuting training. They misinterpreted his craving for a bottle of wine as some kind of snobbery; every choice not mean and ordinary, he found, could be so interpreted. They were brave fliers and jumpers, but they seemed in a hurry to pass their bravery off as a job of work, reach quickly for their bottles and their liquid promise of forgetfulness. Blaise couldn't have expressed it so in his meagre English, but in his view they allowed too little time for the savouring of the experience, they wouldn't understand what he was happy to call the poetry of flight. They just weren't capable of expressing their exhilaration. If they could compare their efforts with the all-weathers drudgery of all the uncomplaining ground support staff, they were content with that comparison. Eloquence was certainly not in their arms and hands, expressiveness didn't travel past their shrugging shoulders. Then, once inside the mess, it was forget, forget. Forget the flaming wreckage of wings and fuselage in a copse, forget the twisted strings and rags of parachute silk shredded in a beech tree; yes, by all means forget those sights for the sake of warm beer, but the swinging and floating down, the wobbling carpet-world of earth jumping upwards and the wonder of being on a clear day able to see everything, see everything, why omit mention of those sweet moments? This was Blaise's philosophy. What on earth, or in the air, was theirs?

He had seen only clear skies all the way up the country. He'd flown over so many birds he couldn't count, could hardly name – gulls, pigeons and buzzards when he took the plane above the valleys – felt the peculiar superiority of this advantage over nature. Birds could be emulated; even bested. But he had his hopes firmly on human efforts – the bold English businessman who possessed the nerve to stage such a spectacle. The man must have read about his jumps in the English newspapers. His imagination must have been excited by the extraordinary French aviator. Not a mere flier, he would have clearly read, but an artiste of rare courage. The man must have seized on Blaise's special daring to attach his own name to. He would be known as the man who brought the famous French airman to town. And Blaise would be the exotic animal, solid, athletic, captured and shipped by plane for the zoo collection, that's what he'd seem like to these people in their grey suits and their loose grey trousers, their braces, their grubby-collared shirts. These people who guzzled hot sugared tea with milk.

His manager was the person who'd been contacted by this fruit importer with the ambition to present a treat for his poor one-way seaward city. Claude said, yes, of course he should go, it was a fresh turn in his career. They had television in London, probably here too; everyone listened to the wireless of the BBC, which wasn't much of a help to him, he really needed to be filmed in action, not talked about and reported on blind. People needed to see him in the solid flesh. The cinema newsreel cameras were bound to be there, they would surely film his flight and bring it into people's seats; he would be seen before the main feature in cinemas in every town in England, there he would stand, in goggles, a wave from the cockpit, when the rising cigarette smoke would cast a grey mystery across his masculine airborne grace.

But this was a completely new country for his career, what his manager called an expansion of business, after which he might reasonably expect to go to America. Claude had already made some telephone calls. Coming to England might be a help with the language. But he must practise more English so that when the right time came he could fly over to America and do his jumps for crowds in Chicago and New York. The Americans loved a big show and they didn't mind paying. This corner of northern England could be looked on as a practice jump for America. Next stop Niagara Falls, or Manhattan Island, he'd even consulted an atlas; and the more he thought about it, the more he believed in the possibility of such a trip. Whereas Francine wasn't encouraging at all. She wished only to sit on a beach in her own dip of sand dune, with a magazine and a glass of wine. She had no desire to share in his aerial excitement. She refused to be frightened for his life any more. So she had decided not to accompany him on this trip – England was horribly grey, far

18

worse than Bordeaux, and after all, this was meant to be summer, and nothing, but nothing, would drag her from her station on the beach. She might change her mind if this was Los Angeles or Boston, Massachusetts, but it wasn't, it had to be England and he was inevitably flying solo, she was sleeping solo.

He could see that it was green below, so many small fields and neat, cosy woods. Narrow hedged lanes wiggled as he flew low to see more closely a miniature herd of black and white cattle gathering at a water trough. Maybe he would decide to buy more land himself and farm his life away in retirement somewhere inland, away from the Landes. Now he had to gain altitude because a sandstone church spire suddenly threw itself in front of him. Yews hugging it darkly, he noticed as he cleared it. This was the only hazard for miles. He wasn't scared. But from higher up even the gentle hills flattened and became plain for a spell, boring plain, wheat and peas, clear uninterrupted plain when the view ahead was a privileged twenty miles instead of five. And the blue outline westward was his first sight of mountains, the coastal range, and before too long he could see the Irish Sea's horizon, and he knew he must be approaching the wide river valleys that signalled the grim beginning of this edge of the industrial north.

Blaise knew he had to turn to due west soon and follow the line of the river. The mill chimneys started appearing on hillsides, and the pit wheels and the slag heaps, next to lines and lines of labourers' cottages. Each grouping comprised a village, each cluster of villages a town, all connected by thin threads of road. Above every town its own cloud. Dark canals connected pits, factories, warehouses; steam plumes seeped from miles and miles of pipes. This was Belgium, only more cramped; northern France only greyer. Blaise had the feeling he was drawing close to his destination.

He had been warned of the dampness of this valley, as he

steered his course towards the sea. But the sky was still clear and would remain so for his attempt for the air show, he was confident. The people would converge. Trams would transport them, and trains and ferry boats too. They would have heard about the show. The promoter, the fruit importer, would have done a good job with the posters and the newspapers. There would be newspaper billboards on every railing at twenty-yard intervals. The man was putting his own money behind the venture. He had connections in Paris, and he said he had connections in New York too. Perhaps he possessed something of the showman instinct himself. Here had to be a man of vision, well able to present a spectacle for hordes of poor workers and their families whose only possible excitement could be soccer, crowded seasides and pubs. First he would see the airport and if he flew a little further on he would see the showground park where the flight by the famous Frenchman was due to have its climax.

Now he could even see small freighters and barges busying at their moorings along these middle reaches of the large river. He could see where the river widened suddenly, opened out into a current-pulled pool. A giant, awkward swing bridge joined one smoking town to another, each fuming with its own competing chemical emissions. Sandbanks, paddling gulls and waders showed that the water was at low tide. Beyond the widening mudbanks Blaise could see more chemical-factory chimneys and cooling towers, all with their strapping of leaking pipes. On the north side of the river's first bend was a lighthouse signalling to no ships. And on the southerly bank where the river ran deep, refinery tanks huddled together close to the waterside jetties.

Blaise was taking his bearings. He always did this as he flew: played the cartographer making a sketch map for a geographical survey. It was essential at the height he would be flying to be sure of some reliable landmarks. An unkind wind could easily blow him off course. His wings could be carried too far for control. He had to have an idea what to expect. He did his homework on the available maps and he added his own notes and sketches from observations of the terrain as he flew over. For landing he preferred water to sand, sand to farmland, farmland to treetops, and treetops to rooftops and roads. The wind alone would decide. He could only try to steer his flight towards a comfortable landing.

The airport was not more than two miles along the coast after the lighthouse. A long old wood and then plenty of the flat ploughed fields that were needed for airport environs. Landing strips started their parallelograms along the bankside and in grand triangles pointing to a control tower. Grey hangars on either side, and rounded camouflaged sheds, still grim-green-painted from the war: hardly a plane on the runway. Blaise banked his plane over the airport area, awaited permission to land, rose again and circled. This would be the place he would make his flight the next day, all being well. This would be his sky. No instructions from the control tower, they had him on radar but they weren't ready, a Dakota in the way, so he circled.

There was an opportunity to gauge the terrain closer to the city. Woods; then immediately the river; straight roads to the docks and to the city; dark red tiny houses close together in strips, back-to-back, they formed the mass of the city right to its uncertain edge of fields, parks, and even in the distance, yes, to the north of the city could be seen sand dunes in the distance, refusing the sea – an unexpected reminder of his Bordeaux home. The larger city buildings pushed on to a narrow point, a neck in the estuary, where a tangle of derricks and cranes marked the busy waterfronts; beyond that the bay and the open sea. Not much green in the city, except a few wedges of parkland in the south side, but otherwise cramped and gathered everywhere. Blaise had time to guess which small patch of park must be the showground. He checked the map, but he couldn't easily see in its

21

shading the density of rooftops and narrow streets that actually surrounded the showground space. Safe landing was possible, but by no means easy. There was no doubting the place was more built up than he'd been led to expect. But the flight was possible – he knew he could steer his wings in a clement wind. He'd have much more time to plan the details tomorrow.

At last his plane had clearance. The Dakota had taxied away to the far runway. He brought the Cessna down, bounce-landed it smartly in front of the control tower, then past the tower and back again. He wanted to allow time for his welcome to gather. He positioned the plane as close to the terminal as he could. He noticed spectators, travellers and their families at a cafeteria window. Blaise sat in the cockpit, loosened his belt, waited. Only one large man strode across the concrete to him, and his raincoat skirt flared in the breeze. A few yards behind the promoter trailed a dark-skinned woman, chic, young, and then, skulking behind her, a single newspaper photographer. The promoter held on to his brown trilby hat – the wind from the propellers blew at hat level. Blaise forced his door open and jumped down to the runway. A firm business handshake between promoter and artiste, the camera made three clicks and the press man disappeared back to the terminal.

Blaise must have shown his surprise.

'Don't worry,' said a firm business voice. 'He's got his deadline for tonight. He's in a tearing hurry. We'll see him again tonight, and of course tomorrow too.'

The Frenchman asked about the others, about the extent of the advance publicity, he expected a bigger reception. He had taken off his helmet and goggles by now, thrown them angrily back into the plane. He was speaking very quickly in French: 'What kind of publicity? Where are the newsreel cameras?'

'Hold your horses, Blaise.' He pronounced the name

'blaze'. 'I've asked the Lord Mayor to pop in and say hello to you at your hotel. Everyone that matters knows you're here, it's a big story, trust me. He will if he can. But tomorrow is the big day, let's be patient for now, old chap. Today you can rest yourself after your flight and you can relax. I have organized a girl from the university as your interpreter. Here, meet Marie-Sainte.'

The girl was tall and bespectacled, shy of him, impressed no doubt by his reputation. She greeted him with an English handshake; he returned the gesture with a peck on each cheek. She blushed with pleasure.

The promoter clapped his hands together: 'That's more like it. Hand it to the French for the women's department, what.'

Marie-Sainte didn't trouble to translate some of the promoter's cruder idioms. She used the time to tell Blaise she'd read about his exploits, though she hadn't seen him in person.

Blaise's instinct to demand more answers via Marie-Sainte from the promoter was thwarted by the man's hand trying to grip the aviator's elbow. 'Now I'm going to bundle you through customs. A tedious formality.'

They walked separately to the small terminal building. Blaise wouldn't sit at the customs table; the promoter boomed and whispered by turns to hurry the bureaucracy. Marie-Sainte edited out the conversation, because she wasn't attuned yet to the promoter's way of speaking, he talked so quickly, she wasn't trained for this. In any case Blaise didn't need at that moment word-for-word.

'I expect you'll be needing a drink, now we've got that little lot sorted out.'

In a corner of the entrance hall, at a pale wooden counter, a large charlady attended a chromium tea urn behind glass. The man in the raincoat ordered a large pot of tea and some pieces of fruit cake, enough for the three of them. The man in the flying suit hissed his impatience at Marie-Sainte. She was busy thinking of the most diplomatic version of Blaise's demand for publicity, when he interrupted her with: 'It is necessary for me to speak to the English press.'

The promoter chose to ignore the request, bluffed some reassurance instead. 'I'm taking you to your hotel next. When you've finished your tea, that is. Can we get your things brought there, your luggage and what not?'

When Marie-Sainte explained, Blaise's sudden panic propelled him to the window, where he watched angrily as two small men in navy-blue overalls were taking his luggage from the plane, including the vital giant parcel marked FRAGILE. He punched on the window pane, screamed the French word *fragile* six times and a phrase referring to his wings which sounded like 'maize eyes'. Heads turned.

The promoter ran, quite athletically, raincoat flapping, out of the cafeteria and on to the runway. He barked at them to be more careful, touched the parcel by way of explanation and pointed fiercely towards where his grey Jaguar was parked; reached deep in his pocket, tossed them his car keys, signalled OK to where he knew Blaise would be at the window. Marched back to his teacup with a certain satisfaction. The airman was gesturing to the interpreter and she didn't need to translate: What am I doing here?

'Are we all clear and ready for the off now, chaps?'

The promoter was on the point of ushering them to his car, but Blaise was ahead of the others, waving arms at the two porters manhandling his precious wings. A box bigger than a parcelled up bicycle couldn't fit in the boot of the car, it would have to be more carefully placed on the roofrack and secured with tough string. He would have to supervise the strapping; he would have to be the one to lift the parcel on to the roof himself; he would have to be absolutely sure it was tied down safely before he would budge from this

24

airport and sit with the promoter inside his fine leather-upholstered Jaguar.

The promoter and the interpreter waited awkwardly by the car, watched the performance. They remained nervous when the Frenchman was sufficiently satisfied to be ready to leave. The promoter didn't know the moment not to ask questions. 'So how do you feel, Blaise, about tomorrow? Collywobbles?'

The interpreter explained that the airman was experiencing some anxiety about the arrangements made for his stay in England, but no, no nerves at all about his big flight.

The car eventually floated them smoothly from the open land of the airport down into all the blackened redbrick villas and terraces sharing their plane trees' frontage in the first of the city's suburbs. A long articulated lorry loaded with timber obstructed their road into the city centre, while grass-green double-decker trams snaked smoothly through the traffic on rails. A girder bridge carried a train of box-like brown carriages noisily above the waiting road vehicles: the city's overhead railway threaded its cunning way through buildings and allowed glimpses between stations of a river's varied trafficking. Blaise started to see the dockland cranes over the roofs of warehouses and became first aware of the presence of the river. Men and women in dark work clothes jostled along the pavements, peered into the car window, grinned, sneered, seemed to shout something amusing as the Jaguar pulled away. Would these people be going to the show? Blaise found himself wondering. How many thousand could safely fit into the park area? As many as at a football stadium, crammed tight and standing? He asked the promoter, through his new interpreter, 'What will the capacity be?' As the two compatriots spoke he was more comfortable speaking in his own language: relieved. He also became momentarily aware of her knees, showing through the opening of her raincoat; he pressed a hand on one knee, squeezed its point gently to elicit her support for his anxieties. It was an absent-minded question.

'Are you worrying yourself about your payout again?' the promoter piped up. 'I've told you, Blaze, I'll see you right.'

He was worrying about everything. Would the girl from the university be a help to him? Would the promoter honour his promises? Would enough English people hear about him and see him in the flesh? Or would these people, he was thinking, have to watch from outside, take their chance that they might see him descend from the sky while reduced to sitting on their own front doorsteps? He dearly hoped they would take the tram out to the airport and pay to stand behind ropes and peer at all the day's planes, but with particular anticipation of his plane positioning itself correctly for the grand moment he stepped out of the plane's hatch, and surrendered his breast and wings to the unpredictable currents of air.

Through the car window: churches, meeting halls, warehouses; they were all soot-blackened brick, front-fenced close by black-painted iron railings, bounded at the side and back by high walls topped with jagged broken-bottle glass. The sloping-down streets finally tunnelled them down to less claustrophobic spacing of buildings – a broad triangle of memorial monuments, station terminal, market hall – then a squash of department stores, shop doorways and narrow-fronted public houses. Here were a few components of civic splendour, civic squalor in an unconvincing configuration. Blaise was fast realizing his idea of England had always been of London and its more imposing, cleaner architecture, its ceremonial processions of soldiers. His own experience of airfields and camps and wartime London had not prepared him for this poor-grand provincial city, which he could hardly hope would serve him the privileges and pleasures he'd known as an allied airman on leave. He couldn't have known another such city as the capital, because such times were unrepeatable. Now the choice of this place was risky, it was, but he just had to trust to the support of others, and if that was something his own philosophy of self-reliance was uncomfortable with, then he could only check and double check all his own procedures again and again. Limited comfort in limited control, but some.

The Jaguar braked silently next to four thick fluted columns of an entrance. The promoter's sudden noisiness and gesturing were all the explanation Blaise needed that the revolving door ahead would whirl them into the Corinthian Hotel.

The promoter tried to usher them quickly into the hotel, but he only succeeded in getting the interpreter to position herself demurely on the sofa in the hotel foyer and wait. Because the airman was remonstrating outside with a waistcoated porter on the safest means of removing the awkward parcel from the roofrack. Blaise refused all attempts to be ushered.

The promoter cornered the hotel's duty manager next to an untenanted grand piano. 'My guest wants a slap up meal now. Can we speed things up for dinner? I know it's not the proper time and all that. But a distinguished French flier is in our midst and he's going on about the press boys not greeting him. Do you happen to know anyone at the *Echo* you can telephone for me?'

The promoter turned to his French lady interpreter for favours, once the manager had mumbled his reassurance. 'Look, I want the man to be happy. Anything he asks for. There's extra in it for you.' He counted out a couple of large pale notes. 'If you can keep him company, you know. The man needs to be settled, even I can see that. And I'm not the person, I ask you. I'll be forever in your debt. You're a good girl, I know. Being Catholic it shouldn't be a problem for you, should it?'

Marie-Sainte was trying to interpret the sense of the last sentence. It might only mean the man was Protestant himself and he was clumsily broaching a delicate moral question. But Blaise appeared from an unexpected direction, giant parcel balanced on one shoulder. The parcel wouldn't fit through the revolving doors, the hotel wasn't prepared to dismantle the door, and he had been forced to enter by the tradesman's entrance at the rear. Now he was careful to position it where he could see it, under the sturdy legs of the piano. Satisfied about that detail, he sat himself next to Marie-Sainte on the sofa and complained loudly to her: 'Where is the Mayor, then? Is he coming to see me?'

The promoter then heard his name mentioned with increased exasperation and decided flannel was his only course. 'Blaze, they do a really nice spread here. I can recommend it myself. Sometimes you have to wait your turn, but . . .'

The airman was pounding his fist on the firm padding of the sofa arm. Then he was tugging at the interpreter's elbow. 'Doesn't he realize this meal could be my last meal? Tomorrow could be my last flight. These problems are truly insupportable.'

'He is getting agitated, isn't he? Steady on, my friend. All under control don't you know.' He tried a consoling hand on the Frenchman's shoulder; decided against. 'I for one have every faith in this particular hotel, which has catered for important visitors to the city for nearly hundreds of years. And as for your aerobatic skills for tomorrow . . .'

The promoter was talking his way towards an exit.

'Anyway I'm going to leave you in the comforting hands of our brainy and I may say attractive friend here – I do believe behind those specs there lurks a dark horse of Gallic passion, no doubt. And rest assured you'll be happy with your room, small but comfortable, you appreciate that rooms are at a premium with the show on this weekend. Other important guests – army and such. I'll leave you, I've got a committee to sit on, final touches for the big day tomorrow.' The promoter had started walking by now and had reached the revolving doors when he remembered something else: 'I'm told they're sending a photographer – as you might say, *tout de suite.*' The continental flourish took him through the door with a wave.

The airman didn't even look to the interpreter for a version of this speech. The treatment he was receiving was insulting. He stepped over to the hotel bar and asked for two cognacs. He placed the balloons on the low table in front of Marie-Sainte.

He spoke to her in formal English: 'Excuse me, mademoiselle. I will return.'

Like the serviceman he had been, Blaise marched across to the piano, hauled his parcel upright, hugged it to his broad chest. There were British army and navy personnel in uniform, he now noticed, in other parts of the room, who glanced suspiciously across to the foreigner causing all the commotion. Blaise collected his room key from the manager and the manager accompanied him together with his boxed and sealed wings up the broad marble staircase to his room. And it was some time before Blaise returned with the key swinging from his little finger to savour his first healing cognac of the visit. Something – the drink or more likely the locked room – had succeeded in calming him. He sat and asked Marie-Sainte rather pointedly about herself. She couldn't be sure if this was another angry enquiry in place of more anxious conversation, or this time genuine interest in her for herself.

She related how she had been born in a colonial military family, in Martinique, where her father had been a kind, stern civil servant needed again as an army officer in wartime Marseilles; eliminated by the SS. Her mother was beautiful, artistic, of mixed descent, ostracized, bravely and still a widow on a civil pension in Paris. Marie-Sainte had studied in Paris, where she missed the heat of the West Indies, but now she only missed the elegance and the heat of Paris. A scholarship brought her to this English city, a sentence thankfully nearing its end. The university provided her with regular translation work for shipping companies – correspondence and legal matters to be translated, meetings needing an interpreter. She took on this work to pay for her lodgings with a dull suburban family who did not, could not, understand why she was so unhappy and withdrawn.

The airman interrupted her story: 'You are homesick I can tell. I understand that feeling myself perfectly. I have been in this same cold wet land of exile before. Before the Liberation.'

He could have told her about his war experiences, his loneliness and more. He would have asked if she was in love. But she wept bitterly into her hands. She dabbed the handkerchief he gave her behind her spectacle lenses. She replaced the glasses firmly, recovered quickly when a waiter appeared and announced a table prepared for them.

Then they were in the pale green dining room. They were served without ordering: nearly ripe melon with Parma ham; roast leg of lamb, *pommes de terre dauphinoises*, local carrots and asparagus in a béarnaise sauce; Bordeaux rouge without having to ask. For dessert they requested more Cheshire cheese to sit on the water biscuits and complement the palmful of white grapes. His stomach began to fill; coffee and another brandy, and he was presenting the interpreter with a complicit smile. They might have been mistaken for a couple by the military guests staying at the hotel, or by the lanky man with springy ginger hair wearing a charcoal suit who stumbled through the revolving door holding a fat camera to his stomach.

'Is there a Monsieur Blaise here?' he shouted across the room. Heads turned again and he directed himself to the manager and on to the dining room.

'From the *Echo*. I just need some names and dates. What time's your flight? Or is it a jump, sir? Must get it right. And what will you be wearing exactly? Wings, you say? Have I got that right? Made of wood, really. And have you done this kind of thing before? Can you understand my English OK? I can go slower if you like.'

The airman was able to answer these questions himself, but he asked the interpreter if it was possible the reporter was not aware of his record. She quickly delivered an abbreviated version of his feats in Europe to date.

'Fine,' the photographer said. 'We might get an inch or two in the morning and afternoon editions. Now all I need is one simple picky – could you tuck that serviette under your collar and hold that wine glass (any left?), have to look very French, and hold the glass high, that's it, as if you're wishing yourself luck for the flight. You get the picture – just right.'

The airman felt foolish but smiled for the man in this picture of an interrupted dinner.

'I've got an even better idea. The young lady, is it Mrs Blaise? No, doesn't matter, you could lift a glass too. Could I ask you to, would you mind, slipping off your specs, just for the picture? They'll cause glare you see.'

Her bare face blushed at being persuaded so easily, and for being mistaken for Blaise's wife. The man was so quick with the suggestions. Blaise was staring at her with increasing interest.

'Now lift the glass, both of you. What is it you say? *Santé. Salut.* Something like that. That's got it. There. Thank you so much, sir. May I wish you the best of luck myself for tomorrow. I'll let you get back to your *tête-à-tête*, shall I?' He was already packing his camera up again. The interpreter hurriedly replaced her glasses.

The airman stopped him to ask about the other newspapers, the national newspapers.

'The London big boys. You'll be lucky if you see them this

far north. Have to go now. Another shot of the show's planning committee at the Town Hall and then I'm done. They're making such a fuss of the arrangements this year – they're really trying to push the boat out. This air show of yours is a new thing, you see, the rest we've all seen before, same every year.'

Blaise needed Marie-Sainte to explain the views he'd just expressed, and then he was glad of the man's haste to go. He wrenched the serviette from his collar, pressed his palms to his temples, blew out an exasperated laugh.

It was her initiative to order another brandy, double for him. He started to tell her about his strange room. The room was without windows, long and narrow as a store cupboard. The manager had given a long apologetic explanation – he'd even used his hands – about how unusually busy the hotel was this weekend. But Blaise didn't need a window view of a brick wall or the roofs of trams and taxis, nor did he require more carpet to pace, just as long as his wings fitted the room safely, that was sufficient for his immediate needs. It would have to be. He was laughing about it now. The girl was relieved at his appreciation of the ridiculous. It was a bemusement she shared, but hadn't before been able to express. Here was a sympathetic spirit. She was about to light one of her English cigarettes, her Kensitas tipped. The airman gallantly pulled his own soft blue pack from a trouser back pocket. Marie-Sainte ripped a match from the Corinthian book, lit two ends together and when they came close, she puffed too eagerly and coughed and laughed in one convulsion. When the sweet smoke danced, she was breathing relief.

'Yes, I remember these well. I have missed them greatly.'

But across the room some military caps turned, faces eyes right, noses atwitch. Their loud coughs were humourless. Mutterings with an official stamp. Blaise and Marie-Sainte were still laughing, for the enjoyment of the moment and as proof against English disapproval.

'Would you like to come upstairs and see my wings?'

The couple waited at the lift doors for the criss-cross bars to sink into the glass.

'Aren't you frightened?' Marie-Sainte asked. 'I mean about tomorrow?'

'This is the only life. It may be ridiculous, but . . .' and he laughed away the question.

The lift door could be opened, the criss-cross was there. Blaise asked confidently for Floor 5. A capped commissionaire with a pigeon chest asked: 'Are you sure about Five, sir?'

The airman folded Marie-Sainte's hand to his as the lift's cables rattled round and up. All the way without a stop.

The commissionaire intoned: 'Floor Five, as high as we go, otherwise we'd be on the rooftops.'

The airman didn't satisfy the supercilious man with an explanation. He directed his key to the second door along the corridor.

'You go in. I have to find the bathroom first. Don't step on the big parcel on the floor, will you?'

Marie-Sainte found the light switch. The wallpaper pattern was tiny single roses joined in diamond formation. The parcel, as long as a tandem bicycle, lay alongside the bed. She barely had carpet space to step before pitching herself on to the pink candlewick bedspread, wedging her back against one wall. Cardboard boxes and paper in rolls had been stacked carelessly at the end of the room; it was windowless, the walls were close: nothing more than a storeroom with one bed. She read the blue crayon instructions – FRAGILE – and the French address repeated neatly at all angles on the packing; every 7 had a familiar line through it, every S was a French S; there was nationality for handwriting, she realized. She tugged at the hairy twine that belted the container, then sat back against the wall when she heard the airman's approaching movement in the corridor.

When he entered, Blaise had most of his clothes folded over one arm. His skin was tanned, hirsute; arms and legs muscled; white undershorts, as if for gymnastics. She had expected him to be athletic in just this upright military way. Not unlike photographs of her own admired, resented, departed father. The airman, with almost religious deliberation, bent over to undo the string, slipped the knot with sure fingers. He unfurled the paper from the cardboard, gently stacked the top packing against a wall; scooped out white tissue paper like foam from a bath. Marie-Sainte could see light varnished wood, cane struts, canvas webbing, brown leather straps. She felt hot in this small room, and had to slip off her cardigan.

The artiste held the balsa pieces firmly together, fitted stiffening canes and webbing behind; he adjusted the length and angle of the wood, looked along the line of all surfaces, like a soldier along a rifle barrel. He looped the leather straps on to the webbing and with a heaving breath hoisted the broad wings, turning in one strong movement so that the smooth machine rested, creaking, on to his back and shoulders, and what faced her finally were his broad chest and proud smile: the French airman and the beautiful geometrical extension of himself, wings of wood.

'Would you assist me with the straps, please?'

Marie-Sainte tightened the straps for the Birdman with the outstretched wings.

2

1990

Graham Connolly had tried life away from cities, away from rivers, in flat places without shape, where groupings of trees were landmarks, where lanes eeled drily through squares and squares of fields and where hills seemed distant, almost accidental. He had tried noisy summers of cut-grass fields, and vicious winters of nothing plus rain. Years on the back of years in a place he hardly knew now, which he looked back on only as the country, nothing more specific. His time there must have added up to a couple of decades – years missed, only partially lived through, or daydreamed. Gray reckoned those years didn't count if they could hardly be recalled now.

An abrupt blast of wind off the Irish Sea suggested to him that memory could be blown clean away; and from where he was sitting, overlooking some sparse busying around the landing stage, Gray was hoping it would be as easy as that.

The grand waterfront office buildings behind him, cleaned so white of their grime, offered no particular shelter to a returnee. Marine breeze made chewing-gum wrappers swirl at his feet and around the legs of his bench, plastered his greying hair up to his crown, and buffeted the gulls in flight. No need yet to grip the railings for balance, but he did have fears for his equilibrium. There was nothing more here than paving flags, litter bins, statues to the war dead lost at sea, a horse-backed king, his helmet soiled by seagulls, and all the space in between. Space. Here had been a bus terminus; now flattening and excavations; contractors' bright orange marker tapes; a worrying absence of shape, when attachment to the city's present solidity was what Graham now wished for most.

Great sandstone blocks of the river wall, mud-slimed as high as its tractor tyres, held back the rising old grey-brown estuary water, and an old fear. The edge of a river bed was exposed, rounded, shit-sticky, the colour of an armoured car, oil-smudged. And now that he had to look down on the bulge of low tide rising, down where a fragile moored dinghy bobbed against the landing stage, Graham's fear was of toppling in, gagging on flooded lungs. Childish.

It was just that the accident of his being here again seemed less of an accident and more of a problem sooner than he'd wished. There was perversity about daring to return to the place you started off and expecting the fact of the place to make no difference. Graham was defying the city to claim him – after so many years away – well, it was all so changed. He would have to test it, of course, he couldn't avoid that: test himself by insisting that he happened to start off here, happened to leave, happened not to come back, till now. And he expected to know no one, or hardly anyone. Expected no one to make a difference. Because this was meant to be a new life, decided upon and executed; career take-off, admittedly a little late in the day. Couldn't he enjoy this phase of his life without being weighed down by old choices, refusals from long ago? Well, he was already making this effort to meet new people, not forcing it, just giving people more of a chance and presenting this adult person to all the faces he met, regardless of new or old, as if he had never been a child here, only an adult tested by too long in the country.

The gangplank of a ferry boat made a washboard rattling and a chain jangle as it hit the deck; then came the rumble of shoes up the boards of the floating stage. Graham watched the kids run up first, then it was day trippers, then the pensioners still clutching their cards, and cyclists in brightest Lycra overtaking the lot. The sounds ambushed him; he wanted to refuse the effort of trying to reconstitute the changes there'd been.

One fat herring gull flapped up from the landing-stage roof below, retracting its wings as quickly as it established its balance on the railing, posing boldly in front of the bench where Gray had stationed himself. Bilious yellow bill, clear demarcations of grey and white feathering; the body was clean and rounded, close up – solid, there – nothing at all like a white-crayoned V in the sugar-paper sky of a child's drawing, and nothing, either, like a sodden rolled swimming-towel corpse washed up on the sand. Black and white wingtips and tail, and no juvenile brown mottling noticeable on the feathers anywhere: so, Gray deduced, definitely mature, or near enough.

But this bird had designs on Graham's snack in crumpled foil: pumpernickel pasted with cottage cheese, wodges of watercress poking out. The gull performed its display of neck stretching, then attacked him with the long harsh cry. Another of those forgotten things to unsettle him further. How was it seagulls weren't so noticeable in other places he'd tried to set down roots? Inland, only in numbers above the markets, the abattoirs, the rubbish tips and across all the broad ploughed fields. An annoyance now.

Since he had started work at the hotel, the week before, he had been putting particular effort into filling his days, getting out more, meeting people. And he wanted to give the place a good chance, in spite of history. He knew it wasn't going to be easy. There would have to be these reversals, like tidal undercurrents against the river's natural flow. When Gray shaped for a kick at the herring gull's tail feathers, the bird's legs dipped, the wings lifted easy, no cry, and up into the wind. Gray overbalanced, then just saved himself, looking round with relief that there were no witnesses. He hurled his lunch hard into the wind and watched the pieces drop down into the grim water for any other gulls to squabble over.

An annoyance with himself, most likely, because parking himself at the landing stage was only one more means of delay; when he knew very soon he would have to make the dreaded phone call to his mother. With every new day he was in the city he imagined he could sense something more of her stored up reproach. Cissie Connolly was in another part of the city, back of a florist's shop, a matter of miles away, but his sense of her, just like his awareness of the river, was getting close to physical the more days he settled there.

No; the seagull was more of an annoyance because it was his father the gull put him in mind of, not his mother. The wind battering his raincoat hem against his legs helped him up the steep streets of shipping offices, insurance offices – his father's world – in the general direction of the hotel. As he passed the gilt-decorated doorway of a corner bar, Gray sniffed the tang of flannel drip mats soaked in beer, didn't step inside, in spite of the temptation of dark and liquid. The problem was the thought that a dapper man well into his seventies (if he'd lived on) might be leaning jolly-for-all against the bar, and say, 'Come in, son. What's it to be? My round.' Graham imagined the drinkers spread along the bar counter: donkey jackets, greased denim, suits, but glowering towards the door, laughing their smoky laughs. London was the last time he saw the man, but a drink with a drunk isn't a talk, and there was nothing to say. One glimpse of his father's smelly little room was enough to cut him off. By the time of the funeral Graham was trying to get away from the city to what he hoped would be the country. He made it back for the burial and wished he hadn't. The last words

38

with his mother on Euston Station had caused the long, long silence.

But, it was unavoidable, he would have to make contact. He knew where she would be. He would just have to pick up a phone and ring the shop. He would have heard if she had been ill. Marva would have to be his intermediary again; she was still there, surely. Gray had phoned the shop in a moment of weakness two years before and heard the bones of a progress report. He had written a couple of postcards to Marva. 'She IS all right, the old woman, isn't she, you would tell me? This is my latest address for the foreseeable. Don't tell her I've been in touch, will you . . . not yet.' He never could fathom how the girl stayed with her.

If he made the effort Gray could actually picture to himself the exact row of shops. The flat behind the flower shop. She wouldn't have moved. He didn't expect the anaemic brick-faced block to be much different. Repointed perhaps, individual window frames different paint colours from the Council's old cream and brown, a few of the windows boarded up, no pet shop, the hairdresser's with another change of name most probably, and, yes, there it would be, same place, the florist's.

As he navigated safe passage through the city shopping centre, Gray had stepped carefully to dodge the nudges of old ladies' shopping bags, the nodding, swaggering approach of youngsters in baggy T-shirts, zippers, baggy jeans. He stamped the herringboned brick pedestrian pavements, he pulled himself up newly constructed steps towards a glass-covered market. And at the top there he was facing the grand half dome of the railway station; it was much too hard to think back, father, mother, all that, easier to walk on, embrace this new, and forget. The station dominated one end of the street – the revolving door of the refurbished Corinthian Hotel, his place of work, his temporary home, was at the other.

He strode into the glass and shine of the station concourse, nearly slipped on the marble where an ice-cream dollop was still melting. He had difficulty recognizing this as always the start of his departure to London, away for good, because it also had that could-be-anywhere newness. The only phone booth free was blue and silver, but shaped like something they used to have in record shops, a hood holding the sound in but allowing the listener to look all around. The trick was, just before the record ended, to disappear from the shop without buying: Little Stevie Wonder, the Searchers. He did remember some stupid things. Only one station booth had a shelf with an unripped set of directories. Gray fiddled for coins and watched queues forming for burgers and milk-shakes, where a beautiful toothy black girl, maybe Somalian, pressed into candy-stripe apron and cap, was parroting her customer greeting once more. Students in ripped jeans hug-ging luxury travellers' baggage, their parents', lolled across a long crescent of benches. Coffee was being sold from a trolley in polystyrene cups and red carnations were ready wrapped into small bunches for quick sale. Here he was, anywhere; or else here again.

Graham checked for Florists in Yellow Pages and worked his way through the box adverts for Blooms, Boo-K, Fleurs, Flowercraft, all offering Interflora, down to the smaller list-ings, which he read upwards: Say it with Ours, Sara Jayne's, Posies, Petals, Orchids, Oleanders . . . In his previous phone call he had heard from Marva how the name came about – a line from a Billie Holiday song she liked. Something about oleanders in June. Apparently his mother had decided the time had come and offered Marva the chance to change the name from 'Cecilia Connolly: Flowers', just as she herself had it changed from 'Bulstrode for Blooms'.

Someone answered at the other end. 'Oleanders. How may I be of help?'

'It's me. Gray. Graham Connolly. Back in town.'

Silent acknowledgement.

'Am I supposed to tell your mam?'

'How is she then? She OK? You'd have told me, wouldn't you?'

'If I'd had an address to send to I might have.'

'I gave you the last one, didn't I, in the middle of nowhere?'

'It's not for me to get in touch, Graham Connolly.'

'Nobody calls me that, Marva.'

'Your mother still does. If ever you come up in conversation.'

'Which isn't often, you're saying.'

'Your problem, Graham. I've got a customer waiting on a wreath. What was it you wanted anyway?'

'Tell her, can you, I'll see her soon. I'm back, sort of. And, yes, thanks, Marva, for keeping an eye on her.'

'Someone's died, Graham.'

The words stopped his blood, because he thought, for a moment, he might have arrived too late. And, curiously enough, it was a sensation he'd been half expecting, by some subconscious self-preparation. The little panic deprived him of words.

'Are you there? Are you in this world? I said someone's died, and there's someone who wants to make a point of saying they miss that person, well they're paying me to weave some chrysanths and roses together tight – that's just their way of saying it. Do you get the picture, Graham? Thank you for calling Oleanders, sir. Call into the shop, why don't you?'

He put the phone down before all his credit digits dropped from sight. Gray knew it was all going to be uphill.

3

1957

The boy, Graham, was playing aeroplanes on the bare potato patch, so he couldn't know the father's satisfaction at being home without having to avoid his wife. A war drama blared on the wireless, extension wire into the kitchen, a bottle of India Pale Ale in hand, backside on deckchair: everything set up for a guiltless bank holiday in the sun. Whereas Mrs Connolly had got it into her head to take her sister and brother-in-law to the showground for the busiest, hottest day of the weekend. For some reason unknown to him she saw the need to be at the Captain's side.

On such a fine day, when all the men in England would be out in their back gardens, stripped to their vests and some no doubt, but not him, baring their torsos, Joseph Connolly settled his back into the canvas deckchair. His own chest was narrow, however heavily hair-fringed, and his belly noticeably rounded for such a slim-built man. Sport, apart from the keep fits of naval drill, wasn't even a memory. He liked the chair wedged in the last and lowest rung, not fixed bolt upright waiting for a front-door call. But then, Joseph reckoned, couldn't people be so divided? The early risers, the late; the brisk bathers, the tub soakers; lip of the deckchair sitters, and flop back loungers like himself. People were just different. Who could say it was a waste to waste the day's rest of a bank holiday with only a pale ale for adult company?

Joseph Connolly supped his beer only slowly, slower than he downed it from the pump at the Coronation, where it was sometimes helped down by a whisky chaser. The Coronation, where people were friendly enough to call you Joe, and ready enough to lend an ear to your tales (and gracious enough not to stop you in your tracks because they've heard the one about the torpedoing before). They tell their drinking friends that you're a gent – they might guess as much by your charcoal waistcoated suit and your naval tie and you prove it by raising the brushed grey trilby for a lady. They appreciate that. There's a contract between you. You arrive, smile all round, a word for all the bar staff, swallow the first Teacher's of the evening. Mr Connolly, the gentleman, appreciated that unqualified welcome. No quarter is given for talk about work or shops or flowers or takings, just the interesting things like people, war, the boats, football teams, tales from round the globe. This lunchtime the talk would all be of the blessed air show – the promised stunts and crowds, and this sunshine, which had agreed to be sweltering for the bank holiday, unlike every year before. The Coronation was the place he went every night of his married life, and lunchtimes at weekends. Slipping out the door after teatime, sauntering home late, where was the threat in that harmless little routine?

But before the father could allow himself to lie back full in the old varnished deckchair, he needed to yank scutch grass from the borders, rake pebbles and brick shards into a pile, hack at a leggy privet eight feet high; he also had to bump the Qualcast roller cutter all across his uneven baked patch of lawn, and now his arms trembled – there was this throbbing in his muscles which reminded Joe that exertion was an unfamiliar activity for him. Was he getting old? He hadn't felt like a shave that morning – he had a head from last night, there'd been words with Mrs C and he would have surely growled if spoken to. Now he looked forward to the smoothness that came from the soaping and razor scraping of stubble, and to the release still experienced by the nightly dressing up to go out. He would feel better then; and better still later on, with glass in hand.

Graham sat in a neat rectangle of dry soil, last year's potato patch from which the yield had been only twelve pounds. His stubby fingers and palms had patted even smoother what his holiday spade had already flattened to resemble an airfield with runways. He made a control tower from bucket-formed sandcastles jelly-moulded together. The airsock is a stick and the foot of an old nylon. Some of the planes are pegs whittled to shape and spliced together with string. His best plane is a long plastic model of a Wellington and he stands up to give the plane its necessary altitude. In his other hand there's a single tin soldier, khaki kit and helmeted, and this man has a six-inch ruler strapped to his shoulders with elastic bands. This special one is held next to the hatch of the bomber as it flies and drones. The boy is doing the sound effects and adding his own approximation of war-film French and officer-sounding English. Now he's making him float, hang in the air as on a thermal updraught. He's going to make him jump, then fly with his wings. He'll float for a while, parachute and land safely at a distance from the airfield. The father hadn't noticed the poor kid so happy in recent weeks.

Joseph scrabbled under the deckchair for his matches, tamped a cigarette hard on the bearded sailor's face on his wide box of fifty; he stood up to stretch the cramp from his legs. He started his walk down the straight paving-slab path. In his opinion a good garden had to be kept simple and manageable. He hardly ever looked out from this end of the garden, but the view was impressive, he supposed – wide fields (wheat, then peas) unbroken by fences, a cricket field bordered by trees announced by a cricket sight screen intensely white, how they all seemed to pull the land to the horizon – and for distant landmarks only one tiny church spire, a glinting glass-roofed building and a colliery slag heap far off. This was a council estate on the edge of the city and the edge of the country too. Space enough for a growing boy to explore. Safe enough for him to wander off into the fields. Had the boy been to watch the cricket before? What else did boys do with themselves in the open air? Climb trees and throw stones harmlessly. Anyway, he could see the chubby knees were permanently caked with soil. Whereas Joseph himself had hardly ventured to the other side of the garden palings, escape being always the front door for him.

Graham was standing and his stubby hands formed pretend binoculars to scan the plain blue sky. A skylark had lifted from the field, twittering hard, and the boy was the first to see it. He was exhilarated by the small bird's strength and daring.

'There he goes – up, up, high.'

The lark climbs high into the heart of the day and out of human view.

'And no one sees them drop – because it's not where they rose from. It's a different landing place from the take-off place.'

'So you're all genned up on ornithology are you, Graham?' Father trying to make conversation. 'I was forgetting you were forever chasing the birds in the Isle of Man.'

The boy ignored mention of their recent holiday. He was informing his father there'd been a biplane earlier in the week, pulling a banner advertisement for the show across the sky, there'd been Cessnas and Avro trainers galore, and a Meteor jet too. He was up again looking for more.

'Graham, why don't you put a cap on? You'll ruin your eyes.'

He turned himself and dropped his hand-binoculars.

'Anyway, son, you're looking in the wrong direction for the airport. It's more towards the river, you know.'

The boy had wanted to go to the airport where all the planes, all nationalities, took off, landed and bounced and parked outside hangars and taxied slow enough on runways for their numbers to be read from the tailplane. It would have been the perfect opportunity. It would have been – if his mother had chosen to go to the airport – instead she wished to go to the show in the park, which was where the Birdman was intending to land. Not so very far from where they were so frustratingly now.

'You don't understand, Dad. The Frenchman is going to float down from a thousand feet, more than a thousand, I think – and fly down on wings. The best place would have been the airport, you'd see him boarding his plane.'

'Well if the Lord had wanted us all to fly, he'd surely have made us with wings.'

'But Dad, he *has* wings. He's made his own wings. It said so in your newspaper.'

'Who does he think he is then, this Frenchman, on a day like this? Blooming Icarus?'

'Who's that, Dad?'

Joseph Connolly knew his mythology from the names of ships. He had taken the trouble to check them once in *Pears Cyclopaedia*.

'He flew too close to the sun and the wings just melted.'

'Melted?'

The boy puzzled with the word but couldn't connect it with anything he knew; dismissed it smartly as a storybook story.

'Mum's gone to the wrong place really.'

'Isn't the showground where your Birdman has to land?'

'After a bit, yes. But he has to *fly* first, doesn't he? And I wanted to see him leap into the air first. It doesn't matter where he lands.'

'I hear they've got a flower show at the showground. All colours and sizes. Your mum's probably gone for that.'

The boy couldn't believe such frivolity of his mother. Yet, even when she'd broken the bad news, she hadn't truly explained why she was going and he wasn't.

'For a start, it's far too crowded for you,' his mother had said. 'There'll be thousands there, as many as a football crowd.'

The boy couldn't understand this adult logic of who was allowed to go and who wasn't.

'You're too young, son. We might lose you. You might get crushed to death in the crowd.'

'Don't frighten the lad, Cissie. No point in that.'

She was in her stubborn, bustling mood and Joseph wasn't really the one to talk her out of that.

'Anyway I'll need all my wits about me to look after Old Jack.'

'What's your fine and grand sister for then? She's going, isn't she? Wouldn't she be sufficient?'

'Lydia's not been a great support to him in recent years. You know very well.'

'And you have?'

'Yes I have. As far as I've been allowed. Who wouldn't for such a man – if asked?'

'Such a man?'

'Oh for goodness sake, Joseph. Give the questions a rest, can't you?'

Cissie's sister, Lydia, had worshipped and pampered the good Captain when he was a younger man and away at sea for most of the time. She made their house by the river beautiful with tablecloths and lace and figurines, and she kept it tidy even though there were so many pieces of furniture and ornament to dust around. She was the Captain's lady and graced numerous onshore functions and as few as possible on board ship. And when the Captain lost his command, when his sight was first faulted, he was forced to stay at home a great deal, sitting and reading, sitting and drinking. He grew heavier, ruddier in colour, and much much quieter. Lydia didn't find it easy to look after the old man – he aged quickly, and he already had ten years on her. So she tried to busy herself by taking on a student lodger from the nearby Maritime College. Cissie, the younger sister, was only too eager to help the couple out when she could. She had by then started part time at Mrs Bulstrode's flower shop and so she was able to take the largest bunches of flowers to the hospital when the Captain had his first eye operation eight years before. 'He needs to be able to see something cheerful, doesn't he?' she said hopefully at the time.

'So why does the Captain have to go?' Joseph had asked his wife. 'He could stay at home if it's so dangerous.'

'He's spent too much time on his own in his chair,' Cissie explained with the fullest sympathy. 'That was why they went to the Isle of Man – for a last smell of the esplanade. He likes to feel the crowds – they're a comfort to him. There's a life in them that maybe he's been missing.'

'He's brave then.'

She had always been quick to defend him. 'He's always been brave – he's had to be in his career – as you well know. So my job is to tell him all about the show, all the dogs and horses and the children's dancing. And of course the plants and flowers – I'll tell him all their colours.'

'Oh yes, you would know all about those, wouldn't you?'

'And that man has some appreciation of the finer things.'

'Does he now?'

Joseph didn't care what they were doing at the show. But Cissie wanted to be the old man's ears and eyes. Now. As if the man's own wife, Lydia, didn't have the wherewithal for the task, and apparently she didn't on her own. But wasn't it too late for Cissie to remedy that – now of all times?

The boy had asked his mother bravely: 'And what about Uncle Jack, how much will he see?'

'Now you know how he's afflicted. He can't see at all now. And it's a special treat to him because of that. Like a last wish, if you can follow that. The man's not got long to live. It's a crying shame.'

'What about me?' the boy persisted. 'I'm the one interested in planes. I'm the one that told you about the Birdman. Well – after you'd told me, anyway.'

'I know, I know, son.'

The boy was blubbing. His mother was in tears too. They hugged and said their sorries. Joseph had to slip out of the room.

Now Joseph wasn't a man who pretended a closeness to family members he didn't especially like. Cissie Connolly was happier far, if she was given the chance, in the company of her sister and brother-in-law, Lydia and old Jack Argent. But this in-law was Yorkshire, stocky and blunt, merchant navy – different outlook altogether. Joseph didn't disguise his antipathy. He wasn't envious. His wife claimed he was jealous of the man's achievements – attaining the rank of captain and his own command at such a young age, and then a succession of ever-larger vessels. But Joseph himself met captains every working day and shared a drink with them as he checked their cargoes and their paperwork. They were no different from any other breed of men, and he himself was always treated amicably and equally. It wasn't his fault if the old man had cataracts and a bad heart. Did that explain his wife's fond attentions, which he could only describe as fawning?

He turned the volume up on his wireless – water was gushing through a breached hold, a barked command, clanging feet of ratings escaping upstairs. Nobody he encountered ever spoke in such clearly scripted lines. That wasn't the sound of panic and cold, cold water. No music of course when a torpedo hits you. A drama on the wireless was the nearest he got to the cinema because he couldn't possibly have taken his wife, not in recent years – even if she'd spared him the time. They couldn't have sat still together nor even shared cigarettes. She had a Ronson lighter, he was a matches man, England's Glory; she Kensitas for the prizes, he Players. They were very different people.

'Aren't you sweltering there, Graham old chap? Take your shirt off, like me.'

The boy looked at his father's drooping sweat-wet vest.

'Or drink for you?'

He forgets his sulk, decides on an attempt at communication. He's hot – the shirt is grey flannel, a vest underneath. 'Can I have a shandy? What time's Mum back?'

'I'll have to go and get some pop from the kitchen. Shall we have a fire, burn some of that grass I've cut? Just to annoy the neighbours?' He was trying to engage the boy's interest again – away from the planes.

'Will the Frenchman be in the air yet, Dad?'

'How should I know?' But he checked his watch all the same. The pub wasn't open yet. He'd have to wait till evening.

The boy seemed tiny, distant, as Joseph walked to the kitchen; like a toddler in beach sand viewed from a promenade, hunched over his play. Joseph reflected that he didn't know the boy. His wife had kept him from him – as if he was more hers than his. She talked to him, he rarely did. He was merely referred to as 'your father'. He couldn't in fact recall the night of conception. He couldn't at the time calculate when it must have been. Penetration and the rest of it wasn't always possible after a night out. But then Joseph was always at work or out at the local when the boy cluttered the house up with his arrangements of soldiers and planes all over the carpets. Breakfast time the boy was subdued, still half asleep, when Joseph himself was touchiest and shouted too loud at the smallest irritation, in his hurry to escape through that front door. Amiability only settled on him evening time and in another friendlier place, not home.

It had been a whole month since they tried a holiday in the Isle of Man for the sake of the boy. The plan was the boy could enjoy the seaside and do the kind of exploring things boys do and Cissie and he would try to be two together, revisiting the old places from their rushed honeymoon. But it hadn't worked; it couldn't have worked. Even if they hadn't met up with her sister, and the embarrassing scene on the promenade hadn't taken place. He had to accept that their differences were probably what were called irreconcilable.

Now he was talking to himself – wasn't that a bad sign? – in the deckchair again, even though this new bottle he was prising open, the one he had after mowing the grass and the one at lunch were all he'd touched since the skinful last night. Now this was a new thing: he held the thought nervously, as he pursed his lips ready for the first sour taste of beer from the bottle neck. 'Your mum and me will have to come to some arrangement. One day.'

How long could he last though? This was his family, but it hadn't worked the way it seemed to for others. Seemed to. He didn't easily understand himself how a family was supposed to be. He had an understanding of what friends and colleagues, comrades in arms, could mean to each other, especially in times of emergency, and that sometimes meant at the expense of the family. He understood that he went to work, and she, like all the young wives in their street, kept the house shipshape while the boy was at school – except for the odd day helping out at the flower shop or visiting Lydia, more often of late, it's true. His wife wasn't interested in him. Romance had only been shaped very briefly by the rushed circumstances of war. She was actually embarrassed by him, yes. When he tottered up the wrong path, pushed his key in the wrong Yale lock, fell down on the pavement outside – and she had had to pick him up out of the hydrangea, that was when she felt her neighbours' pity so bitterly. She couldn't forgive that.

Now the boy was whimpering.

'What's up? Someone had a nose dive at your airport?'

Joseph looked to see if it was all part of his play on the Home Service – a drama – or if the boy was really crying.

'No need to be upset. We've already gone through why you can't go. Do you want to kick your ball around? I've got two left feet, but I'll play in goal if you want to take pot shots at me.'

The boy stared as if he relished something like that, then shook his head.

Colonel Bogey chimed in the street outside.

'Want a cornet?'

'What time's Mum home? She's late.'

'It'll take a long time for the crowds to disperse. Remember she's got an invalid with her.'

'She left me behind though.'

'You shouldn't think too badly of your mother – she's had a lot on her mind lately. Uncle Jack's not well.'

'It wasn't fair. I wanted to see the Birdman fly – Mum knew that.'

He turned away to his game. Still standing, he hurled the toy soldier with his wooden wings down into the dust of his miniature airfield. He wasn't listening to his father. He ignored him as if he wasn't his father. He had to crouch down to pick up the broken figure – the wood of the six-inch ruler had cracked on impact.

'I wanted to tell you something, Graham.'

He couldn't be sure he was listening, but he would say it anyway. It was only like affirming it to himself.

'The shipping line might want to move me away. They're talking about a transfer to London.'

The boy wouldn't understand. No, he definitely wasn't listening. He was too busy trying to repair his toy airman.

'Would you mind if you didn't see so much of me? You've always got on better with your mother – you have, haven't you?'

No answer. The boy stood and squinted up at the sky again. All blue. The skylark must have landed somewhere, because the air was without its relentless twitter. He steered himself more in the direction of the river. But his movements made the father nervous; now he wished he hadn't said anything about going away to London.

'Are you sure you don't want that ice cream, Graham?'

He wasn't reaching him at all. The boy shook a fist of cold annoyance and stared hard into the distance; a plane might be circling in the sky at any time.

'No,' he cried. 'Not fair.'

And Joseph squinted in the direction the boy looked, saw the dull horizon – fields, trees, cricket sight screen. However determined his utter indifference to cricket on any other summer day, this day he still wanted to save for the sake of the boy. A father could still think up distractions for his own son, surely.

'What about you and I walk up the fields as far as the cricket ground? I'll have to put a shirt on first though. But what do you think of that for an idea?'

The boy muttered, 'Not the same.'

'No, but we can stretch our legs a bit. There might be a game on – on a day like this. Sunny – just the weather for cricket. I'll buy you a drink of Orange Crush. What do you think of that?'

The boy moved at last. They would walk and find the cricket game, the two of them together, and he would make his own guesses where the airman might be now.

4

1990

The darkness of the small windowless room next to the lift surprised him every morning. The head would always swirl; this was as bad as jetlag. Clean clothes still lined his suitcase. Thank goodness for the white kitchen uniform. Fifty covers on a good night. The new job was making him sleep hard. What else was there to do? Relaxation wasn't an easy trick.

The first morning Gray lay in bed and there had been someone in the next room practising guitar. A sequence of well-rehearsed sixties tunes, a strong nasal voice singing out the first few lines before changing key for the next. Gray had tipped back his head on the pillow with something like a grin, because of the familiar edge to every strange, new thing in this restarted life.

On that first day Peter the manager had shown Graham round the kitchens, got him to shake hands with the other staff, Grant, Jamie, Yvette, Siobhan, then walked him down every corridor, along every metre of carpeting, opened every door, given him a full and personal tour of the building. For every face the manager had a nod, a genuine nod of recognition, which also asked how each was fitting into the team, any problems, anything for the suggestion box, etc. He gave Graham to understand that his interest in improving the menu was personal and he'd had a personal stake in

Graham's appointment. 'I'm assigning Grant to you, to show you the ropes. I've an idea you'll want to get down to talking food, won't you?' But they hadn't, had they?

Under Grant's direction – Graham hadn't any particular plans of his own, except that he knew he needed to get out sometimes to fill his lungs with fresh air, well, air from outside – he had taken to drinking slowly at the bar. He might have to find somewhere of his own soon, if he decided to stay; if the hotel got busy and they needed to let his room, or more likely, use it for storage, fill it to the ceiling with toilet rolls or bargain bed linen. His room had been a very swift stop on Peter's induction tour, a place to lay a head, surely a matter of no importance in comparison with the priority of seamless service presented by a committed and happy workforce. When Peter claimed the room had been taken out of guest commission expressly to ensure new staff could be close to the centre of operations, Gray had believed the man. He had accepted there and then that he would be happy to live in for the time being, until, that is, he found his own place. Yes: if this was a real job; if moving from the country was wise; if this was actually a new start and not a return; if he had any choice in the matter. But it was too early to be sure on any of those matters, and Gray decisively postponed all his ifs.

The second night there Graham's new colleague gave the door a thump, before walking in.

'Fancy a bevvy before we get cracking?'

'Isn't it a bit early, Grant?'

'Never too early. Aren't you brassed off yet with the floor show next door to you? Myron's his name. Myron. Says he's from Memphis, I know for a fact he's from Cleveland, Ohio. Which isn't the same thing, is it now?'

Graham didn't dislike Grant. He'd been guarded, a little suspicious, but that hadn't stopped his new colleague offering to be hearty and very nearly friendly. Graham wondered if the time he'd been away had made him mean-spirited, too distrustful of talk.

'You mean he's not a hotel guest. He's on tonight? The guy next door is?'

'The manager thought he was good, better than the last twinkle fingers we had: Gordon Mr Piano Handley. No, he wants the young people in. With plastic charge cards and fat wads of money.'

'Myron sounds OK through four inches of plaster. The young wouldn't go for his stuff though.'

'Well, I want to know what happens to the big black grand.'

In the kitchens that evening Gray was chopping the rooty ends off five bunches of leeks and washing Cyprus potatoes for a soup, fennel bulbs and tomatoes for something else, while Grant was dressing three legs of lamb with rosemary and, more reluctantly, raspberry. He shouted across to Gray: 'The boss reckons you have to be able to cater for veggies professionally. Are those people special nowadays? Whoever heard such horse shite?'

'I'm not doing you out of a job, Grant, don't worry.'

'I fucking hope it isn't going to come to that. I'm not nouvelle, but I'm good on the basics. Which is what people have always wanted.'

'You are, Grant.'

Grant had served his time in the merchant navy. He'd squeezed into tiny galleys on cargo boats and tankers. He'd cooked fried eggs and chicken curry for indifferent crew across most of the widest oceans. He'd been dressed up as steward, white collar buttoned to the chin on cruise liners in the Mediterranean, served up with middling panache steak chasseur from their cramped kitchens. But found all boats everywhere pretty much the same. When he'd well and truly got his sea legs, he decided he wanted to come back home. No reason: fewer boats; ships' sides closing in. Before the hotel job, he'd done three years in a burger bar. Now he drank whisky in moderation somewhere and ate seriously in the city's Chinese restaurants.

'There's a couple in tonight,' Grant continued. 'Giving the waiter grief over the wine. Showing off. He's skin and bone and she's got a skirt up to her arse. Did you know they sent a steak back last night? Uneatable. Bloody nerve. Any bets they're from the fucking art gallery or somewhere. These new people.'

'What hope for my vichyssoise do you think?' Graham held up a ladle of soup to Grant for tasting.

'What's so special about leek and potato all of a sudden?'

There were other customers, the passing business clientele, the bread and butter of the hotel, all as important as these, but more easily pleased. There was always all the flurry of getting the starters and the main courses ready, then the anxiety of waiting for the first impressions verdict passed on by Jamie the waiter, and then it went quiet while they all ate. Each time the kitchen door swung open, snatches of the quieter Beatles songs could be heard. 'Michelle', 'When I'm 64'. Inside they concocted a few desserts. Grant watched the profiteroles didn't explode; Gray experimented with mango and passion fruit in filo-pastry parcel, drizzled with yoghurt and honey. It had been added as a special to the menu; he'd handwritten it himself on all the cards.

Afterwards, out of uniform, off duty, they drank spirits – Grant was on whisky chaser with a lager – against the bar. Myron, the floor show, was trying to persuade the few diners who remained and the drinkers, most of them non-resident, to throw him all-time favourite requests for fielding. A half-drunk woman with a mane of wet curls shouted 'Donna Summer' several times. Myron avoided answering her, but talked in his down-home stage drawl to his audience. It didn't matter that some of his beginnings got no further than four lines of lyrics, broke off with a discordant strum of defeat. His showpiece finale could have been his way of silencing the requests. Graham and Grant listened idly, then intently. Myron had somehow managed to reproduce the inflections of the sweet voice on 'Yesterday'. He was a careful mimic, with a very serviceable voice.

'You wouldn't really remember this, Grant. The tingle on your neck when it first came through on the radio.'

'What are you drinking that I'm not? It's not old songs gives me a tingle, I can tell you.'

'Myron's actually not a bad recycler.'

'Please yourself. Half the time I can't be bothered.'

Grant nosed closer to his whisky glass.

Then in stepped the girl, jolly-eyed, self-possessed, right into the dim-lit bar area, two Japanese men in tow. She seemed still to be at work, but enjoying it, peered quickly around the tables for faces she might know. Smart in black polo-neck, black tights, short tartan skirt, shiny Doc Martens, she was the same height as her two men companions. She squinted towards the performer even as she ushered her guests through the tables to the bar, talking, explaining all the time. She cocked her head to hear the extended instrumental passage in the middle, clapped loud when the guitar went still. Graham applauded louder, smiled at the girl. Myron bowed, unclasped something off his guitar neck, stepped in the direction of appreciation. Gray tried to offer Myron a drink.

'I'm your next door neighbour, apparently. Graham Connolly.'

'I can't hear you.'

Gray repeated his introduction, fearing the bar noise drowned him out.

'I mean you're like a mouse in that room, man.'

'Only just moved in. But I can hear you OK. Loud and clear.'

'That's cool then.'

The girl was explaining something more about typical nights in the city to the two very interested Japanese. Myron swallowed his beer straight down, walked away to the toilets.

Graham nudged Grant. 'Who's the girl? Is she regular here?'

Grant offered a surly answer over a shoulder almost. 'How should I know? I'm not a girls' man, and you're not her age, are you, dear? Be honest.'

'I just want to know who she is.'

'Probably another one of the new people.'

'Everyone's new people to me, didn't you know?'

Nonetheless Graham hopped over to where she sat.

'I'm Graham Connolly, I'm a cook here, off duty, actually, but I could put a word in for you for some bar food, if you're peckish.'

Introductions – he was getting used to them, and better at them. The four of them – Grant stayed where he was – were all soon talking about boats and the Beatles, then somehow it was sushi, then it was whales and Michelle got more annoyed than was professional and Graham had to steer the surprised guests back to the crucial difference between noodles and pasta. Michelle made a promise to Graham to bring visitors more often to the hotel to eat. She quizzed him about meat substitutes and protein and cruelty, and he was in his element expounding his theories, such as they were, not much more than fashionable what-passed-for-wisdom, but he blathered on regardless, natural ingredients, organic vegetables if at all possible, and he was pleased to see how she listened with interest. Gray thought she looked at him with interest too, and he was forced to wonder if his age would be a turn-off for her, or the thickening of his torso. Even as he spouted he was able to resolve that he really ought to try to look more the picture of health and fitness himself. But there would be time for exercise wouldn't there, when he settled in, didn't she think? Michelle let slip she was involved in some environmental campaigning, locally, which didn't mean there wasn't a global effect. Gray said he was interested. Where he used to live he'd been a supporter of this and that ... The tunes were getting quieter, and minus the lyrics: 'Blackbird', 'She's Leaving Home'. Myron glared over. The guitar stopped. With just the right touch of moodiness, he rested his voice and his fingers. The Japanese businessmen, who'd also gone silent, nodded to Michelle they wanted to leave. Michelle offered Gray something like a date, a morning assignation at the waterfront, to continue their conversation, and she led her visitors to the revolving door.

Gray rejoined a surlier Grant at the bar.

'I knew you were a tosser the moment I clapped eyes on you.'

'You flatter me, Grant.'

'Anyway, where did you say you trained?'

'Somebody I worked for paid for me to go on posh courses. That was after she'd taught me everything she knew.'

'And not only about cookery too, I bet.'

'No. We got on very well. Upmarket guest house. For walkers with cash. And I got to do their ratatouille, their couscous and their assorted risottos.'

'Shut up about food, will you?'

'And then somehow – it all got too difficult. Her man in the city, I called him her venture capital. Giles. He appeared back on the scene. Dragged her off to France.'

Myron had resumed playing ballads the FM stations wouldn't allow their listeners to forget. His novelty was lessening. 'Jealous Guy'. 'Hey Jude'. 'No Reply'. But at least he sang them as if they'd just come to him in his shower.

'So you came late to the business?' Grant was still insinuating shortcomings in Gray's training.

'My mother had a great effect on me, of course.' Gray

found from somewhere a note of fondness to soften his sarcasm, before smiling and continuing. 'If it hadn't been for her watery ham-bone soups I wouldn't have had the incentive. I figured food had to taste of something. I should really be grateful to her, shouldn't I?'

'Yes,' Grant joined in the praise to mothers. 'Me ma started me off too. She won't let me near the cooker even now.' Grant lifted his glass, held it up to a water jug and chinked it. 'We have some giggles, the countess and me. I go up the bingo with her some afternoons. I try and win her these little presents – stupid ornaments. She knows where I go late nights.'

'Here, you mean?'

'I mean the friggin club, don't I, soft lad. I'm expected there now. I couldn't drag a bastard like you along, I don't suppose?'

Gray shook his head without quite registering the request. Before he could think of any suitable excuse Grant was lumbering off, squeezing past chairs. Before the swing door he mimed a seaman's wave, as if from a peaked cap, over in the direction of the bar. Another wrong-footing. Blame it on the brandy. Order another and make the fuddlement worse. Myron had stopped playing now, gone without him noticing. Or start on fruit juices, clear the fog. Somewhere in the mixture of lucidity and drifting it was possible to think straight and concentrate on a serious matter. The trick was catching whatever it was going to be by surprise.

It was Grant's fault for raising his glass to his mother. Next thing Graham would be back worrying over the whole who-was-to-blame business again. First time since when? The bar was closing up. Yes, he'd made the call. He would have to go along there next, pretend some apologies, offer some begrudged help, go through a few of the worst family misunderstandings, dredge up his father's name, talk about his own disappearance: all that. He was old enough, brave enough, now surely, to face the old lady. When he was more settled.

Graham recognized Michelle at the art gallery shop from the way her basin-cut thick brown hair shook as she reached up, then crouched down for a postcard of a painting to send a friend. He pressed a hand on the card of her choice, turned over a cartooned and screen-printed face in hope of reading the name: Warhol.

'This'll give her a laugh,' Michelle explained.

Over her shoulder he read what she'd written – *Still searching for him. No luck* – and it was a mystery to him.

'Because of what you write?' Gray asked.

'No, because of where I am. I told her I'd get away. Other people have it in their head to go to America. Not me.'

They sat on bar stools to drink cappuccino coffees. He spooned the froth to one side of his cup, disturbed the sediment of grounds and unmelted sugar granules so that they floated to the surface and pulled froth down again with them. It impressed him that she was someone who knew her own mind; raised a worry of his own that he himself might not always be. Gray probed her for the possibilities of the morning. She was meeting two Spaniards outside the museum at eleven for a quick walking tour of the moorings, then a return trip on the ferry, spot of maritime history, as much as they needed to know – sinkings, the Atlantic liners, etc. Her morning so far had been a beat boom talk to a party of Germans outside the site of a cellar club, which she'd laced with allusions to the significance of Hamburg.

'You must have done your homework.'

'It's like learning lines. Easy.'

'In all those languages?'

'I try to simplify the history anyway.'

Gray nodded energetically. 'Yes, history can weigh you down, can't it?' He attempted some elaboration. 'Least said—'

'Who are you sending yours to?' Michelle asked him.

'This is decoration for my room. It's in dire need.'

Just then Gray couldn't think of anyone suitable to nudge by post with a fondness for paintings. Certainly not the regulars at the pub in the village; they stopped speaking to him in the end because of his affair with Vivienne, the woman who'd been his boss. She wouldn't wish to be reminded, not now, not in France. And none of his exes, all married at least once.

'You're not from here, are you?' Gray wanted to quiz the girl further.

'The accent not good enough for you then?'

'I'm listening closely, can't quite catch it.'

'I'm doing the best I can.'

Then she translated the phrase into French, German and Spanish. And added: 'Who gives a shit? What's so great about authentic anyway?'

Graham guessed that this was not an invitation to debate, just a closing-off.

'Right,' she announced. 'I'm off.'

'I was hoping we could meet another day.'

Michelle made her move, started striding off down the gallery stairs, Graham following. Her patent-black Doc Marten shoes bounced her across the cobblestones to the next museum; Gray fixed on the point where her leggings stopped mid-calf. He caught up with her outside the museum. She shouted against the wind all her bookings for the day, and the next day too.

Michelle had to meet her next group just inside the glassed entrance to the museum. Graham leaned against a display case, while she chatted to the man in the souvenir stall.

'Heard anyone talking in Spanish, George?'

'I haven't seen no one with a big wide hat, girl. No.' He doffed a captain's cap to her.

Gray decided to wait. He enjoyed watching her in action. He leaned over quietly to study a dredger in a glass exhibition case, all the ropes and capstans, all the portholes, the painted plumb-line, the shining brass screw – all modelled meticulously to scale. The engraved label informed him that this dredger had been active on the river until 1964, then replaced by something that sucked the silt more efficiently through a vacuum-cleaner hose.

'No sign of your Spaniards then.'

'They're late.' Michelle fingered her watch.

'I was having a look in here earlier.' Graham wanted to begin one of his sly queries, they could be tin-openers. 'Those dredgers must still be fighting a losing battle. I mean the river doesn't get any cleaner, does it?'

Michelle needed to check he was serious, not teasing her. 'Let me tell you,' she started her piece. 'I've found out about years of criminal neglect. All the chemicals out of the pipes upriver. And oil straight into the water. Who would notice? Totally blind to the danger.'

'Do you ever sleep? Or shouldn't I ask?'

She ignored the question. 'You might be interested, I don't know if you are, but some people I'm in the campaign with, we're doing a big clear up of one so-called beach, upriver.' She pointed hard into the glass. 'It's no more than stones really, below the promenade. One low tide, don't know when. We need all the help we can get.'

'Well, I'm a willing body.'

She checked his seriousness, searched his face for innuendo.

'I mean I'm interested, of course I'm interested, I care.' Gray was believing in his own commitment even as he claimed it. 'I try to do my bit for the environment.'

Michelle stood more squarely and seriously than the amenable tourist guide of five minutes before. He could believe from this intensity she'd been a student not so long ago.

'We can sometimes get the press along if we manage a good enough stunt. I know a few of the reporters. It all depends how much other news is breaking that particular day. Last time I made page five with an oil-soaked cormorant across my breasts.'

Gray tried to imagine the picture. Her breasts.

She was going on. 'Gulls just aren't so pathetic, are they? Too common.'

'Too stroppy,' he added.

'But it's very valuable to us if we can raise some awareness with these photo opportunities. New membership, even sponsorships, that's what we're interested in.'

'Yes.'

His flat response woke her out of the recruiting speech. 'And you say you're still interested?'

Graham would have to consider how far he wished to follow her, give her support. He would also have to gauge how much she might wish him to. He'd only been in the city a matter of days; he couldn't be very sure of people.

'I'm still trying to hear that accent.' He threw at her: 'Is it Ireland somewhere?'

'Not in the least bit important where a person starts off.'

'Quite agree.' She was a mobile and ambitious person. But Gray was thinking as much of his own accent, flattened by years of other places, blunted by anonymity and now only sharpening again with the first warmish honing of curiosity. 'So how do you find the time to clear beaches?'

'Nobody finds time.' Michelle was sounding defensive. 'You have to make time. All completely voluntary. If you want to help out you can come along. Only if you want to though. Nobody's forcing anyone. It's just that I'm planning a look round next week – halfway along the old promenade. I'm hoping to fit it in with my running training.'

'Running too? You've got it all organized, haven't you?'

He admired Michelle's energy and purpose, she had this serious side that complemented the professional fun person. Nonetheless he had a desire to tease her, press her towards change, slow her down to his own speed; just as he wished to speed himself into change too, if possible.

'In fact I'm not sure if I quite believe you sometimes.'

She hadn't heard him. Before she could even notice his attempts at pressure Michelle had swivelled hard on her heel at the sound of Spanish voices.

'Ah, Señores González y Martínez. I'll be seeing you, Graham, yeah? The so-called beach by the promenade, you know it? The railings by the steps. Wednesday morning.'

Gray thought he might care enough. The sunlight through the museum's glass walls made him squint. He knew the promenade she meant and the silted rocks of a beach. The model dredger put him in mind of his father; they must have watched one on the river together, shifting the silt in an elevator of buckets, dumping it later at sea.

Michelle was back working now and oblivious to him. He slipped his postcard into a jacket pocket. He could always drop his mother a line, let her know in writing he was here, give her a shock. But what would she make of a rust stain by Rothko? No, for the time being the postcard might as well stay on the wall of his narrow room next to the light switch.

At the hotel that evening, late, after the end of his shift, Graham was scurrying down the top-floor corridor, needing the toilet. A cowboy-rangy figure with a guitar by the neck turned a corridor corner.

'I want a word with you, Mister Mouse.'

'I'm just off to bed, Myron. Whacked, you know. "Hard Day's Night".'

He expected the guitar to be hiked horizontal and a song to start.

'Are you trying to get inside little Michelle's pants?'

'I find her quite intriguing. Is that the same thing?'

Myron's hand made a fist and stroked the wall. He was thinking, reconsidering. 'Anyways, Gra-ham, take it from me she's a prick teaser.'

'You're telling me she's teased yours? She took you half the way there.'

'Just my warning.'

'I'm waiting for my slash, Myron, OK?'

Myron stepped back. But when Gray had adjusted his clothes and walked as far as the lift door, Myron was still standing there.

'I can tell, you know. The twang, just sometimes I can hear it. You people say we haven't got an ear for them. You *are* from these parts?'

'As if it was a birthright.' Gray's reply came out sharp, almost resentful. 'To have started out in the same place as someone famous. OK, I was born here,' Gray told him with more equanimity.

'Is that all you can say? When so much – I mean – began here.' Myron fingered his guitar head, twirled it twice.

'Purely accidental. The history and the geography, it might have been Memphis or New Jersey. It might have been Ohio.'

'I came a long way, man, to experience this place. No shit.'

'You've come nearly thirty years too late. I thought I was stupid turning up again twenty years behind.'

'I'll stay till the great man comes here.'

'Who might that be, Myron?' Gray would tease him. 'Christ himself?'

Myron could give murderous looks. Then he set out his request. 'I heard he's visiting soon. Look at me. Go on. Everyone back home tells me I'm like him.'

Gray looked over Myron's chubby face, wide eyes, his helmet of dark hair.

'You'll have to give me a clue.'

'You listen to my songs, don't you?'

'Your songs? Not yours, Myron, someone else's surely.'

'Yeah, go on, that's the clue, asshole.'

'I think I might have guessed.'

'Right. You've guessed, so why not straight out with the name? How you go about things, you people, round and round. So I'm saying: when McMichael himself, as if you didn't know already, comes here on his visit, I want to meet him and talk to him. I need to get close to that guy. It's imperative.'

'You want his autograph, is that all?'

'I haven't come this far for a name in an autograph book. I'm not just a fan. I need more.'

Gray was beginning to gauge an unlikely seriousness about his interest.

'Get this, Gra-ham. You know the manager better than me. He talks to you. So you have to find out the details, I need to know. Right?'

Myron poked a thick finger hard into Graham's chest. He noticed a metal plectrum still attached to one finger.

'You just bought my services, Myron.'

Gray wished to keep the joking going because there was an earnestness in Myron he took exception to. Myron dumped his guitar behind the door of his room, pulled his brown leather jacket out, without actually stepping over the threshold, pressed for the lift – the elevator.

'I don't even mind your singing really. No, I mean that as a compliment.' Graham's truce offering.

'A shower is what I really need, Graham. And a room that has one. You can stay in a shithole like this. I can't. So long.'

The windowless room was narrow, it was true, the ceiling was high. It was always dark without the lamp switched on.

But it was somewhere he could try to sleep when his head was still buzzing from the day. Because the day's objects passed before his eyes once and then ghosted again when he drank, when he tried to sleep and again when he woke early. He reached for the exercise book he'd bought from the shopping street, made wholly from recycled paper. Switched on the lamp. He didn't have much energy to scribble more in the notebook than a few notes about gulls at the water-front, some sentences about other people, the new ones, and the odd phrase – Douglas, IOM – that might be the start of some hard recollections that pressed: his father, his mother, all that. Light out, try to sleep instead.

5

1957

The view from the first-floor bay of the Isle of Man boarding house looked right on to the prom: vista of the bay, glimpse of the harbour. The boy had to wait for the green-grey vegetable soup to arrive; fatty swirls would open and close like the pulsing of amoebae. He played at unfolding olive-green linen napkins from their tarnished silver amulets. Lunch was always an interruption to any day's possible explorations. Afternoon might include his bare legs dangling from the harbour wall, and with each lowering into the water he might be folding lengths of green hand line over and over the frame – if only his dad would buy him one now early in the holiday, not at the end, and he'd be happy, he'd be a fisherman, hook, line and ledger weight. Or could Dad be persuaded to pay for a boat trip into the bay to jerk mackerel flippery into the dinghy? And then they'd be one of those brave little boats you would see when you looked down from the headland, matchbox-size, making arrowheads on the flat water.

The boarding-house formality of the table setting gave the three of them an encouragement to talk.

'When we're looking down from the headland on to the water,' the boy was asking, 'do the dark bits mean shoals of fish?'

'They're reflections of cloud, most probably': the father,

only half engaged, nibbling at the dry triangle of bread intended for soup-dunking.

'Even when it's completely blue sky?'

His mother was trying to secure her napkin nervously at the collar of her blue flowered frock.

'Wind, then.' His mother wished to settle it quickly. 'Ruffles of breeze on the water. Will that satisfy your blessed questions, child? Or seaweed. Or different depths. Or rocks underneath. Take your choice.'

The father was surprised by his wife's agitation.

'But not fish?' the boy persisted.

'No of course not, not fish – how many do you think there are in the sea?'

The boy hadn't given fish numbers a thought, but all around the harbour were stacked mackerel in crates, herring boxed for smoking, crabs in pots, flat fish he didn't know the names of, dogfish slapped across the cobbles for herring gulls to rip at. Fish was the smell of the harbour; mixed with coal smoke from the ferry boat's orange funnel.

'Did I tell you?' The mother began her announcement with a cough. 'Lydia and Jack came over on the boat last night.'

'Your sister, why? When was the diplomatic mission?'

'We had tea and a cake in Reece's a few weeks back. We're sisters. Eight years is too long not to speak. But Jack's not well at all. Not his eyes this time: it's his heart. Anyway she said we'd be sure to bump into them on the prom. This afternoon probably.'

'Is that an appointment you've made between yourselves, without telling anyone else?'

'We all know you were never comfortable with Jack. This is a special trip for him, maybe his last, you never can tell. The boy's never seen him, has he? He was, I mean he still is a fine figure of a man.'

'Whom we've all had to look up to – and did you realize that comes hard to some of us?'

The mother was trying to piece together some picture of the man, while the soup bowls were carried away: 'But he was an educated man. You never saw such books and pictures. I should know, I dusted the things. Fat Charles Dickens books and all of those others. And a long row of grey and blue James Conrad's.'

'Yes, you skivvied for your sister, didn't you, and cast covetous eyes on her possessions.'

Lamb with large new potatoes and carrots arrived.

'Thank you. I didn't mind helping Lydia out, being only part time at Mrs Bulstrode's shop. And she'd a lot on her plate with Jack. Remember, I always liked nice things quite as much as Lydia. It's not my fault I married a Philistine.'

'Don't get biblical with me. I remember, don't you go thinking I don't. Because then it really was Exodus, wasn't it? And you got your marching orders.'

She had expected a reliable lack of interest from him, and now she was surprised at this sly attention to detail. 'Don't talk soft, will you?'

She never addressed her husband by name. Out of habit she turned to her son: 'Carrots make you see in the dark, you know, Graham.'

'That was always a mystery to me,' the husband said. 'I never did find out exactly why you were ostracized. Just accepted it.'

'Everything's a mystery to you – in a pickled haze all day, what do you expect? If you must know, she didn't like me talking to him. That was the up and down of it. I was being too familiar. The man liked me to talk to him. And I was a good listener. The man's sight was poor at the best of times and starting to get worse. And I didn't mind reading to him from one of his books. Oh yes, he was always asking me to read the one called *Youth* – which I found a bit boring, all ships and no love, and another one which made him cry, made me cry, a couple of softies for five minutes, he cried about this captain and his daughter in Malaya or somewhere having trouble steering his craft, his craft, that was the word, because of his eyes, you understand. Lydia didn't have the patience. I did. And let's face it, she wasn't the Brains Trust. Third one along he'd say, always the same, James Conrad you know.'

'Joseph. Joseph.'

'What do you mean? You're Joseph, if you need telling. What do you know anyway? Finish up them potatoes, Graham. Lydia went funny of course. Started saying things, didn't want me in the house. She couldn't accept that his eyes were going. I told her. She told me to stop interfering. That was it. Things were said. Not my fault she was barren. I felt sorry for him, didn't I? Are you listening to me?'

'Oh I just let the record play. A good thing you were banned if you ask me. Less trouble with Lydia. But then there was ructions over visiting him in the eye hospital – without her say-so.'

'What was so wrong about that? I took him some flowers – he reckoned he could just make them out – bright yellow. Where were you anyway – the Grapes, the Prince, the Coronation? Take your pick. Years ago.'

'Eight. Some people still remember.'

'Water under the bridge. Some can forget too. My sister's talking to me again. Wonders will never cease. Hello stranger, I say. All in the past, she says. I say I should think so too. Me, I'll be pleased to see Jack again.'

'I bet you will.'

'And a chance for the boy,' Joe suggested. 'The poor man's old now.'

'He's not interested in a blind old man, is he? See, he's staring out of the window.'

The boy had heard arguments like this at mealtimes before. It didn't mean they were talking properly. It was only another sparring match – but more rounds because there was a subject, the Captain, for a punch-bag. He didn't even listen now. His attention was on the promenade where a toast-rack tram had stopped to unload more holidaymakers. The passengers hopped off the running board. The horse pulling the tram rested while he waited, extended a hosepipe dick and peed a torrent on to the rails. The boy giggled and covered his mouth as he turned back to the table.

'It's not funny, my lad,' his mother pointed out. 'Your Uncle Jack's a sick man. You wait.'

They waited mid-promenade – halfway from the harbour and headland. They claimed a bench set in the sea wall, placed a *Daily Express* and a plastic mac on the wood. The boy was impatient to step down on to the pebbly shore. The father had his eyes on the pub tables of the seafront hotels, open all day, Manx law; they were already beginning to fill and conjure their easy friendliness for him. He talked to the deckchair seller about custom and they both consulted their watches. A ferry had just manoeuvred out of the harbour and begun the voyage back to the mainland. The mother scrutinized every walking handholding couple, every family with arms linked for solidarity strung across the prom; every elderly couple especially, every person having to be helped along the walkway; every person in glasses; everyone short. The boy had resorted to counting how many of the children, whether in khaki shorts or yellow cotton frocks, were licking ice-cream cones; they couldn't cost very much.

She knew her sister's hair, its parting and its bun; she also knew the height similarity of the two; she'd been searching the oncoming faces for a stately couple, him upright, her busy; him agreeing to be guided, her drawing attention to her leading. Everyone else had open-necked shirts or floral frocks and gave themselves to the breeze. Lydia wore a cream cotton raincoat and Jack's was a heavy navy gabardine, double breasted, belted tight. His face was rose, his nose only pitted and purple.

'Here they are.' She attempted to share her excitement with her family: 'You didn't believe me. I said they were coming.'

They were intent on ice creams and deckchairs.

'Yes, we're here. We made it.'

'Was the crossing rough?'

'Well, *he* wouldn't notice. The rest of the ship could have been vomiting into the wind and he'd still have his Guinness.'

Captain Argent was half turned away, face to the sun. Not laughing. As if embarrassed at his blindness, or at his wife's words.

'Jack, you know who it is, don't you?'

'Course I know who it is,' he wheezed; then whispered: 'The voice is Cissie's.'

'It's me. It's Cissie all right. Bless him.'

She wanted to reach forward and pet him, but her sister stood in front and questioned her first.

'So where's Joe hiding? And where's the boy?'

'They're sitting right here. Joseph. Graham. It's Lydia and Jack. Come and say hello to your uncle. Don't be frightened.'

The boy was hesitant. This didn't look like a fine, much photographed, bearded man in uniform. This was a slow fat red man in a belted raincoat in the middle of summer.

'Are you my Uncle Jack?'

'According to your mother I am. Yes. Let me shake your hand.'

Two purple-pink hands like work gloves clasped the boy's bony fingers in a shaking jellyfish.

'Is he growing?'

'We hope so. He's starting to give cheek, I know that much.'

'That's good. Is Joe there? Hello, Joe. I'm here one last time – in heaven where the pubs stay open all day.'

'I'd have to agree, Jack, it's a great convenience for someone like me too.'

'Plenty of people all around. I like that, but you see I don't have to look at the faces in the crowds.'

Lydia spoke up for him: 'He's lost all vision now. And his heart, you only need to look at the colour of him. Blood pressure.'

'No – don't say – Lyd.' The boy's mother had been quiet and having difficulty joining the conversation again.

'Cataracts, Joe. Did you know? Can't see a pint glass in front of me now.'

Lydia tried to divert them from the subject of health. 'So, how's the holiday working out, Ciss?'

'Oh shut up, Lyd, will you?'

The Captain had finished his politeness to Joe Connolly. He turned his bulk more towards Cissie now. 'It's Cissie I can hear, isn't it? Is it the girl?'

'Yes, love. I'm here, Jack, it's me again. You remember. Let me give you a hug, dear man.'

The boy's mother couldn't help but weep as she pushed herself into his raincoat belt. She seemed like a girl at a dance; her body lost all its weight. The old man's fat red fingers pressed firmly the flower print of her frock.

'I can't see you. How have you been, child?'

'It's been too long.' She cried into his shoulder, sobbed out her next confession – 'Too long' – to the blind man standing in the middle of the promenade. Their loud embrace blocked the promenade traffic. Passers by wondered if St John's Ambulance should be called. The boy's father's silent embarrassment became a turning away. Still people walked at him. He looked to their faces to mirror his own dismay. This wasn't a holiday scene, the boy shouldn't be witnessing this, it shouldn't be taking place on this promenade in broad daylight in full view of hundreds. The holiday was meant to heal. A special effort by man and wife to be in one place with the boy and not tear at each other for advantage and blame; the boy surely deserved better.

'Come on, Graham,' the father urged. 'Let's go for our long walk. Your mother obviously needs some time to talk.'

She was still convulsed with grief and speechless. Lydia helped her sister to the bench they'd been sitting in earlier. A bewildered couple decided it was time to vacate their seat of the day. Lydia went back for the old man, stranded mid-promenade. She led him carefully to where Cissie slumped, and positioned herself firmly between the two of them.

'What a show you made of us, Cecilia. In public. What's got into you? Are you not well? You've really cooked your goose with Joe now. Don't you even think about the boy? Or me, for that matter?'

Lydia pulled a ball of knitting from her shopping bag and resumed her brisk finger work silently.

Father and son strode away harbourwards. This direction was better than failing to sit still while adults talked about nothing sensible. The boy chose his moment to ask some questions he'd stored up.

'Can we go to the harbour? A fishing trip doesn't cost much, you know. Or will you buy me a hand line? I've seen one in a window just along the front. I can sit there on my own, you wouldn't have to watch.'

They neared the quayside. The father tried to explain to the boy: 'Don't worry about your mother – she gets upset sometimes.'

'I wasn't, Dad.'

'I don't especially want to stay where all these people are.'

'Why not? There's always people on holidays.'

'Right. I'm not made of money, but you can have an ice cream. Let's walk up to the headland. I'll race you.'

That was more like it. What was called holiday. The father

started a sprint and the change bounced in his pockets. It stopped him stretching his legs properly. The boy pulled away steadily, won easily, pumped and puffed his way to a pleased red face up the incline. He gained height without realizing. Houses, boarding houses, all with steep garages and short gardens – chimney tops busy with jackdaws. A gull lifted from over one edge, greeted the boy. Cry: the boy was exhilarated. The higher he went the more he was able to see. A cormorant jumped from its rock perch below, pitched into a level flight diagonal out to sea. The mystery of the patches on the water again. He forgot his father, pushed on to get first to the top of the headland – and look back down at the grand ferry at its mooring (Was it really as big as a Cunard liner? It was the same colour funnel), the sailing dinghies, the fishing boats, the kids in miniature trying to fish; and then underneath a gull's gliding sweep perhaps then, his father eventually, head down, all worried-faced.

The boy pressed aching knees down with his hands to force the last climb to the top. Where was his father? No matter; there appeared a hut on the promontory's grassy edge, a hut unattached to other buildings, exposed and isolated above the height for buildings. Finches and gorse, yes, stonechats and heather. But not a hut like a garden shed, flaking green paint. There was a notice board. And when the boy reached there the lettering read: *Camera Obscura – Panoramic Views of the Bay*. Curiosity made him pull open the shed door into the room-size cinema dark.

He positioned himself on the bench inside with a reverence both for the dark and for the broad colour picture spread on a white table like someone's proudly completed jigsaw view. Except that the grass moved, the gull's flight cut across it; this was cine camera sharp, moving pictures. Next to the table he found a lever contraption; the table could be adjusted. There must be a swivelling lens somewhere above, a mirror somewhere, somehow, but it was so dark he couldn't see. He only knew the outside could be inside, with photographic clearness, only moving, never stopping. Finches darted faster, gulls swept more swiftly than ever he'd noticed before. He lifted the table slightly. He fancied he could see the movement of the clouds, the movement of the water in the bay, and the shivering the breeze made on every blade of grass on the headland. By accident the boy moved the lens out to sea, without control of the direction he was taking, not really knowing whether this would be a scene behind him, behind the hut, or to his right, or to his left. But he jerked the machine closer to land, where the rocks were roosts for cormorants, then suddenly up a foreshortened cliffside where rock doves and jackdaws trafficked; on to gorse and bramble thickets, and goldfinch swaying on the gorse, and he could see the yellow. Now he knew: this was a bird-watching machine. A fulmar wheeled its bullet body over a dark blue chill sea.

But he wasn't cold in the Camera Obscura hut. He felt warm with excitement at the secret of his hide and view. His father he'd forgotten. Now he turned the table 180 degrees for the path he'd run up, caught the backs of people. His mother and uncle wouldn't be up here. The old man could hardly walk. She'd be tending to him on the promenade, crying probably, while her sister knitted in the next bench seat. The boy caught sudden sight of his father though, walking wearily, pushing fingers through his sparse hair. The man didn't know he was being watched. He couldn't call to him. Sad. His hand pushed his hair ends and the wind gave them a waver. In fact, the wind's influence exaggerated the quiet. The boy began to feel uncomfortable, hot inside where outside seemed so breeze-cooled.

He wanted another focus and tipped the table to hold something other than grass, blown grass, disappearing over every edge, grass agitated by the day's breeze. And then he held in his panorama two adults sitting on the cliffside, as if picnicking, in fact half lying, about to kiss. He wondered why he hadn't caught them before in the grass. Now he's frightened of the control he's found, to have this advantage over them, when he doesn't know what their canoodling will amount to, the man's shirt white and billowing, her frock flapping. He decides he won't move the lens again, won't look for parents, but instead he'll fix this position, the one he's found by accident, in case he loses what he might see. He magnifies the focus and the girl reaches forward to the older man, paws at his shirt, presses a hand inside to his stomach. The boy can see the man's head drop, he's nearly bald, older than her, old enough to be her father or uncle. The man laughs and on this screen the laugh is silent. Their every movement is slow in spite of the still speeding grass by their legs and the sea over shoulders, shadows all across the surface. She leans herself forward, appears to adjust her own clothes before spreading the material of her frock over his legs. He has a grip on her arms at the shoulder, her arms are tanned, his skin sunburnt red. She raises herself to him slowly, then jerks down, jerks up; his fists pull her up then down, jerking, the boy sees, and not a sound from the clinch, but the boy's palpitations and a hot sickness all through his body. She falls sideways next to the older man, as if happily to roll down the cliff with him and into the sea. His arm now presses over her, she's cemented to his arrangement of legs. The boy doesn't know what he has witnessed: a beautiful torture, a touching death scene in a film; or some other betrayal that adults contrive.

The door clunked hard and spread right open. Light from outside intruded suddenly.

'Is this where you are? I thought I'd lost you.'

The boy gave the lens and table a hefty push, sent all scenes kaleidoscoping. Breeze, grass, water, gulls thrown into sickening motion again.

'Bird watching, Dad. Is that all right?'

'You look white. Are you OK?'

'It's hot in here.'

'It's much too dark, Graham. We should be getting back to see what malarkey your mother's up to now. Back to the promenade. Never mind the birds. When I've got my breath back at least. Makes you dizzy up this high, doesn't it, Graham?'

6

1990

After closing the shop for the day, Marva made her usual call to the flat at the back of the shop to see the old lady. Dozing in her chair. She pretended to complain loudly to her about the temperature she had to keep the shop so the blooms didn't dry out.

'A good day?' Mrs Connolly asked, with an attempt at interest.

'Not nearly as exciting as the radio,' said Marva.

'The radio is quizzes about pop records. The TV is horse-racing. What do I want with any of those?'

'Ask me another, Mrs C.'

'If business is quiet, why don't you try for the hospital pitch again? I used to do it when I was your age. Just a little stall at visiting times.'

'So how do I manage to be in two places at once? In the shop and at the hospital.'

'You close up the shop and you take your bum down to the hossy, sit there for two hours a day and you sell the poor visitors flowers already wrapped in cheery paper. That's what you do, Marva.'

'Not today I won't.'

'I'll keep on at you.'

'You do anyway. What's the difference?'

Marva stepped into the kitchen and slipped Mrs Connolly's boil-in-the-bag beef into water, opened her tinned carrots, and mixed her powdered mashed potato. She was wondering whether to tell her about Graham.

'How was the meals on wheels today?'

'It was pork and it was dry. And untouched by human hand. Whereas whatever you make for me, Marva, is ambrosia, believe me.'

'You've only had rice pudding once that I know of and that was out of a tin.'

'Don't think it's not appreciated. Just because I don't hardly touch it.'

'You mean you like it really. Even though I'm throwing it away and scraping it into the bin?'

'Yes, Marva, that's what I mean.'

'You could have fooled me.'

She placed it all on her tray. Mrs Connolly pushed at it with her fork.

'Pass us my teeth, Marv, they're in a cup by the bath.'

She stepped into her bathroom. Rails around the toilet pan, rails along the bath side. Everything so she could manage herself now that her health was leaving her.

Marva decided to tell her. 'He rang me today. A call out of the blue yonder.'

'Who did? Another fancy man? What colour this time?'

'No. Your long-lost son. You remember, the one who rang me from the country a couple of years ago.'

'Well, you're honoured, aren't you, Marva? He hasn't spoken to his own mother for twenty years. My husband's funeral.'

'Just checking to see if everything's all right, he said.'

'That's thoughtful of him, I must say.'

'It's a start, let's look on the bright side, Mrs C.'

Her mandarin oranges and evaporated milk were placed in front of her.

'There's better ways I can think of getting in touch. Like in person, for instance.'

'But I thought you were oil and water, you two.'

'I can say with my hand on my heart I have wept buckets inside.'

'You're the water sign, of course.'

'Listen, Marv, maybe I don't show it, but my emotions are currents that run deep. Not so much nowadays, I'll grant you, but years ago, yes. Tears, and plenty of them.'

'Which must make him the oily one. Or does he think of himself as more refined?'

'That's a laugh.' Mrs Connolly pushed her glass dish away.

Marva raised her laugh.

'And you can shut your cackle, Marva. When do I get the royal visit?'

'He didn't say.'

'Oh yes? What else didn't he say?'

'He didn't say nothing.'

'Well I've got nothing to say to him either, Marv. Except he might be interested in one little item I happened to see in the In Memory column in the paper.'

She cleared her dishes away for washing up. She'd be going up to her own flat upstairs in the same block soon, to watch her own TV.

'You and the deaths, Mrs C. Give them a rest, can't you? In their graves or wherever they are. In your state of health you shouldn't.'

'I brood on things from yesterday, daft things from years ago, like they were now. Old people do. You wouldn't understand, child.'

The Corinthian Hotel hosted conferences in its function rooms. Men in suits and women in suits had name tags dangling from their lapels. Visitors from other countries, specialists in their field, came together and exchanged business cards discreetly. Local businesses made use of the rooms and facilities for their training sessions. The large airy room

Graham walked into had been carefully arranged according to the manager's stage directions. Flip chart, screen, OHP and a perfect circle of chairs, none larger or more important than any other. The front-of-house staff were smartly suited, but the kitchen workers and the entertainers helplessly scruffy. One large table behind had a tray in its centre, and a chandelier of Perrier bottles topped with tumblers for self-service refreshment breaks. The arrangement might have been for a televised summit conference anywhere in Europe, not an in-service one-off training gimmick for catering and front-of-house staff in the hotel.

One of the flip charts had already been written on in orange felt tip, neat and large: What is Quality? Underneath in smaller letters: Performance and Service. Peter appeared from a side door, leaned easily in front of a small table, inspected his shoes briefly before announcing the start of his presentation with two brisk coughs. 'The reason I've arranged this session today is simple. It gives me the opportunity to say well done for the good work you're already doing.'

Grant muttered as he chose his seat, 'That means we must be getting the sack. Or else the boss is moving on.' He peered into the bright green envelope folder on the chair.

'You'll see from the outline in your folders . . .'

This had the effect of making Jamie, Grant, Gray, Yvette, Siobhan, the cloakroom staff reach with interest for their instruction, then smile at each other.

'So to warm up I'd like us to try a little brainstorming on: Quality.' Peter spoke with a relentless cheerfulness. 'Not as hard as it sounds. I'll write your suggestions on this flip chart. You tell me in a word or a phrase what you understand by Quality. Bit like a word-association game really.'

'Bit like a waste of time,' grumbled Grant. 'Are we getting paid for this?'

Each time the manager uttered the magic Q-word, he

85

paused and pronounced it as if introducing a special usage from another more successful country. Others would become accustomed in time to its significance. The word itself made the manager's teeth project a self-satisfied grin. It was a transforming word. It had been for the manager, and could be for his staff too.

'Yvette? Can you push the boat out for us?'

The receptionist wasn't confident about her suggestion, but she was happy enough to offer something, as Peter well knew. 'What about: the best you can do?'

'OK. And Siobhan?'

'Pretty good, I'll say.'

'Jamie?'

Not as ready with an answer, but not unwilling. 'What about consistently high standard?'

'And right round to Graham. Let's hear your yardstick.'

He felt smug as he spoke it; it sounded as if he'd given it a little thought. 'Striving for something special.'

'Grant? Are you with us?'

'Good enough to keep your job.'

Laughs all round the table.

'Interesting answer, yes, Grant. Myron? Any inspiration from you?'

'Answering the call of your talent and destiny, number one. Holding the torch that great artists have passed on to you, number two. Three . . .'

'That should give us enough for our present purposes, I think.'

Peter picked out with felt-tip rings the definitions most conducive to his theme. He had written the others in smaller writing and in corners of the chart. The particular configuration of the circles on his chart gave him just the evidence he needed to speak further about Excellence and Commitment to it. As his sermon gathered momentum the hotel employees showed their first signs of restlessness. Jamie stood up and poured water for the others; they sipped and hoped it would give them the look of concentration. Watches started to be consulted.

'I want to make it clear' – Peter called his audience to order – 'that there may be some opportunities ahead.' This had the effect of forcing their attention. 'A very large event, or series of events, I'm told, where the Quality of our Performance and our Service is going to be vital. We must be able to hold the custom we already command and offer something extra on top.'

'Can I ask what this special event is?' Grant asked. 'Are we getting taken over?'

Peter deflected the question with a show of generosity to the round table. His face offered up an invitation for suggestions.

Myron spoke up loudly: 'I guess you've been given a date for the great man's concert? And he's staying here in this hotel. Michael McMichael here. That would be great – in my book.'

Graham, recalling something Michelle had mentioned when talking about her tour-guide work, guessed: 'Are the big sailing ships coming again?'

This elicited one of Peter's smirks. He tugged at the cuffs of his blazer, left then right. It was evidently the-right-thing-to-say.

'I've already seen all my chamber staff separately. And cleaning staff. We talked more briefly about this very same issue, about Waterfront 90. Everyone makes their contribution. We depend for business on our good name. This may be a window of opportunity. Which is why I've got you all here.' He coughed, poured himself a glass of water without hurry. This was his punctuation.

'Now then, with the person sitting next to you I'd like you to discuss your personal contribution, your personal performance with respect to Quality vis-à-vis Waterfront 90.'

Myron, who was paired with Yvette, stood up noisily. The chair was sent backwards two feet. 'Am I hearing this correct? We have to answer to you for our performance now as well as our pay cheque.'

Peter's chin pushed out in the most diplomatic gesture he could give of defiance. 'It is only voluntary, of course. I think you'll feel the benefit. It will focus your aims in relation to the general effort.'

Myron hooked his thumbs in his jeans pockets, gunslinger between shoots. 'What you could tell me about quality, man, I could write it on my ass. You could start by getting down to the bar to take in my act.'

'Obviously I wouldn't presume to advise you on the musical content. That is quality-stamped anyway. With the little beetle seal of approval.'

'What are you talking about, man? I do my job well. The audience applaud. That's my performance. I go out and get stoned. Everybody must get stoned.' Myron snorted a laugh as he made for the door.

The manager pushed his tie closer to his collar. 'Myron has reminded me of something else – we must save for another occasion this question of the use of bar facilities by hotel staff. But for the moment in your pairs you'll need to address your own experience of Quality. List in which areas you consider you're reaching a high standard, giving your best or providing what the customer expects. You might even think about how your present performance fits into your overall career pattern. Testing times ahead.'

A telephone call was paged to the manager. He made a crisply worded excuse, motioned them to carry on with their group work, signalled Yvette to take over if necessary.

'What career pattern, I'd like to know,' Graham complained to his pair partner, Siobhan.

'My performance is quite adequate,' Grant was claiming to his partner. 'I never spit in the soup.'

'Myron took a bit of a risk there.' Graham started to worry.

'What was it Teacher just said?' Siobhan was asking a regressive, blank-faced Graham. 'I hope you know what we're supposed to be doing?'

'Knees under a desk, I feel like I'm eight years old again. I mean I don't mind cooking, I enjoy it, but all this stuff . . .'

The training session had only applied some extra pressure to Graham's uneasiness about work. He was putting all the effort he could into this change of scene. A gamble. It was a larger undertaking than any he'd had before. More responsibility. He'd seen it as an opportunity. It was. Calling for commitment, which he was happy to summon up. Vestiges of ambition must have been somewhere in there too. This striving that he'd mentioned in the seminar must have been a submerged wish to make good. To make good what had been not good before. Self-esteem was a hard enough state of grace to reach, all the harder when the working route was running parallel to the ageing process. What Peter had called career path had always been a wiggly track for him, a cliff path steep up and steep down, indicated on an OS map by a broken dotted line. He had determination enough to stick to the path.

But Graham had imagined there would be next to no distractions. Which was partly why he'd taken so readily to the poky room without windows on the top floor. He had intended not to become too interested in the city, or entangled with its people. He had expected to get by without reference to his own former life. Did a new start always have to entail an accommodation of old starts too: all the false starts, the conceivable lives, the paths away, setbacks, falls, uncompleted relationships? He placed such faith now in the new things he tried. Running would be a challenge. Michelle, too. They had some shared concerns. Campaigning, as if certain things mattered in the world. Perhaps not running, just jogging. Easier for someone his age. Jogging back into shape. Jogging along and putting off the inevitable meeting with his mother. Jogging along regardless.

Peter marched back into the room and asked for verbal reports from each pair.

Top deck of the bus, Gray faced the flatness of the high department store walls, anonymous rooms above all the shop-front windows. He could look down on all the boarded up windows in churches and terraced streets. It surprised him that he was level with foliage most of his journey. This side of the city was nearly half parkland. The green spaces were all so close together a runner could connect each piece and hardly touch the city. The river promenade was only a walk from the park with giant gateposts, no gates, a boating lake, no boats, ducks, a few anglers, burnt bandstand, no band.

The road that he started down to get to the river was parkland too and playing fields on either side. His Auntie Lydia had lived not far from here. Just off from the river, but within sight of it, the glint visible between buildings. Her lodgers studied at the mercantile college that overlooked the river. Gray skipped down the broad steps to the promenade, stopped to take in the land opposite; what everyone called 'over the water'. Too far to read any activity except cloud movements, weather signs. Welsh hills beyond, faint as mist. Straight ahead: the river's deceptive width. A patch of woodland, a run of roofs, the oil terminal. Movement and stillness around jetties and tanks. Michelle and her friends wouldn't be scrambling on the mud of the shore to inspect any spillage or damage today. The tide covered over all the debris of the river bed, the slimed and silted bricks, the broken cakes of concrete. A heavy oily skin over everything, brown-grey water.

Track suits jogged towards him and past him. He converted his walk to more of a trot in response. There were other fools on the promenade. He searched the railings as he trotted, the lamp posts, benches and shelters for a group of young campaigners, or just Michelle waiting. All the shrubs in the embankment the length of the prom were overgrown. Council gardeners hadn't had time to cut back the broom and dogwood. Squashed beer cans, fire charcoal, Durex in the undergrowth. He walked closer to the water, hit the wire of the railings with the butt of his fist, twice between each post, until he had a rhythm going. The river wasn't any cleaner. Graham peered down for the gulls' dip and splash after the most suspicious flotsam; their heads weren't black at all, more like white with a brown spot, awaiting their full brownness next summer. Each had the business of flying round again to reclaim some more from the current.

Michelle in finest running gear was posted next to a life belt, thighs gleaming. Gray had never seen her still before. Then as he approached she was stepping on and off the kerbstone nervously. She waved in a sulky way. Head down. He hurried himself across to her.

'Believe me, it's filthy underneath, totally contaminated and disgusting. No, don't say it, I know. We got the tides wrong. It was a.m. not p.m. So no checking the shore for us today. Pissed off, you know.'

Her running shoes glowed with a fluorescent yellow flash. The black ski pants and running vest made a life-sized animated poster, plastered against the life belt's Day-Glo orange.

'You look like an advert for breakfast cereal.' Gray wanted to compliment her.

'Do I? Do I really?'

She might have been insulted. He was wanting to say something about freshness and cleanness.

'Something Swiss.'

Each of her appearances was hard to place in a sequence, though she was dressed and groomed right for each one. Graham searched for the connection.

'Obviously the others haven't come,' Michelle explained. 'I get a phone call an hour ago. Too late to let you know. We try to organize people, but it's all voluntary. A holiday comes along, or a drink or a game of football, something better, so-called, and this happens.'

'Thankless.'

'Not looking for thanks. There's too much to do.'

'Just someone,' Gray suggested, 'to check the tide times?'

'The problem doesn't go away though, does it?'

'Meaning the problem of people?'

Michelle turned to search the lines of his face, as if pressing a hand on his forehead to test his temperature. The quick looks she could give were like squeaks of hurt, pricked every time by crassness.

'Graham, I don't believe you're saying all this. The problem is the river. The filthy river, Graham, is the danger.'

She walked across the path to the railings, arms outstretched in exasperation; then gripped the top bar with an impressive anger. 'And the people who allow it, of course – if that was what you meant.'

Graham heard his name repeated like a child's classroom name, and here was a just accusation. Michelle kicked the stiff wire mesh that filled the gaps between the bars, which prevented children and balls from bouncing through; her running shoe kicked loose a fall of rust.

'Who are these people that help you, anyway?' Graham asked her.

They started to walk together, a friendly stroll to discuss a problem.

'Our group? Anyone – students, nurses, teachers, house-wives, lonely men. Do you want to join us? Add your phone

92

number to the contact list? Someone else to send their apologies.'

'I don't have a phone number at the moment; only the hotel. Soon, I hope.' But he wasn't in a rush. He hadn't given it much thought.

'Do you have much time to commit?'

'Not evenings anyway. The kitchen is always busy. I have more time in the day. But I might be interested in a general sort of way.'

Another of her hard looks. He could feel the wateriness of his 'general'.

'Anyway, Graham. Are we running or not? That's what I'm really interested in.'

Michelle was beginning her sequence of warm-up stretching exercises. One arm was a speech mark and it was jerked sideways; then the other arm. She stepped on her own foot and motioned to bend to the ground; reached with her fingers, not quite touching. Stepped off her one foot and immediately on to the other and reached again without even scraping the concrete. Straight to attention; a grimace to show it wasn't a random set of moves: this was a routine. Graham was trying to guess the next. But her last position was a knee thrust forward, a leg pushed back, palms pressing down on the thigh, one, two, three pushes from the pelvis; and change legs, one, two and three. Finally, and with triumph, Michelle smiled her readiness.

'What's so funny, Graham?'

'I couldn't think what you would do next. Like watching yoga. Or positions for sex.'

Michelle had a selective deafness. Heard or didn't hear. She looked down at his shoes. 'So they're what you're running in?'

'My country togs. I've got nothing better.'

Caked mud still on the uppers, laces once wet had dried

hard. Graham's training shoes had the roundness of worn cricket boots: shaped but not giving; potentially painful. His jeans were too snug for running.

'You'll be hot in them.'

'That's what I'm expecting.'

Michelle's first steps were those of a dancer miming running, lightness pretending effort. Graham shuffled his legs into a mechanical start. To begin with he was surprised that however graceful her steps were, he somehow kept level with her. The soles of his shoes thumped the ground, the inside of his jeans legs rubbed and the sounds that came from his mouth were grunts. He noticed he was noisier than Michelle.

'Did you do your running on the farm?'

One leg forward, then the other: it would get easier. Gray kept the effort going with concentration. He needed extra time to answer questions.

'What was that you said? Michelle?'

Concealing the effort was an effort in itself. He was aware of people walking more quickly than he'd seen them before. He was having to think about dodging them. There was the river, a space at his shoulder, moving in an opposite direction. There were the clouds, also rushing. And there was the weight of him squeezing breath from his lungs too quickly. Two feet padding the pavement too heavily.

'Are you not comfortable, Graham?' spoke Michelle a few steps ahead of him, evenly, as if from an armchair.

Gray could feel every join in the roadwork of the promenade; each little ramp between concrete slabs was a new clue to its construction. He pressed on the patches and strips meant to be level and seamless. But they weren't. That was the problem he had his mind on.

'I can slow down for you, if you like.'

'No.' Then as his right foot stamped: 'No.' And stamped

again: 'No, you go ahead.' Stamped: 'I'm fine.' Stamped again: 'Honest.'

A bundle of people were approaching. Young mother with pushchair. A broad-chested man with his dog. A priest and a girl student. A wheelchair was some way behind them. A dark-skinned woman pushing a pensioner. Gray slowed down to walking speed. The woman in the wheelchair was pointing.

'Are you OK?' Michelle asked without stopping.

Gray waved her on and stopped.

'See you then.' Michelle pranced off. An antelope, he'd lost her again, a sight to behold in oystercatcher colours.

Gray stopped to cough. Felt the clanging like metal in his stiffened legs. Head down to get the breath. The wheels came closer. Hot forehead, scalp liquefying.

'You should have known you'd never catch her.' A familiar growl. The wheels parked in front of him.

'I wasn't.' Gray couldn't complete a sentence. 'I wasn't even.'

'I told Marva to stop,' the old woman said excitedly. 'I said to her I think I know this person. Or used to. Never forget a face.'

She turned back to her young woman companion. 'If I'm not mistaken this is my son. Talk about me and my heavy breathing, Marv. What about this performance then? You want to be careful, my lad. You're not a youngster, are you? Let's not kid ourselves.'

Michelle had sprung clean away down the promenade towards the city. He couldn't catch her or stop her. Graham's head stayed down, the oxygen wasn't getting freely through yet. He could see knees covered by a tartan blanket, Hush Puppies on the footplate of the chair. A very familiar voice.

'I'm not in competition.'

'Didn't you see us then?'

'Let's say it was an enforced stop. I couldn't actually go on.'

'I'm glad we haven't held you up, then. Actually.'

Gray needed the time between questions to breathe easier. He raised himself to full standing height, heaved the chest, breathed through his nose again. It could get better with perseverance. He stood nose to nose with the young woman. The flare of her nostrils, snaking locks.

'You must be Marva. I knew you'd tell her. I just didn't expect us to meet so soon.'

'And shouldn't a mother know? Aren't I here? You have to tell me how you're keeping – leaving aside the wheezy chest which I suffer from too.'

'I'm OK, Mother. I thought I was anyway.'

Marva was slimmer, taller, finer, older than he imagined her. A woman more fully adult than the awkward young person he'd first surprised on the phone some years before. And she was amused, not cowed by his mother's tartness.

'Are you going anywhere special? Are we keeping you from some kind of tryst? Or shouldn't we ask, hey Marva?'

His mother had to be pushed round in a wheelchair. She had always been thin-faced and narrow-framed. Now her body seemed stooped and crumpled. But her voice, though perhaps huskier, retained all its former strength.

'What your mother means is, would you like to walk with us? We go this way – to the end and back – every week once a week. She doesn't walk much. My van's in the car park.'

'Is that really what she said?'

'Come on, Graham,' his mother said. 'What sort of witch am I?'

He was fighting for his breath again. There was always the struggle for oxygen.

'I'm your mother, remember me. I'm seventy years old now.'

96

'I'm sorry. Yes. You took me by surprise.' Graham bent to pat a hand lightly on her shoulder and brushed her cheek with a kiss. The hint of a wince from her; close up on her ageing body. 'Yes. Hello. Mother. I was going to—'

'That's better. I can shut my gob now. I'm not supposed to get myself excited, am I, Marv? Let's just the three of us enjoy the view.'

She did seem happier with the son's eventual greeting, however begrudged it was.

'Time to pipe down, Missus. Just because your son appears from nowhere after twenty years doesn't mean you're allowed to get excited. No.'

Marva laughed her high hoot of a laugh, open-mouthed then the teeth coming together in a winning wide smile. Mrs Connolly wheezed along too. Graham offered a conciliatory smile.

'It's not a great view though.'

Across river a succession of long tankers moved in on the tide, then queued for a mooring at the terminal. They anchored where it was deepest, waiting to unload their crude for processing. Gray found it difficult to judge how far away they were. The gulls and boats asserted different claims on the changing water.

'It's something to do, out of the flats. There's always something going on here.'

'Well, we bumped into *you*, didn't we?' Then Mrs Connolly coughed heavily and hawked something grey into a handkerchief.

So much that could be said and it wasn't the time or place. Graham had got his legs loosened enough to stroll. He strolled; Marva pushed; Mrs Connolly sat recovering from exertions, smiling to herself.

'I'll walk with you but you'll have to excuse me, I have to get back to the hotel, honest. I'm sorry.'

'We're honoured, aren't we, Marva?'

'I'm parked just at the end here,' Marva offered. 'We can give you a lift into town if you want.'

'I'm best on the bus, thanks.'

They reached the car park where her lightweight van shone clean pink and brown, next to a yellow and blue ice-cream van.

'See. Can you read the name?' said Mrs Connolly. 'A proper sign writer did that.'

'O-leander.' Gray thought about it. 'Sounds like something from Shakespeare.'

'Why ever not?' Marva defended her choice. 'Billie Holiday, if we're being precise.'

'No, Graham, this girl's got brains.'

Gray looked at Marva again. 'Apparently.'

The large field next to the car park hummed with the noise of aeroplane engines. Gray knew how close the airport was, upriver a mile, perhaps two. He looked up for DC6s flying in, dropping altitude suddenly from Jersey, Shannon or the Isle of Man. A teenage child twirled a brightly painted biplane in lifting and lowering circles. His friend held a transmitter like a mobile phone, swung another fragile model into flight, started up the same drone again. When they landed they bounced; when they ran out of fuel the silence was intense. The three of them, son, mother, companion, stopped to watch the aerobatics: no crash landings.

'Look, I'm going to have to fly, myself,' Graham offered nervously to his mother in the wheelchair. 'Due back in an hour. Sorry. Mother.' He turned to Marva: 'I'll arrange something. Soon.' Attempted a reassuring touch on Marva's shoulder. 'I will soon.'

Across the grass someone's border collie stiffened and directed himself to meet a soft black labrador close up, sniff round her. A hunched track-suited woman tugged on his choke leash, put a halt to the encounter. There were no children at the ice-cream van in the car park, only a white coat stretching out of a window for custom.

'Marva tells me you're at the Corinthian,' a voice from the wheelchair seat broke out again. 'Very grand. Is that what you always wanted?'

'Ambition' – Graham was immediately on the defensive – 'does sort of come into it a bit more now.'

She hadn't invited an explanation, but he started on the theme and immediately thought better of it.

'Obviously, before . . . before was very different.'

Still awkward, and it didn't give his mother a chance to find her own way through to kindness.

Marva waggled her car keys from her coat pocket, wedged the van door open, pulled the wheelchair back, hoisted Mrs Connolly across into her seat all in one movement before Graham could even offer to help.

'I'm keeping quiet,' she muttered to him. 'Can't get between a mother and son.'

Gray was resigned to the multiplying misunderstandings, added another for good measure. 'I'll come and see you both at the shop. Been meaning to anyway.'

'Don't rush yourself on our account.' The voice again, this time from the front seat. 'Nobody's any younger, are they?'

He jogged away, flat-footed. A vague wave meant to cover everything.

7

1957

Plane trees shaded the street and softened the pavements with foliage, their damp triangles littering the gutter, and always their cardboard bark patches unpeeling like the back of old jigsaw pieces. The boy's fidgety walk from the bus stop between, slightly ahead of, his two silent parents, stepping on the edge of all small puddles, didn't distract enough from a stomach still nervous. He had been led to expect a riverside mansion, not one of these narrow-fronted, deep-backed town houses, only differentiated by door colour, net curtain or brightness of brassware.

His mother tugged at a gate catch, then it was only one pace up to a step. The three of them crowded the space, his father tottering backwards with the boy's small black suitcase. His mother pointed out to him an arrangement of roses above the door, an oval of cut and bevelled glass. The boy's sideways view of the square bay window exaggerated the dark of liquid glass. Lydia's door knocker carried on bouncing after his mother's gloved hand let go; the boy thought he could hear an echo inside the house.

'Let's hope her ladyship's at home to visitors today.' Joseph Connolly broke silence.

Lydia pulled open the door wide enough to let the family in. The grey paisley whorls of her powder-blue housecoat caught the boy's eye.

'This is the day then. The boy packed off to his old auntie – and she's a stranger to him. The child's seen a ghost. Don't worry, I don't bite, son.'

'Graham's fine,' Cissie explained. 'He understands. I've told him what's been decided. He knows and he'll do his best.'

'The child's terrified. What a thing to put him through.'

The father had already taken the boy through to the dining room. A fire was building in the hearth, a smoking parcel of potato peelings to hinder its flames.

'Never mind all that now.' Cissie forced some cheeriness into her voice. 'Any chance of a cup of tea now, Lyd?'

The sisters walked to the kitchen: another fire, a black range with kettle steaming.

'I didn't think it would come to this state of affairs. I didn't. A couple of nights, you said, while you both get things sorted out for Joseph in London.'

A stout black teapot was at the ready, three scoops from the Chinese tin caddy, and the leaves were given their dousing; top on, then brown knitted cosy to muffle all the heat. Lydia wouldn't accept help with the tea tray, and the crockery was already laid out in the dining room.

'Here we are, Joseph. My tea is on the strong side, maybe not the kind of strong drink you like, but it's my house, isn't it?' Lydia pressed the tray hard on to the bottle-green chenille tablecloth.

And in the minute they all knew to sit tight while the tea brewed, Lydia coughed out her terms of business. 'As long as you know I'm not used to children. I can't give them any special quarter, it's not in my nature. He'll have to eat what we eat. I can't have fussers.'

'He won't give you any trouble.' Cissie defended the boy. 'I said already.'

'As long as it's understood, that's all.'

'So how's it working out with the lodgers, Lydia?' Joe tried to change the subject. He was reminded that even before Captain Jack's recent death she had begun taking students from the local maritime technical college.

'To be honest with you, Joe' – Lydia was addressing her remarks at the boy's father – 'it's easier without Jack. He wasn't very patient with them. Thought they made fun of his blindness. Truth was they were in awe of him.'

'Weren't we all?' the boy's mother chipped in, as she moved to comfort the boy. 'And wasn't that half the trouble?' Her voice rose. 'And nobody got near him.'

'Behave, will you, Cissie?' Joe shouted across the room. 'It's past, your fine Captain's gone.'

'Your man's right. I was only saying Jack felt overtaken by all this modern equipment that you see now. Maybe he envied the boys. I mean he'd seen sailing ships. Imagine that.'

'How can you say "your man" to me?' Cissie broke in. 'How can you, when you know very well that we are separating – legally? How can you pretend and chatter away about Jack like that. Honestly, Lydia. No wonder.'

Lydia began to load the cups on to the tea tray again.

'For pity's sake, Cissie.' Joseph fumbled to get a cigarette lit. 'Drop it, can't you?'

'What time's your train today anyway?' Lydia shouted from the kitchen. 'We won't go into all that again, will we, Ciss? No we won't.'

The boy's mother was still smarting. 'Why don't you go in the front room, Graham?'

'That's a good idea of your mother's,' conceded Lydia from the doorway. 'Any children that come here usually end up getting the cigarette cards out on to the rug. As long as they clear them up afterwards. But he's been here before, hasn't he, Cissie?'

The front room had all the early evening's light from the bay window. The glass doors of the rosewood bookcase reflected shapes back into the room. One large gilt-framed painting occupied an alcove's wall: long-horned highland cattle drinking, not a galleon, not a dhow. But it was a squat wooden cabinet the boy was directed to, with its own oval mirror and a drawer packed with cigarette packets, playing cards and a cribbage board. The boy pulled out the sets of cigarette cards; they stuck to his fingers as he peeled them from the safety of their boxes. Grim-faced footballers and boxers pulled on his finger skin; smooth-shaven music-hall stars shone in their top hats and wide smiles. The names meant nothing to him, but their faces were proof of some history before his own life. He marvelled at the brilliantine plastering down the centre-parted hair of so many smooth-faced cricketers, caps and county badges floating somehow in the air, signatures diagonal and unreadably wiggly. He didn't read the tiny blue print on the sticky backs of the cards; the information would have been meaningless. He arranged the sets, piled them and spread them, shuffled them and packed them, all the subjects, back in packs: the household hints, and lastly the most battered by use, the ships of the British Navy, all battleship grey, but different shapes when seen in silhouette. He wasn't interested, he couldn't find a single set for birds or aeroplanes.

The adults were watching him now. They had stepped into his room. His mother was looking fondly over the blue and grey book spines showing behind the glass; she read the titles without comment and turned to the boy. She had her raincoat buttoned up.

'We're going now, Graham. The taxi's come. Be good for Lydia. I'll have everything arranged for you and me in a matter of days. Stand up and say ta-ta to your father properly.'

Joseph Connolly stepped forward with his awkward formality. 'Well, old son. This might be it from me for a while.' The father pulled hard on a cigarette, breathed in through almost closed lips. 'Maybe quite a while if only you knew. I'll keep in touch, of course I will. I don't know.' The smoke was exhaled hard. 'I could just shake your hand, there, and give you a pat on the back, and then neither of us will embarrass your Auntie Lydia with tears.'

He turned to Lydia for help.

'Oh, I'll make sure he doesn't let the side down. I don't want my lodgers getting the wrong idea.'

They both turned to the boy's mother. Her white gloves and white handkerchief were greying, going pink with the wet at her nose and lips.

Lydia called from the doorstep. 'Let's leave the emotions to your mother, shall we? She's the expert. Go on, your taxi meter's running. Let's hope London's the answer to the whole how-d'ye-do.'

The door closed on the taxi's turning circle; the knocker repeated on its chrome sounding pad.

Lydia showed the boy how she could help replace each pack of collected cigarette cards and press them properly back into the wooden drawer. She knelt down on the rust-coloured rug, gathered cards to her. He thought she was making friends.

'So what did *you* think of the Isle of Man? Not as bad as your mother made out, surely? We haven't talked since then, have we?'

The boy did feel encouraged to talk. He didn't remember her very well, or talking to her; though he did the blind Captain in the raincoat.

'Well, I didn't get my fishing line. But I saw a Portuguese man-of-war floating in the harbour and it wasn't dead. And I saw two gannets and hundreds of cormorants.'

'You're the bird watcher, aren't you? Your mother said. Fancy that.'

'I've got really good eyesight. I don't need binoculars.'

Lydia hoisted herself up, pressed her housecoat flat. 'Lucky you then. What time do you go to bed?'

The light had gone from the room, the pink had turned grey. And she moved him to the other room and sat him in the rocking chair, while she pulled the curtains. The wood of each runner creaked on the linoleum. She poked the fire and stood up to adjust the two Dresden figures on the mantelpiece: a young shepherd in breeches and hose, a maid with a dove not far from her hand: none of them quite touching.

'What shall we talk about now? You'll meet my lodgers later. They want to work on the big tankers. They're probably out drinking now. They're going to be my comfort in my bereavement.'

'What's believement?'

'It's how I'm supposed to be now Jack is gone. I'm supposed to be distraught and beside myself with grief. And I'm not. Your mother's more upset than me. She can't help herself. No moral strength. But he died on me years ago. Your mother has no idea, just because she saw such a lot of Jack this summer. Luckily I've got my little job, this big house and those boys to see to.'

The boy was gazing at the heavy black clock in the shape of a Greek temple which squatted on the mantelpiece. The casing was carved with dome and fluted columns like a giant smoke-charred city hall. The white clock face had delicate metal fingers, roman numerals, but in separate windows were smaller dials that recorded the phases of the moon, and other inset sections with miniature skies in pastel blue and cloudy white to suggest the seasons. The minutes, the hours, days, months, years – the boy started calculating, backwards across the summer, then he tried forwards, before giving up.

'Your lodgers, Auntie Lydia. Are they like children, because my mum said you couldn't have any?'

'Did she? Well it was never proven. You wouldn't understand, you're too young.' She muttered the next part. 'But I'm glad to say Jack didn't bother me too much in that way.' Lydia coughed and poked the fire again.

'When he was older' – she spoke audibly again – 'he sat just where you are now in that rocker. And he never moved and he hardly spoke. He put weight on and he had the daftest of ideas. Trouble was he'd been too many places and read too many books. Gulf of Siam and such. Dissatisfied really. I mean: what did he want with that city show – all those tanks and horses and aeroplanes?'

Mention of the city show aroused the boy's interest; he understood what Lydia was referring to. 'That was the day,' he reminded her, 'the Frenchman fell from the sky.'

The boy had been playing planes in the dirt. He'd been on at his mother to take him instead of an uncle he didn't even know, and only heard of all of a sudden, it seemed, since their holiday. Which seemed particularly unjust. His mother wasn't interested in planes, nor his Auntie Lydia, and worse still, this uncle was blind. It was a waste of tickets, and he was the one who ought to have been asked, but nobody was listening. He recalled that strange day and especially the long shiver of fear that turned into hot panic by the cricket sight screen. Something had happened. Walking back over the fields with his father hadn't been any reassurance.

'I wasn't allowed to go, Auntie Lydia, but the Birdman from France jumped from the sky and I didn't see it properly.'

'Well, I'm sorry for you son, I am, but listen: my husband died that day. I'm afraid I haven't any tears to shed for some French pilot.'

'He wasn't just a pilot though. He was an airman. He was a Birdman. Everyone said so. He had wings.'

'Wings my eye. Angels have wings and no one believes in them, do they? There were all manner of foreigners doing daft stunts on that day, I know that much. I gave them no attention. And I can't say I'm very sure what my husband's interest was in a city show and all those people. In his state of health indeed. What got into his head I'll never know.'

'Mum wouldn't let me go. She wanted to go herself, she didn't say why. Not really.'

'Your mother, she's a clever woman. She had her reasons. And soft lady here, your Auntie Lydia, tagged along for the ride. She was so friendly with me all of a sudden . . . and I had no inkling. But we're sisters, aren't we? So that's all above board, isn't it? But it isn't, you know. Not in my book it isn't.'

Lydia was looking straight into the fire, mesmerized by the melting of the opening orange core of coals. She was fingering the pile of the chenille tablecloth and when her index finger pushed one way the green was almost silver, the other way the nap showed almost black. Different greens, this way, that; back, forth; her finger worried over the sudden changes.

'She's got this idea about a flower shop, and my husband's money, this special codicil whatever they call it, given over to her in his will, well, that's all very well. The solicitor says so. I suppose I have to wish her well. She's my sister, but people don't change. Meanwhile I have to look after these boys for the grand old merchant marine. I'll keep myself busy, don't worry.'

The boy didn't understand the half of what she was saying. He was tired. He was staring at the clock on the mantelpiece again, the clouds and blue next to the miniature columns of the temple.

'And you'll have to move house. A flat above a shop, if I know my sister. She's got such ideas.'

He knew that during this long summer everything had somehow changed; the complexion of everything, and mostly for the worse.

'Anyway, you get yourself ready for bed, and then when you're ready you can come down for your Horlicks. This is what I give my boys. See, I'm not such an old stickler, am I?'

The boy unclasped the black cardboard suitcase, unfolded his spearmint-striped winceyette pyjamas, never so ironed before, and took his gingham draw-string toilet bag to an eau-de-Nil bathroom. Squat brass taps forced a gurgling in wall-hidden pipes. Flannels and loofahs had a different smoothness, soaps were more carbolic; the chill of her water was a colder chill than home's; the towel he reached for rougher. Discomfort was what he must deserve, but with new smells. Milk boiling was the latest smell, he even imagined he could hear the hiss of milk bubbles on the pan sides. He took the steep staircase with enthusiasm, caught Lydia off guard, because all the rooms were dark except the kitchen where she cheerfully cursed her pans.

'It's you. You had me worried for a moment there. I'd better put some light on the subject in that dining room.'

The fire still gave the walls some friendly light. But the lightest scratching, sliding noise on the linoleum could be heard inside. Lydia stepped ahead of him, and he faced a steel-grey spread of her hair across her back; her bun was loosened and she was forcing on it a nightly brushing.

'You're not frightened of a few creepy crawlies, are you? I'm certainly not.'

The sudden dazzle of the electric light sent beetles in numbers scurrying back under the wainscoting.

'Every morning when I open the curtains here. Away they scuttle, the armies of the night, my husband called them. He couldn't see them, but he wasn't deaf as well, was he now?'

Lydia looked vulnerable at that moment: her hair, the beetles, the half-empty house.

The boy sucked the froth on the Horlicks, sipped the hot drink with some care.

'I don't blame your father. Don't you think too badly of him.'

The boy had almost succeeded in forgetting the arrangements being made by his parents. Looking ahead to the days after this day was beyond him, in spite of Lydia's attempts at reassurance. He stopped hearing what she said.

'My boys are late tonight,' Lydia concluded fondly, with a hint of disappointment. 'You won't see them after all. You'll be well asleep, by the time they roll home, the worse for wear I'll bet.'

The light switch was brass, not Bakelite, and made no click when the light went out. The boy was propped uncomfortably high on clean sheets and a weight of blankets. He was in the very dark room and only the occasional car passing brushed the cracks in the ceiling, brought half light to where he had to rest his eyes. Something to see, think on. A taxi turned; its chugging was the night noise of someone going off, escaping. In a strange bed the boy was trying to think: Was that the same as when someone died? Did they just disappear from your life, or stay as shapes and shadows across all these variations of darkness, as reminders?

8

1990

The tweed-overcoated man in the seat in front was reading
his appointment letter a third time, and folding it back into
its manila window. By leaning forward Gray could make out
the exact time – it was sitting on a dotted line in the middle
of a paragraph; the man would be two hours early and listen
hard for the names – all the wrong names – called indistinctly
into outpatients before him. Graham's bus stopped outside
one of the hospital's indeterminate entrances. Mostly elderly
passengers swaddled in coats, only the women gripping
overwrapped bunches of flowers. Someone needed directions
to a different hospital, she'd caught the wrong bus.

Graham walked away from the main road, towards a
parade of shops. Along the line of shop fronts – a news-
agent's, a wine shop, a minimarket – it was easy to spot
the name Oleanders, because its lettering and the colour
scheme (pink on brown) had been so neatly painted. The
shop was the end of the first block; a paved gap before
the next block. Gray glanced inside the flower shop as he
passed, but he could see only two female backs, shrugging
in unison, appraising a bouquet. In the gap two boys, ten-,
eleven-year-olds in training shoes, kicked a World Cup plastic football against the shop's high windowless wall, taking
turns to head and kick. Gray easily found his mother's flat,
ground level, adjoining the back door of the flower shop.

When he'd lived in the block himself it was a flat upstairs. He knocked.

The door took a time to be opened, and the pale-skinned face that glared out had the greeting ready. 'Ah, stranger,' Mrs Connolly remarked to her son, archly, 'I wondered how long it would take you to get yourself over here.'

The old lady hobbled forward, as if to walk past Graham and outside. 'I've told those blooming kids eight times already. Their mothers will get to hear from me.'

She managed to turn circle by gripping the door frame, picked up her walking stick from the umbrella stand, stalked quite sprightly up her hall.

'Yes, I made it. It's been difficult for me to take time off. I work funny hours.'

'I know: you're a galley slave, aren't you? Just as long as you don't drink the rest of the time. Like Joseph Connolly.'

He couldn't have expected her to speak warmly of his father, whom he could hardly remember. No photograph was visible, not even in a framed family group on her sideboard, taken at her elder sister's wedding, a grand reception at a hotel before the war: herself fashionable, gigglesome, looking up to Graham's Auntie Lydia and her seaman husband; Captain Jack and Auntie Lydia, both much more dignified. Also one portrait of the same man in naval uniform, with naval beard. Captain Jack, much mentioned years ago by his mother, and always an icon in the household. He remembered shaking hands with the Captain on a promenade once. Nothing else. And Lydia was in Graham's memory chiefly for the time and the place when he heard she had died – he had been trying to be a student in London. Was death in another place, reported in a letter, and read on a number 134 bus, was that really a death you could be expected to grieve over? Because it was only a matter of months before his father's. He had met up with his father in a pub in Muswell Hill and next thing you know he was dead, in his squalid rooms. Then the funeral, and his mother said what she said, and he didn't feel he could speak to her any more.

Mrs Connolly steadied herself at her settee back, pressing a red, swollen hand on her embroidered antimacassars (windmills, tulips) before lowering herself down. One armchair from the three-piece was missing; the room would only allow two and a small portable television set, magazine rack stuffed with out-of-date newspaper supplements, *Woman's Weekly*, *People's Friend* – somebody else's – and the current *Radio Times*. Two coloured prints edged in passe-partout on one wall either side of a perfect oval mirror. Lady in a yellow dress, toy dog in the folds of her lap; another called *Peonies*: patrician lady pensive with flowers. Graham had some recollection of most of the objects in this crowded room, in the rented council house they all first lived in, the one with the garden.

'So how many years is it here, Mother?'

'In this block since you were little – how long is that? Think back, will you? When did Mr Palm Oil up and off?'

'I don't want to, thanks.'

The contents would have been moved down once from upstairs to make it easier for Marva to service the shop; Marva would have moved in upstairs to be on hand.

'Marva carried down all my bits and bobs. My pictures, these old photos.' Mrs Connolly tried to stretch an arm back to motion round the room, hurt somewhere at her chest, winced. 'The few ornaments that Lydia passed on to me – the old clock, of course, the shepherdess. You know I always had my eye on them. And all my jigsaw boxes, naturally.'

Gray liked, actually liked, that about his mother, that she worked away at these picture fragments and took her time to piece them together whole, or as near as manageable. The thought of her jigsawing was his moment of weakness.

'I could try and come to see you more regular.' Gray

hadn't intended any apology to pass his lips. His visit was to demonstrate he could, and no hard feelings. No hard feelings, when most people's feelings, his own included, were just that: hard. Neither did he want to blame the woman all these years on for his difficulty in settling. Here he was attempting a kind of peace, no more than that.

'You could put a kettle on; it's three hours since my last. Marva's been neglecting me.'

'How's your health been? Apart from your legs, I mean.'

'It's not my legs, who told you it was my legs?'

'I saw the wheelchair on the promenade.'

'I've got no puff left, son. My lungs aren't taking in the air properly, too many years of this.' She pointed to a gold cigarette pack. 'The doctor tried to tell me and I said to him: Too late, I said. Damage done.'

Gray looked at the chest area where her lungs might be located. Yes, she hunched her lungs into herself.

'I'm OK. No need for you to worry yourself. Didn't you see from the bus, I've got the hospital just round the corner?'

'Are you under any treatment?'

'No. It's very handy though. I just wave a hanky out the door and they send an ambulance for me.'

'But you haven't had any serious falls, have you?'

'Any?' Mrs Connolly laughed. 'They were talking about fitting me with a cord I could pull, like a lav chain. I wouldn't hear of it.'

'What about a phone? Never had one fitted?'

'I don't need one, do I? The shop's got one. I bang my stick on this wall here, and Marva, my manager, can lock up the shop and come and see to me. She's my treasure.'

Mrs Connolly must have seen surprise in his face at such an admission of affection. 'But I can't go telling her, can I? I don't want her going soft on me.'

Gray knew soft wasn't what his mother liked to allow herself to be.

She changed the subject. 'That blooming ball. Listen. Bang blooming bang. There's a park around the corner. But they haven't got the energy for that, have they? Oh no.'

'It's only the same as I used to do. A kickaround.'

'Yes, and now look at you, reduced to making an exhibition of yourself puffing and blowing in plimsolls the length of the promenade. Chasing after a spring chicken too. Embarrassing your old mother and poor Marva.'

Graham winced again at the scratch of irony always in her voice. 'Do you want this tea or don't you?' he challenged her. 'I don't even know where you keep your teabags.'

Gray stepped out to the kitchen.

'Graham,' she shouted through. 'If I'd known you were coming I'd have baked – no I wouldn't, I never bake. I'm so close to the shops I can easy buy a cherry slab if I get a visitor. Big *if*, mind you.'

'I'm not hungry.'

'Good job. It'd be a fine how-d'ye-do if you went hungry – working in a big posh kitchen. I'd never have guessed that you'd have ended up with a cook's apron round your bum.'

Gray placed a tray on to her invalid's table-on-castors. Left side and perfectly discreetly like a table-waiter.

'That was my change of direction. A career in catering. And certificates to prove it. Felt right.'

Gray might also have been proud of his positive presentation of himself, if it hadn't been his mother he was trying to convince.

'I wasn't aware you ever had a career. I thought you were going to be an art teacher?'

'I was. I might have been. That or something else.'

'And you were good at English, weren't you? I was telling Marva. She's a great reader, you know. You should see all the dog-eared books in that shop. And wet through, some of them. But some days I quite understand she has to read, she'd die of boredom otherwise, because the doorbell just doesn't jangle.'

'What were you telling Marva? The way I remember it you never took much interest before.'

'Who had time for interest in those days? Remember I had my troubles with the man I married. And with my own sister as well, but you don't want to hear about that, it was before your time.'

'You're right about that.'

Graham rubbed hard with frustration across the furrows of his corduroy trousers. So much not to say. The visit was sufficient progress in itself.

'Pass me that ciggie packet, can't you?'

'I don't want to, Mother.' Gray felt peculiar saying that word to this naughty child.

She glared and threatened to raise herself from her chair. 'Pass it. We're beyond all that bad-for-your-health stuff now.'

Graham passed the Benson & Hedges. She smiled her satisfaction.

'Can't have tea without smoke.'

'You can,' dared Graham.

She was sipping tea from a rose-pattern mug.

'I know what I meant to ask you, Graham, when I had the chance. What was the name of that teacher, the blind one? He encouraged you to read too much and you helped him down the school corridors, you said.'

Gray could never tell if the mix up of information his mother could create was mischievous or accidental. He could never tell, he could never ask.

'Prof, you mean?'

Gray had been encouraged in his reading by the teacher's courage; the man's presence in the classroom offered a teenage child the example of an adult intensity. He dictated notes

115

from Braille folders. He seemed to look hard inside his head at every question.

'I saw his name in the paper. Benson. Benson, Herbert ('Prof'). In my usual place. The lists of names. Classifieds. It's like poetry to me.'

'Are you telling me he's dead?'

'Dead ten years, that's all. If my Latin's correct. The In Memoram column, that's right, isn't it? What would he have to say about you a cook I wonder?'

'Ten years.'

Twenty years away and Graham hadn't thought to write a note, report on his progress. Because he figured that straight-line success stories were always required in such letters, not the wiggly line of fail and change. He hadn't wanted to disappoint small expectations of ambition, decided by default to wait until a triumphant letter could be sealed and sent. To wait a life for a life to take shape. Gray's stupidity had gathered definition.

'I remembered you'd said he was blind and you won't remember this but I knew someone who was also blind. I told you but you won't recall. Your Uncle Jack, he was blind. Not all his life though. A shame and a tragedy it was too. But you mustn't get me on to that.'

She gulped her tea, sucked her cigarette. She was indulging herself. 'Oh yes, I like to read the papers. All the break-ins happening on my doorstep.'

'You haven't, have you?' Gray had a sudden concern for her safety.

'My turn will come.' She quickly lost interest in burglaries. Thought of another name to offer up to him, like a cat a dead bird. 'And another one, that footballer friend of yours. He was in trouble over his wife. Meagan. Beagan.'

'I didn't know. I wasn't here.'

But Beagan was the right name. Solid, low centre of

gravity. In the school football team, signed professional forms, didn't work out; then went to sea.

'Of course, with having no address for you. See what you've been missing all these years?'

Where to start? With a tower of old local newspapers? There was no catching up, never. Had it been remiss to stay away so long? Thoughtless not to have kept in better touch? Or was it all only free choice anyway, with attendant risk?

'Is it too hot for you? You can turn the gas down a notch. No? Or do you want to see the paper? You can if you like.'

The kindness in her voice came unexpected. She probably had no notion of the effect on her son of this news of an old life – surely not the same life. It wasn't possible that she had been waiting to pass on the information, to see how he reacted. If so, she had disappointed herself by tiredness. He looked again. Her always thin face thinner if anything, face skin looser on the bones. But no mischief. Just talk, perhaps a beginning to candour. Sleepiness, a weakness that almost won his pity.

And Mrs Connolly was suddenly, comfortably asleep, head against the settee arm. It seemed like a compliment she was paying him. Which he didn't know how to take. He would have to stay till she woke. Or he could slip next door and talk to Marva on her own. He watched his mother in innocuous sleep. He was in a classroom at his grim old school, the blind teacher, Prof Benson, intoning, the class taking notes. Then Graham tried to read a profile article in the *Radio Times* – a disc jockey with a garden, a day in his life, no help at all. Watching someone asleep was something like watching a blind man, the freedom it gave from the query of eyes. Weirdly comfortable. He hadn't been in touch with Beagan. He hadn't tried. Nor troubled to reach the teacher who'd helped. When Gray had gone, he'd gone and he hadn't come back. He'd gone to London and things didn't

117

materialize there. He'd gone to the country and stayed too long. Now in another small room he was back, and some of it was being remembered for him by his mother, the rest he was starting to remember himself. Late in the day.

'Did I drop off? Are you still here?' Mrs Connolly sat herself straighter. 'I nearly didn't recognize you. You weren't the person in my dream. You don't have a beard.'

'I was thinking I ought to write to his wife, to his widow I mean. I wish I'd have known at the time. I don't know where I was then.'

'You can say that again. I don't think anyone knew where you were. Or who you were chasing. What changes? No, I think you should try and make amends. Say it with flowers. Twenty years is a good spell – as I know myself.'

'I don't feel I need to make any amends.' Gray had bristled at her suggestion. 'It's just a gesture – you know, freely offered, like any other.'

Mrs Connolly lifted herself forward and pulled her stick to herself: a practised movement, but pain in there somewhere. She got herself standing and started shuffling towards the door.

'Go along and see Marva in the shop. She'll sort you something out for the old man's widow, if the poor woman still survives him.'

'You mean now? Are you throwing me out?'

'Don't be soft, Graham. I get tired easily. It's my age and imperfect health.' She pushed at his shoulder shakily. 'Anyway I might have other visitors – there might be a rush, you never know. Just come again and make sure it's soon. Now, on your way, I've jigsaws to add to.'

Graham gave a promise to his mother that he would call on her again. The following week would be soon enough, would it? Mrs Connolly pointed him round to the front of the shop in case he ran off for the bus without seeing Marva first. Her insistence was curious. She seemed for some reason of her own to need him and Marva to get on; some healing might happen. But her energetic pointing to the flower shop had to pass for goodbye. Graham waved, she pointed. And as he rounded into the paved area where the two boys still thumped their football hard against the brickwork – it was shooting practice, a hearty swear for each well-hit shot – Mrs Connolly tracked her son every step. One arm waved stiffly at them, the other holding her stick steady, she shouted her threats. The concentration of her anger impressed her son. He remembered it too. Again a goodbye was diverted. The taller, slightly less insolent boy flicked the ball up into his arms and led the march away from the shops, muttering. She'd vanished when Graham turned to look back.

But Gray hardly knew Marva. She'd been in the picture the last ten years or so. He'd sent cards to her via the shop. He'd telephoned and spoken to her a few times. But he hadn't met her before his jogging exploits on the promenade when he'd run into them both. He'd hardly had time to register what she was like. Except he'd immediately felt comfortable with her. And he was certainly impressed by how she handled herself. She ran the shop and she kept an eye on the old lady. And nobody had asked her to, it was her choice; evidently it suited her. Nobody would have been surprised if she'd run off with a man, considered the option of children or instead worked seriously at clubbing. No doubt she had her own separate life.

There must have been reasons she enjoyed the company of his mother. Because she more than tolerated her sharpness. She seemed to bask in it. Gray had to wonder what kind of woman could bear the daily tussle of talking with her. It wasn't possible he envied the knack. How to handle his mother and still live a life on her own terms. She didn't seem attached to any man. No mention had been made. Yet she was a handsome woman, and grounded in a world he only part understood.

The cowbell against the door clanged heavily. Marva was laughing into a wall telephone at the end of the shop. She was speaking to a friend. She pushed the palm of her hand towards Graham, an instruction that he should wait. She returned to her hilarious conversation. He turned away to allow her privacy – was it man or woman? he wondered – stared out to the pub opposite. A large semi-circular building pleased with its bright doorways and generous car park. A lorry was unloading cardboard boxes – crisps of all flavours – and bar snacks stapled to cards. A saloon called Parker's Bar marked out by a small neon saxophone shape above the door.

It had irritated him – as it had infuriated his father to the point of surrender – that his mother could introduce names into any talk at any time. She could plant the names in a place they hadn't been seen before. The surprise only made a person think again about the name, when maybe that wasn't what they wanted to do. Prof, for instance. Was it glee in her eyes that dredged the name up and tipped it in front of him? Surprise attack. A sudden thought she had. He never could determine the tactic as innocent or mischievous. The name on a plate: an invitation to curiosity. She started it off. Now Beagan.

Beagan had been one of the boys Gray had grown up playing kickaround with. He'd played in the same teams as Graham, different position, more attacking, more of a striker. Gray had imagined himself creating openings, threading the passes, giving cover, dribbling himself out of trouble, tackling back so that players like Beagan could mount a more straightforward assault on goal, receive, turn and shoot. Beagan had been particularly assiduous at weight training, ate at every opportunity, guzzled school milk by the bucket, counted press-ups in tens and built up tight muscle. Gray's approach had been less determined, and what he considered his natural energy and fitness were no longer adequate for the fast and earnest game the senior school teams had begun playing. More swottish interests caused Gray to drift from the football imperative.

'So what's with the long face, Graham?' shouted Marva's cheerful voice. 'Got a cob on 'cause it wasn't open arms with your mother?'

'I had no great expectations, to be honest with you,' Graham defended himself. 'No, I've been set to thinking about someone. And I've come to see you about arranging something floral.'

'Did Mrs C send you?'

'Not really.'

Graham started to finger the chrysanthemum stems in pots on staging. Pale yellow spider, autumny amber, big white heads with looser petals, and tight white heads too.

'You're not going to tell me you didn't want to see your own mother?'

'No. That's right, I'm not.'

Graham pulled a stem from a vase of purple, and dragged four more stems to the lip of the vase, pushed them back in to avoid spillage. He smiled without embarrassment.

Marva wore denim jeans for warmth, but with a certain style too. They fitted tight on her high haunches, made her legs look longer than they were. Ribbed purple polo-neck under a leather bomber jacket. She had rings on a number of fingers, but not on any fingers that signified attachment. Gray now stood close to Marva for a second, waiting for her to speak. She had an advantage over him, knowing about his family difficulties. It seemed inconceivable that he for his part had not known anything of her before. She walked briskly over to her work desk. He tried to bring her back close with a question.

'Would you believe I need to buy some flowers myself?'

'Who's the lucky lady? Ingrid Kristiansen?'

'I don't understand.'

'The runner on telly.' Marva expected quicker wits from him. 'I mean *your* runner, soft lad.'

'Oh no.' Gray clicked. 'No. The flowers aren't for her.' Graham's disappointment at not keeping pace with Michelle, running on the promenade, his shame at having to stop, being seen, at the very moment he bumped into his mother, travelled again to his face. 'No. They're for a teacher I used to admire. He was blind. For his widow, I should say.'

'Would you be wanting to deliver them to her in person?'

Marva's business voice, the one Gray had heard on the telephone. He pictured the gloomy front room of the semi the couple lived in, no children, no need for light inside and further shadowed by cypress, yew and unclipped privet.

'There was a memorial piece in the paper, apparently. Ten years is a long time. I didn't know about it. I mean I didn't even know he was dead.'

'Out of touch for so long. Tut tut.'

Another reproach for not staying in the city. Marva fiddled with wire and green ribbon, shaped the crimson and white roses round a horseshoe, a miniature white soccer ball attached and dangling.

'It's not for a wedding, is it? Or is some loony football supporter going to name their child after the whole team?'

Marva looked up with regret. 'Only another memorial. You must have seen the papers even where you were, wherever that was. Did they have a telly in the countryside? Did they have electric there?'

'Marva, I didn't realize. Football. I'd clean forgot.'

Graham walked away and started to examine the ceramic vases and hangings on a shelf. Limp bunches of white silk flowers failed to fill them. Small vases in swirled glass. He picked up a heavy-bottomed vase and feared to drop it. When he figured enough time had elapsed since his latest gaffe, he turned round to Marva with a shrug for apology.

Didn't say *daft*, *insensitive* or *sorry*; changed the subject. 'But you see, Marva, that man had high hopes for me.'

She continued her work on the wreath. Her fingers pushed and fiddled behind the face of the flowers, changing the depth and shape with each touch of adjustment.

'Great expectations,' Marva muttered to herself. Her face kept the calm of a gentlewoman busily embroidering in a painting. Her cassette player spooled through a worn Billie Holiday tape. The music was her privacy, and a part of her work too. She looked up with a smile.

'*Great Expectations*. I read that book when I was at school. "Wot larks, Pip." '

She laughed her high hoot. Graham was beginning to see it as her cheery trademark. She stood up and walked to the large sink with one cold tap, filled her electric kettle.

'You wouldn't be taking the piss, would you, by any chance, Marva?'

'Not really. You ask for it sometimes. But do you honestly think you're the only person to have had encouragement from an English teacher?'

Graham searched her brow as she bent over two mugs and pulled the lids off a clay pot of teabags and an instant coffee jar.

'Tea or coffee, Graham? Black or white?' Her crinkly hair fell forward; she combed it back with fingers swollen and dirtied by wires and stems. 'I'm coffee, of course. Brown sugar.'

'White coffee, please. Well, more grey really.'

Marva smiled as she poured from the kettle. Gray again couldn't be sure if she was kidding him. He fingered the feather lightness of maidenhair fern in a bucket of foliage, only three red carnations left for working with or selling.

'Did you do A level too then?'

'Why wouldn't I?' she countered. 'Adult education, you know.'

He pushed his hand down in a vase holding two comical gerbera, tube stemmed, daisy headed; something from a child's painting book perhaps. He made a show of laughing at two bright pink joke flowers. A diversion.

'Evening classes. You're surprised, I can see that.'

'And you've trapped me. I don't know why I'm surprised.'

Marva's look of mischief was replaced by brief satisfaction. The shop was her space, her territory. She took her coffee back to her workbench. A collapsed pile of cassettes next to her radio. Graham twirled one gerbera like a clown with a water-pistol flower in his buttonhole.

'Listen, if you've set your heart on these purple chrysanths, I could deliver in the van as long as it's in my radius.'

Graham told her the town not far away where the river narrowed then broadened out into the wide estuary. Where two smelly chemical industrial towns fumed at each other across a great bridge. The bridge was the one to carry the railway south, and through a carriage window every student would look down through trellis-like grating at the dirty currents and the calm islands of sandbank and know the shapes of what was being put behind; thereafter fields with hopes of future – either individuality or anonymity.

'Either that or I could phone the nearest Interflora and then I dictate for them the shortest of messages. They'll throw together a bit of everything from the leftovers of the day. And you'll just have to pick up the tab, sight unseen. How does that sound?'

'That would be great, Marva. I think I'd be happy to stick with Oleanders. Such service.'

'To be honest, Graham, delivering gets me out of this place for a few hours. So you'd better get writing your card then.'

Gray pulled a fountain pen from his inside pocket. He shaped to write on a card headed *In Memory*. He struggled to think of the phrases. *A former pupil. In appreciation of. A*

124

small token of esteem. Much welcomed encouragement. Always held in fond memory . . .

'Having trouble? My advice: don't try nothing fancy.'

He combined the stock phrases into a shorter message of conventional sympathy. Marva was right: it was easiest.

'But she mightn't even remember me. What then?'

Graham wrote the dates of his school career in brackets after his message. He passed a £10 note across the counter while Marva calculated delivery costs.

'You don't think it would upset her to be reminded after all this time?'

'She was the one put the advert in the paper.'

'Are you sure the flowers are for her, and not for you?'

'I feel I ought to. I only just heard. There are things I haven't done.'

'Do you ever listen to yourself, Graham? The world hasn't stopped turning because you disappeared for years on end. Your mother's got older. This city's a new place and you're an old face – it's going to be difficult for you, but we've got lives, you know.'

'OK. I'm sorry. It's just a shock.'

'What's a shock?'

'My mother's an old woman all of a sudden.'

'Sudden isn't decades, Graham. How long is it?'

'Leave off, Marva, can't you? I think I've had enough with my mother this morning.'

'Ah but, Graham,' a joking voice was being tried out. 'Have you given her a chance?'

'OK, I know. She starts things off. Why does she want to rub my nose in the past?'

'Just be patient. She's not had it easy, you know that. You're saying she's getting under your skin already? After two days?'

'After two minutes, Marva. I mean how does she know

about my school mate Beagan? *I* don't even know anything about him. Why is she so interested?'

Gray realized he could actually talk to Marva. That was something, painful or no. He was asking her things. As if he'd always known her. Because of her closeness to his mother – his chief problem.

'I'll tell you for why. Because your friend that was, Mr Beagan, he is a regular in here, poor man. He's not well. You think you've got troubles, well you haven't. Plus he gives me some stick and I don't like that.'

'Beagan comes here?'

'Yes. You could actually come and see this Beagan of yours, if you really wanted. Fridays four o'clock, the cemeteries close at five, don't they? But you could take him off my hands – anyway he's become something of a nuisance. I know he's lost someone and it's terrible and all that, but all my customers have, unless they're getting married, everyone has a terrible loss and what I can do with my hands is meant to be a balm to their grief – which is OK by me, I am able to witness it and say the right rubbish.' She paused for more breath to fuel her indignation. The anima impressed Gray. 'But what I don't need is all of their grief weekly.' She ran out of breath, or decided against further elaboration. 'It's too much for one person.' Then realized how serious that sounded. 'Sometimes.'

Grief hadn't touched Gray so hard, not for his Auntie Lydia, neither for his father, strangely enough.

'Is my mother all right? Her health, I mean. What does her doctor say?'

'What do you think, Graham?'

Gray coughed. 'Obviously. We'll have to talk again soon. I have to thank you for everything.' He couldn't emphasize the gratitude enough. 'For everything.'

'You did pay me for the flowers, didn't you?' Marva smiled. 'It'd be stretching a point to say family business. I'm only thinking what your mother would say.'

126

'Marva, you know her better than me,' Gray admitted, half in relief, half defeat.

Gray noticed that Marva laughed as she pulled the last lengths of white and red ribbon out for a bow. Her conviction that he was only getting what he deserved; his that he wasn't getting a chance to present his own case. The shop doorbell clanged with his leaving. Marva shouted after him, 'Do call at Oleanders again, sir.'

'I have to, yes.'

9

1957

Miss Farragher, the boy's teacher at infant school, kept a blue globe on a table behind her desk; above it she'd arranged painted tourist posters of harbours – New York, Sydney, Kingston, Jamaica, Lagos, Nigeria, Hong Kong – all stapled to a grey sugar-paper frieze. The posters, supplied by local shipping companies, showed off the ships' hulls and their peopled decks more than the background ports and cities; but the colours brightened up her large room, and brought the wide world inside. She said to the children, 'You don't just live here, children. You live in the world too.' The boy didn't quite understand her; he wondered how it was possible to live in two places at once. Two places, one place first and then having to go to another, even though you didn't want to: yes, he understood that.

Her blackboard had the date neatly chalk-written in one corner: 24 October 1957.

'No one's birthday today?'

The boy had a few weeks to wait. Since the summer, everything was waiting, because everything had changed. Waiting for his mother to sort everything out; for the move; for the shop to get started. He'd had to wait nearly a month before starting school properly; his mother had taken him away to stay with his Auntie Lydia; then back to the new flat.

On a broad tile shelf next to the high windows, well away from where the hooked window pole lay, the teacher had arranged objects brought into school by children in the weeks he'd been absent. The boy knew that the children weren't allowed to touch the two pairs of brown cowrie shells, or the heavy bush of white branch coral; or the crusty, dried up, sharp-skinned seahorse; they weren't allowed to play on the bongo drum or the calabash, or pull at the stringy casing of the fat coconut, or trail sticky fingers over the weighty slab of teak; or spill the coffee beans or cacao beans from their ash-tray containers. They could just look and read the label on a pink card, the name printed in rounded letters in royal blue ink explaining the country of origin. No mention of the child who'd persuaded a parent to let the curio out of the house; but the teacher had already made one lesson from that mystery. Miss had asked them about their parents and relatives, and the jobs they did for a living.

The boy had been frightened of the teacher's question: 'And what's your dad's connection with the sea, Graham?'

'My uncle was a captain but he never had any foreign things in his house – I stayed there and my mum says it's all best English furniture and some German ornaments, Miss, nothing from Africa or places.'

'So where did you get the coconut from?'

'My dad worked in an office and he always went down to the docks and had drinks with all the ships' officers, that's what my mum said he did. One day he showed me these ships that had come from Ceylon and Jamaica, getting ready for unloading. The coconut came from there, I think. And then he went off to London after our holidays. That's where he lives now. And that was that. I told you, Miss, before, in my composition. I wasn't kidding, Miss.' The tears came because he thought he hadn't been believed.

'Oh, you did. I was forgetting. You said. I'm sorry now

that I brought it up again. Use your hanky, son. I am sorry, Graham.'

Miss Farragher had forgotten, something a teacher wasn't allowed to do.

'Have you been abroad, Miss?' another child rescued her from further embarrassment.

'Good question, Avril,' said Miss Farragher with relief. 'Not me personally, you understand. People in my family have travelled. Like many families here, I'm sure.' She turned to check on Graham. 'As we were just saying, weren't we? But I hope to go on a voyage one day, don't you, children?'

The class kept their own record of trade and travel on the back page of their yellow rough book, which they entitled their Empire book. A Mercator's projection from an ink rubber roller unfurled a wide world map and the children marked in coloured pencil where their objects had first been taken from as souvenirs; the teacher insisted they shade certain areas in pink to indicate the British possessions still on the map. And she asked them to get their rubber erasers from their desks when she knew for certain the country had gained something called Independence.

'When the Union Jack comes down and a new quaintly coloured flag is run up the pole instead. Haven't you seen the ceremony on television?'

All the children with televisions in their family homes pushed their arms diagonally in the air. The boy wasn't able to yet.

It was the day after half-term, or teachers' rest as the parents called it, and Miss Farragher had rested by rambling in Denbighshire, where she sifted through some new ideas and some old ones as she walked and sheltered from the rain.

'For our next project I want you when you get home to ask your parents for any stamps torn off any old envelopes or postcards – not British stamps though – but stamps that have

130

been sent from abroad. Who can tell me where abroad is – anyone?'

'Foreigners, Miss.'

'Nearly there. Anyone else?'

'Foreign countries, Miss.'

'Yes. Now, if you all bring in your stamps we'll see where on my globe they come from. And next week we'll mark the places on your maps in your Empire books.'

Luckily, before he'd gone off, the boy's father had saved stamps for him, asked a secretary at the shipping office, slipped them into an envelope, and passed them on to him without explanation. He assumed the boy would be interested, perhaps when he was older. He left stamps from the United States for the boy, from South Africa, Australia, the Argentine. This was another of the things the boy was starting to think about – the few quiet favours his father had brought about. A couple of surprise Dinky cars, one Airfix kit, Hawker Hurricane, boxes of fruit pastilles and Quality Street – he tried to list the only presents, not including birthdays, his father had brought home. Not many.

He had, though, taken the boy to his bank one Saturday morning. The counters were so high and wooden; the quiet of a church just for men, like a posh pub but without the smell of beer. Then he'd had to wait at his father's untidy office and he made his guesses about what his father actually did from walls covered over with calendars – freighters mid-sea mostly, and from a desk and chair entirely hidden under bills of lading, correspondence, and back issues of *Lloyd's List*. In a corner one cardboard box of empty whisky bottles; on a windowsill his telephone. Evidently his father didn't sit down much. They were soon outside again in the narrow street that sloped down to the landing stage and the docks. But instead of catching the tram straight home, his father hurried them up a dark flight of wooden steps to a dingy wooden station.

The railway was track raised on stilts, high above the streets, above the green double-decker trams and, best of all, above the river. The cranes and wharves were below you, all the dockside sheds. Each blue or red funnel would announce its bright colour suddenly like a piercing hooter through the morning grey. Their carriage was the size of a cattle truck, each compartment a dark brown lacquered-wood box, each small carriage window held down by a stout leather strap, and yet it was comfortable when the boy smelt the full mixture – the carriage smell and his father's smoker's scent. The man was talking to him, telling him things, and he could sense underneath the latest cigarette the sweetness of whisky breath – even though the boy hadn't seen any bottle, no matter. No, because all this, all this was the best of his father – Joseph Connolly had found from somewhere an enthusiasm for showing to his son each ferry boat and dredger, each channel marker buoy, and especially the only loaded up freighter from the shipping line he worked for, all ready to sail for Buenos Aires. Binoculars would have helped, but still you could see clearly down on to the water, as the toy-sized train rattled them, two men together, along slow – one side the city's buildings; the other side shining and important, the dirty brown tide-full restless river.

The boy would try to hold on to that feeling – the coconut didn't matter, the school could keep that. A herring gull had flown level with their carriage, looked sideways to the boy, he was convinced, with a kind of recognition, then swooped away down to the landing-stage roof. Something of the boy wished to travel that flight with him, just for the ride, just for the view, for the experience, he didn't know why. But whenever he tried with such difficulty in later months and later years to call to mind his father, it would be a gull from that morning he would end up remembering instead.

*

When it came, two days later, Stamp Day was a day when drizzly rain confined the children indoors, and the drying gabardine raincoats draped on radiator pipes caused condensation all the way up the high windows; finger drawing in the wet reached only as high as the first window. The room had an unaccustomed warmth on that day; it might have seemed cosy, but it soon became stuffy.

One serious boy whose father was something high up in a sugar factory brought selections of bright mint-condition stamps, triangular and oversize, from countries such as Monaco and San Marino, arranged neatly in folders and booklets. They were on approval before sale, and the boy was selling them for shillings around the class, as well as, for pennies, his own not-so-mint selections in wage envelopes from his father's office. A small boy with blond hair and a deep brown tan had stamps from Sudan, because his father worked on a ship that went to Africa. For six months a year the whole family sailed safely through the Suez to Sudan and lived there. A tall girl whose father was a supervisor at a football pools sorting office arrived with a thick brown envelope bulging with paper like a sack of leaves. They opened it on to the teacher's table and tumbling out came the gambled hopes of Bahamas, Jamaica; Australia, New Zealand, Malaya, India; Nigeria, Gold Coast. So Miss Farragher had the class sorting the stamps into their different countries, and there were so many she was able to allot a country to every pupil. They each drew a line on their rough-book maps, a long thin line like fishing gut, which started in their stamp country and hugged the coast and came around the Irish Sea to the city where they lived.

'Now which ones do you think came by boat and which by plane?'

The boy was trying hard to think about that question, and

thinking that probably planes carried mail faster than ships, but the problem with planes, even when you were only thinking about them, was how the land underneath wobbled and juddered all of a sudden, and made your head swim round in the air and not know which was straight and which was gozzy and made you have to stand up to clear your head, it would surely help make things clearer.

'Is anything the matter, Graham? Do you want to go and see the nurse?'

'No, Miss. Er . . .'

But he stood up from his chair only slowly, his head nodded forward and his shoulder slipped half sideways and the knees folded. Everyone in the now silent room heard the rubber of his shoes buckle and pull across the floor, in a short fart sound. And one grey steel chair leg clattered into a desk as the wooden backrest tipped noisily on to the floor.

'Miss, look, Graham's got sick on the floor.'

A small triangle of vomit would need the caretaker to scatter sawdust across, a shovel and a mop of disinfectant-smelling water.

The quiet-spoken nurse asked if she could telephone his mother to collect him.

'No, she can't come and fetch me, she's started work at the shop now . . .'

He was persuaded to lie on the metal-framed couch that folded up and down, to rest. She walked from the room. The sweet stinging smell of methylated spirits stayed. Wool curtains were drawn. It was the kind of almost-dark you think in – it holds no fear. He'd missed some work while he'd been off school. He had contributed a coconut to this lesson and now Miss Farragher had gone and asked him about it. He remembered now what his mother had said: 'Yes, get that thing out of the place – it's not what you'd call an ornament, is it?' But the boy thought it did look like an ornament in

134

their classroom, along with the shells and beans and such arranged on the tiles.

Miss Farragher had promised to keep an eye on him that first strange day back after his summer, after he'd handed over a note from his mother together with his 'What we did in the holidays' composition:

I didnt like my holidays much. We all went to the Isle of Man and I didnt go fishing proply. My mum got all upset because we met my uncle whos blind. And anyway when we came back my mum went to the city air show with aunty Lydia and the captin Uncle Jack and I couldnt go, when she knew that I wanted to see the french birdman jump from the plane. He can fly and she knows I always want to fly. But Uncle Jack fell over and he died and mum was late home and she was all crying. And I was crying because she told me the bird man fell in the field and that wasnt important, but it was.

And also my dad went to London for his job and hes staying there and only coming back every so often like my birthday he promised me. And I had to sleep at aunty Lydias and I don't think she likes me but I don't know why. I slept seven nights in her different bed.

The boy must have slept all the way through school dinner hour, but he wasn't hungry. The nurse sitting in an upright chair in the next room reading *Woman's Weekly* stood up and escorted him back to class.

'Only if you're sure you're OK now. The caretaker doesn't want to get his sawdust bucket out a second time today, does he?'

The nurse peeked through the wire-strengthened window, and with his shoulder the boy pushed on the long tubular handle of the classroom door. He could hear the teacher was saying: 'Anyway, this afternoon we'll be doing Nature again.

And if the weather keeps up we'll go for a walk outside and see what trees we can see. Will you be better by then, Graham, I hope?'

When he was sitting at his desk, the boy immediately wanted to hike across his fields, and he'd show them past the high elms; and where the wren's nest was, the hedge sparrow's, the best horse-chestnut, and especially the stumpy beeches whose boughs he could reach and climb up; he loved to swing and jump down from them on to the grey grass soft landing, just as if he was a parachutist.

'I said, are you going to be well enough, Graham?'

Then he realized quite suddenly that he wouldn't be able to today, he wouldn't be able to show them now because he didn't any longer have access to the woods. He was forgetting where they lived now. To get there they would have to go by a different path. He'd been deprived of his escape route to the fields and woods, his countryside. All because he'd moved house, and the house was now a flat above a shop, not a house, and it didn't have a garden. And everything would change from now on, as his mother had threatened and his Auntie Lydia had warned. It had changed already.

'I'll try, Miss.'

It would be home time soon, and he'd begun to be nervous about going home, home to the flat and the shop.

His mother had started setting up the shop. And it was still mostly empty: empty shelves, empty floor space, with a couple of too-big buckets of carnations, Xanths, next to the window. She'd installed a second-hand counter, with glass casing missing, and made do with a cash box instead of a till. A chalked blackboard by the front door announced the flowers in stock. The next-door greengrocer had agreed to collect them from market for her. She wasn't supposed to leave the boy alone, yet.

'It's early days, but I'm doing it. It'll all take as long as it takes.'

136

At nights the boy sat on his own and with his mother. He wanted to be outside, but the surroundings weren't familiar yet. She smoked her Kensitas and she still managed to work on her jigsaws in a dining room stacked high with every stick of furniture from the house and tea chests too. In the living room, where a brown settee was the most comfortable place, his mother would come and encourage the boy to play cards with her, show him some games: Patience, and Clock Patience for variation, Rummy for halfpennies, and Strip Jack Naked. Because the boy made such a display of being bored.

'We could always play Happy Families, what do you think, son, eh?'

'You're joking,' the boy had said bravely. He was indignant because he'd watched his mother smoking one after another cigarette, rubbing her eyes, yawning and walking round the flat aimlessly; he'd even caught her crying. He pressed on: 'You miss him, don't you? I've seen you crying. I have.'

Now she cried. She let him see that she was having difficulty.

'He was never here, was he? Don't be soft, Graham. They're not tears for him.'

The boy didn't enjoy the confusion that his mother's recent behaviour caused him; he wondered if his father wasn't right to go.

'You wouldn't understand. You're not old enough yet.'

He didn't; he wasn't, evidently.

'Listen: I've got my shop now. Early days, like I say. Things'll settle down, you'll see. Worse things than all this have happened at sea, you know.'

The boy left the room and sulked on the landing. He didn't always like her jokes; or was it the way she said certain things? He leaned on the rounded windowsill and looked out through the porthole window. He watched adults returning late from work and children still kicking Frido footballs against shop walls, and opposite he could hear drinkers waiting to step into the pub for the night. The nights were all starting earlier, smoky mist was beginning to hang in the air. The week before bonfire night. The first bangers of autumn had started and he was indoors. No garden, no bonfire. The boy thought it might be a good time to ask again about a television set because his next birthday was approaching, as surely as the cold nights were.

When he went back inside he asked her: 'When can we have a television, Mum? Our teacher says it's really good for Independence.'

And his mother laughed; and the boy started to laugh too, not knowing why though.

'You'll have a long wait for that, sunshine. Independence can take years.' She laughed more heartily than he'd heard her for weeks, maybe months. 'But we could try and save for one of those small sets, I should think.'

She passed him a biscuit, as if it was a kiss.

'Something else too, Mum' – because he could see she was in a better mood now, and he was pleased to accept the biscuit. 'I've been thinking. You know when the Birdman from France was killed and crashed in the fields and died before he got to the hospital?'

'Ye-es,' his mother said, folding her arms tight. 'Well, actually, Graham, I think of it as the time your uncle died. Isn't that strange?'

'Only, what I want to know is: was his body sent back to France by airmail or by sea?'

This time she didn't laugh. She was thinking about someone. She said in a serious voice: 'You think too much; forget him. And forget your father. This is supposed to be our new start.'

And then she laughed. More biscuits.

10

1990

Graham had taken the trouble to telephone the Prof's widow to ask if the flowers had arrived safely. And how she was. And he wanted to know how it happened. And for her to tell him something, something that approximated to wisdom. Some message for him in return for his own thought. A thought to remember the old man by all over again.

'Oh yes, the flowers. Lovely. I put a notice in every year. It surprises me how many people think of him.' Surprises was a surprise. 'I can't remember all the names of course. You may have been one of the ones he talked about. Connolly? It does ring a bell, dear. I just can't be sure.'

Disappointment was about to appear in his voice. Because she would have handled his essays and read them out to Prof. Then she would have written in red biro the judgement served on each boy's work. She would have noticed the ones who were getting the compliments, surely.

'He didn't always like it at the school. If he hadn't had his accident he would have been a proper professor with books to his name. And crowds of students in a lecture room. I have to tell you it wasn't always easy living with a disappointed man.'

He was a strong man, surely. A teacher of exacting standards, with a cutting wire for windy words. Books you could call literature, he'd intone in an angry voice, Dickens, Conrad and so on, were of far more value, far more helpful to you than James Bond rubbish and beat music. Why waste your time on twaddle?

'He was a guiding light to me. He helped me.'

'Yes. I know he helped a lot of people. And at least half of them have written to me. From all corners of the globe – I can hear him now – how on earth could a spheroid have corners? But, yes, Australia, London, Africa the letters came from – see what travel makes people think about. Old teachers stuck in a smelly place like this.'

'Would you mind if I came to visit you, just a short visit? I wouldn't take much of your time.'

'Come on a day my husband's playing bowls. That's when I always have my young men to visit.'

Graham tried to extricate himself from the misunderstanding. He hadn't imagined she was anything less than devoted. He hadn't guessed she could marry again and sound so happy about it. How could her servitude to the man's braininess have been unwilling? Why the In Memoriams if he wasn't fondly remembered?

'What are you doing now, anyway, Connolly?' The question he always hated and tried to evade. The way she phrased it was threatening, like the ghost of Prof's memory. Good question.

'I'm in the catering trade. A hotel, really quite large.' He tried to build it larger than it was. He tried to make trade sound dignified. A job sound like a career. The anxiety felt adolescent again.

'Now I don't want you apologizing. You've probably found out what all the bookworms find out sooner or later: that being happy is more important?'

'I can't say I've arrived at a conclusion yet.'

'Of course you haven't. You're young yet. You come and see me. By all means. I don't mind telling you about the teacher you think you remember.'

And Graham wondered if he did, or if this was instead a completely different person, and a mistake. He decided quickly to excuse himself from any arrangement. He'd made the gesture, sent the flowers, with Marva's help, that was probably sufficient.

'I will come, I will, but some other time probably. A few problems here.'

'Never mind, Connolly. I did appreciate the flowers – better than the usual bunch – and so did my husband. Bye, dear.'

Graham had joined the bus at the circular terminus in the city centre, where the buses never rested but started round and out again, outwards from the river, always inland. He settled himself in snugly with the overcoats, the dampened raincoats, cotton, PVC, plastic, and a few that parodied country wear, waxed cotton, olive green. No umbrellas dripped, but clear plastic hoods glistened with droplets. His mother had kept a collection of them in a shopping-bag pocket, probably still did, folded in rolls not much bigger than chewing-gum strips. For one more rainy day.

But it wasn't only for his mother's sake that he began finding reasons to visit that part of the city again. Marva, for one; and now this name of Beagan. There wasn't a high street or a significant grouping of shops. A Methodist church, a Catholic church, an underpass beneath the first length of a motorway. A park that had been sliced in two by the raised and cut carriageways pulling the traffic away to another city, other kinds of work, across a spine of hills into even muggier weather, blowier hillsides, and all the other possible sides and corners of the country. From the top deck Graham watched how the silver cars drove the fastest. How slow vans were the local traffic, going nowhere else except a different part of here. And speeding at the start of the motorway was a determination of escape.

Next to a slip road spread the hospital grounds, its refurbished barracky layout a fixed point of convergence. A place for people who planned to stay. Who had no choice. Those stuck in the limits of the district could always direct themselves to one of its corridors. Appointment card to be checked in at reception. You won't be going very far, will you? Not going abroad for a while yet?

As he turned from the hospital bus stop, crossed the road to the row of shops where his mother still lived, Graham considered the strange man called Beagan who came to Marva's shop every week. Was he pestering her? It needed investigation. In case it was only a coincidence of names. His mother had a prodigious memory for names and it annoyed him that she wouldn't be wrong. He would check this Beagan mystery, and give himself another excuse to talk to Marva, to offer recompense for the unadmitted favour. She helped his mother; and indirectly that helped him, no doubting it. He owed her something. But how to offer in the correct spirit, always risking rebuttal?

When Graham had installed himself on a chair behind Marva's counter, he might have looked to other customers, if any had chanced inside, like an assistant to the manageress. It felt comfortable enough.

'Some kind of nutter, are you sure?'

'I get the lot here. I have to be on my guard. Two kids pulled a knife on me last month. Wanted the takings. "Don't expect to get yourselves high on what I've made today. Try the chemist's, why don't you, with your penknife." I kept them talking long enough to set the handbag alarm off. Blasted their little eardrums. They shouted, "Black slag, we'll be back." But I know them, don't I? They practise the art of hanging around. But no one's invisible. Except the police. Those poor boys can't go far, can they? But anyway, what's your excuse, Graham?'

'I want to know about Beagan.'

'I did wonder if he was from the hospital. But I can't see anything wrong with him. Looks very fit and healthy. Big square shoulders. Must have worked weights at one time.'

'Like me, you mean?' An attempt at teasing, joining her game.

'You?'

Graham didn't like the way she came back on his self-mockery so quick. 'I may have been fit myself at one time. Not all cooks are fatsos. In the country I lived quite an active, healthy life, really. But then who worships muscle? You don't, do you, I hope?'

Marva smiled. Graham looked again to read the meaning.

'You want to know about Beagan. He's bought at least five wreaths from me already. In the last year. Always red and white.'

'Perhaps he's got a crush on you.'

'No; I don't think so. I know how to deal with the sort that fancy their chances. The red-rose boys. The smarmy boys. Anyway they're already uncomfortable about being in a flower shop in the first place, it's not difficult.'

Gray was impressed, again. 'You're used to handling men then, and putting them in their place?'

'Basically, customers come for the flowers, not because of anything I do. Their reasons are usually good and I don't pry. But this guy Beagan wanted to discuss the subject. He plops his arms on to my counter, to show off the tattoos and his two hard-worked fists. One side of his face is caved in. "Do you do footballs?" he says. "A flower shop," I told him. "Florist's is the whole thing, you know." "Don't, love," he says. "Don't, please." And this stocky square man starts to moisten in the eye. I say: "Someone a football fan then?" You have to try to help.'

Marva seemed glad to unburden herself of the tale. 'I waited and I had to hear about his son, fourteen, who'd died in a terrible crush. I assumed that was where it happened.

I'd heard from others of the terrible guilt, people who might have been at the match too if they hadn't been buying a shirt that afternoon, or waiting for the phone to ring about a car advertised in the paper, and now they felt guilty for not being there. It was understandable. A few came to me to buy their flowers; or some other shop. Trade improved for months afterwards.

'I said: "I can show you photographs of the different wreaths I do." So I get out the portfolio: Dad, Mam, Love, Pop, Memories, Always ... "And any name you care to mention – even football teams, daft as it sounds."

'"It doesn't, love," Beagan said quickly. "What about goal posts? Do you ever get asked for them?"

'So I have to humour him. "I do get asked for hearts and pillows and stuff – I could always cobble together a football for you. A bit like kitchen tiles, aren't they, diamond shapes, white with a few black. Except black's a problem, of course." And I must have looked at him hard. "You said it, love, not me."'

'Florally, I mean,' Marva had explained.

Marva told Gray that Beagan had taken a photo to the stonemason's of the school Under 15 team in full kit. 'Same colours as the boy's favourite team. Yes, he was told, he could have it laminated so the rain wouldn't wash it off. A colour photo fitted in the top corner of the headstone. In addition to the words. More people were doing that nowadays. More expensive of course. "So why not just flowers in the shape of flowers?" I told him in the end. But I wish I hadn't. He threatened me: "You wouldn't be trying to take the piss, would you, because this is serious, this, girl." I think I realized how serious he was.'

Marva said she'd seen how most flowers ended up in the chicken-wire baskets at the cemeteries. All the greyed stalks and dried heads got squashed flat against opened out sheets of florists' pink wrapping paper. And Marva had even sorted through the wire baskets, she said, and she'd fished out dried out floral templates, she admitted, borrowed them, she said, the bunched woven flowers dead in their shapes, leaving only bleached lettering, DAD, MAM, like bones.

'But I've seen the men who haunt those places. Frightening. The women are calmer. But then Beagan has his good reason, doesn't he? His own event in history – the thing that happened to him.'

'He can't be that much of a nuisance. The way you speak of him.'

'Yes, I respect his grief. I don't have to like the way he talks to people.'

The Beagan he'd known through school had been confident and strong, not afraid to speak up, cocky. Good at football. Ambitious. 'It might be the same one. The one I knew. I'll just have to wait, won't I?'

'He'll be here.'

Then Graham stood up and walked around the shelves and asked her about the names of the potted flowers. He needed a plant for his room. Something that was his.

'What light is there?' Marva asked.

'Very little. Nearly none.'

'Well, what do you want plants for? You want bug-eyed fish instead.'

Graham didn't know what to do with such a lightless place. Except switch the spotlight on, stare into the dark, listen to the radio, pretend to be a blind man, feel your way past your own shoes. There were narrow streets outside the revolving door which caught the sun one side only and where taxi drivers waited for station passengers. Returning *Gastarbeiter*. Tourists, for one day only. Girls wagging school in amusement arcades. And daytime drunks.

Marva carried on making up an Interflora order. 'Aren't you going to see your mother today?'

'Do I have to?'

'What else are you here for?'

'I told you, I'm looking for Beagan. Isn't it his time yet?'

'Are you pretending you don't care how she is? She's not been well.'

'I know she's not well, I could see it with my own eyes. I'll see her, in my own time, but you know yourself she's not easy.'

'Be brave then.'

'Piss off, Marva.'

Marva sniggered. Gray picked up her newspaper. Read about court cases and the thriving business of the liquidator; football analysis; the yachts on the river, pleasure boats were replacing the merchant traffic; Waterfront 90 would bring some giant rock names to the city.

Gray dropped the newspaper in his lap as soon as the customer barged in. The stocky man in windcheater and sports casuals, fair to grey neat-cropped hair – Marva nodded that this was indeed Beagan – made straight to the counter and Marva. The man smiled charmingly at Marva, looked suspiciously at Gray.

'Is this the new man in your life, then?' Beagan shouted. 'Forget I said that, Marva.' Then he changed his mind. 'No: he's a bastard.'

'Hello again, Mr Beagan, sir.' Marva joshed along with him. 'What a pleasure it always is.'

Gray halved, then quartered, the paper so that the close-print Classifieds were folded inward. The man didn't frighten him. He was feeling defensive – for Marva, for himself too.

'How can you say that?' Gray spoke up. 'You don't even know me.'

'You're a bastard, simple as that,' Beagan started his rhetoric. 'They're everywhere, aren't they, bastards? In solicitors' offices, in banks, in hospitals. Everywhere you look. Sometimes they wear ties and sometimes they're scruffs like you.

They don't say much. They watch you, but they don't say much. They couldn't give a fuck actually.'

'I'm not having language in the shop, Mr Beagan.' Marva's complaints were half-hearted, scripted parts in a game performed regularly. 'As Mrs Connolly would say. Now usually you just ask for your blooms and we have a chat and then you go.'

'Isn't that what we're having, a nice chat?'

Beagan grinned at Gray, clearly enjoying his role of rogue. He smiled again, at Marva now, then let drop a denture plate with two strong white front teeth attached. A routine intimidation.

'See those. Lost those in a scrap. Fucking fat bastard in China. Bevvied out my skull I was.'

'Oh yes?' Marva asked in playful disbelief. 'And when were you ever in China?'

'I was learning my trade in the Merch, wasn't I? First port was Hong Kong. And losing my cherry. And falling downstairs. And getting my teeth and cheekbone pushed in by some fat bastard in a doorway. Someone off another boat – Dutch bastard probably, but I was in no fit state.'

'I'm wondering if we can skip the beer talk and get to what flowers you're having today.'

Beagan turned in Gray's direction for support. 'Soft lad here is interested, even if you're not.'

Gray nodded noncommittally. He'd heard something he could connect with. Beagan quietened himself.

'OK, Marva. I'm looking. I'm looking at these red ones here and those white ones there.'

Beagan knelt down at the carnation buckets. Three dozen of each from market and two dozen yellow, a dozen peach and a dozen mixed. He examined the buckets, lowered his head with some reverence. He might have been sniffing the scent; but no breathing sounds. The heads went to his nose while his fingers felt the flesh below the petals. Then he counted off the stalks methodically: twelve, thirteen, fourteen, he was muttering. When he was certain of the correct number he pulled the reds out, stood up and shook the dripping stems hard.

'No pinks for you, then? I've got some nice blue-dyed.'

Beagan didn't wish to be interrupted in his rite. 'Who'd want blue anything, Marva?'

'Well, more of a turquoise. Cheerful though.'

'Button it, Marva. You can see I'm concentrating here.'

He laid his fourteen stalks on the marble-effect floor tiles. His movement was studied and grave. The kneeling position was adjusted slightly, closer to the next green enamel bucket. And the choosing was repeated at the same painful length for the bunched white carnations too. Gray folded his newspaper over again. A reminder he was here, in body at least, should Marva need protection. She didn't. He was supernumerary. But Beagan seemed familiar to him, he was thinking. The shave of hair at the nape of the neck, small flat ears, or something else that doesn't change much through to manhood. Or possibly a square head seen from one desk behind.

Marva and Gray didn't dare a whisper, a cough or a yawn, before Marva broke the silence: 'So it's red and it's white. There's a surprise for us all.'

'I don't expect judgement on the friggin flowers I buy off you.' Growling was the way he talked to people, straight at them or into his chest. He turned straight to Gray. 'You. Who are you looking at in that tone of voice? Sitting there. I'll stick a gob on you.'

'You just remind me of someone I was at school with.'

'Not me, pal. I don't even remember school. I only remember growing up. When I became a father – that's when real life began. And this, this is now – something else again.'

'You forget, but I do remember those false teeth. It wasn't China, was it? They were for frightening the girls really, weren't they? It was here and you were ten. And I used to sit behind you in class.'

Beagan glared hard.

'Do you need more? Graham Connolly mean anything to you?'

Beagan stared in something like alarm; 'No, you don't, sunshine. You don't. Wrong bloke.'

'Bobby Beagan. I know it is. My mother's probably got the photographs somewhere. You weren't in Miss Farragher's but you were in Mr Baggeridge's and you went on to the same grammar school, I know it.'

Beagan forced himself on to the offensive again. 'Right, good guess, son. But this cheekbone was China, it was. OK, it was bullshit about the teeth. But . . .' He breathed in at the unfairness of the ambush. 'But shit, I mean, block it out. Do what I do. Who do you say you were anyway?'

'Graham Connolly. Same class as you right through the school – apart from sixth form.'

Beagan pulled a few steps from the counter, closer to the door's escape.

'I don't want to know. I can't be having any more ghosts.'

Moving backwards, Beagan remembered just in time his smart-arse act for Marva, wanted it reinstated before he left.

'Who's your friend the head-the-ball, anyway, Marva? I don't know him. He one of those been let out in the community? Listen: I've got an appointment, you know.'

Marva nodded. She knew where he went with his flowers every week.

A clean £10 note was left. Beagan's hand reached for the wrought-iron frame on the inside of the shop door, pulled it and held it open so that the bell rang hard, and rang and rang like a car alarm and didn't stop. Neither Marva nor Gray could move to close it and switch the ringing off.

Beagan slipped nimbly through the door space with a practised triumphal smile. Another successful annoyance. He punched the flowers in the air like a match trophy, waved the bunch as he turned, then broke into a bow-legged trot in the direction of the cemetery.

'Don't worry, Graham. He'll be back. He'll be asking me all about you.'

'How could he deny all that? How could he?'

'He has his reasons. You're not much different yourself, are you? You've got your own blind spots.'

'Well, my mother's setting me a trail.'

'Are you going to see her today? You should.'

'I might.'

'She needs you.'

'Funny way of showing it.'

'You don't see, do you? You don't see why Beagan's like he is. Or your own mother. You've got things all mixed up.'

'Have I now? And you've got it all sorted, have you, Marva?'

'I'm not saying that. Don't underestimate your mother. Go and talk to her. Borrow my key.'

Gray walked reluctantly round the corner to his mother's flat. No footballers. Let himself in. Listened for movement inside the sitting room.

'You back again?' She feigned surprise. Didn't shift from her armchair. 'And so soon. I must have seen you, why, only last week. What can I have done to deserve this?'

'I saw Beagan – thank you.'

'And is it the same one? The one that went off to sea? A brave lad I always thought.'

'Yes, you always wanted me to go to sea, didn't you? But I didn't.'

'No you didn't, you followed your English teacher instead of your uncle.'

'That must have been disappointing for you.'

'I've got over it. You're back, that's what matters. So, what have you got to say for yourself now, son of mine?'

'Why are you so interested in them? Beagan and Prof. One went to sea, the other was blind – any connection?'

'Maybe there is.'

'You didn't even know them.'

'Just thought you'd like to connect with some of the people you left behind.'

'Thoughtful of you. So now I can take up where I left off, can I? You know how many years it is.'

'You don't need to tell me. I've lived them. And now I'm on my way out.'

'Don't talk soft. You're not.'

Because she had never wanted pity from anyone. And she'd certainly not expect pity from him. He was back, all very well, and the world had changed and her best years in the shop were behind her, she wasn't especially bitter about that. But she goaded him, he wasn't sure why. She wound him up, always needed to catch him out. So he had to have his guard up. She might have been testing him, to see if he would weaken. And if he did and asked for some forgiveness – for something he didn't feel he'd done, then would she agree to weaken too, or would she catch him and fling twenty years of disappearance in his ungrateful face?

'What has the doctor actually said?' Gray tired of the games playing, wanted some information.

'Nothing to me. I know what coughing means. He asks me if I've lost any weight. Course I have. I have a lot of worry. And you haven't arrived to save me from that.'

'I've already told you I've arrived here only because I got a job here. Just one of those things.'

'I'll believe you, but I'm your mother, I would, wouldn't I?'

'You don't though, do you? I'm trying very hard, I am. The doctor, you were saying?'

'All he said was: I couldn't get you to give those things up, could I?'

They both looked at the cigarettes.

'Anyway what about the teacher? Did you do anything about that?'

'I sent flowers to his widow. Marva helped me. She thanked me, that was that. But why do you have to dredge all that up for me? I wouldn't have bothered myself.'

'Maybe you should.'

'Maybe I should, but just won't. Is it the lungs then?'

'You've heard me wheezing.'

'Haven't you always been like that?'

'How would you know?'

'No, seriously, Mother, how have you been?'

'I'm not frightened of dying. It's already started. My age.'

'Don't talk like that.'

'No, and the living, well, you just have to prepare yourself. My sister Lydia was sudden. Dementia, but thankfully swift.'

'Yes, you sent me a letter. I was in London.'

'And poor old Joe Connolly slid down into his own ruin, we expected that, only not so quick after Lydia.'

'I was there for the funeral, wasn't I?'

'Everyone has their own way of going. And Jack of course—'

'I don't want to hear it. I'm not interested in Uncle Jack.'

'He was a kind man. You seem nothing like him.'

'I'm sorry then. I wish I felt kinder. But.'

'More like Lydia. Or me. Hard-faced.'

'It's twenty years on. I'm a different person.'

'I'm not sure that you are. You're still my son, aren't you?'

'This talking, it wears me down.'

'Poor thing.' She coughed a laugh. 'Not used to it.'

'I have to go.' He turned for the door, fiddled Marva's key out of his pocket. 'Busy, Mother, you know.'

152

'Thank you for taking the time to visit me again.'

'There you are – sarcasm. It makes it harder.'

'Get away with you.' She was still laughing to herself. 'Don't burn any dinners now, will you?'

11

1957

Cissie caught three buses to get to Lydia's house. She strode
up that street of planes, their continental canopy offering a
pleasant shade from the warming up sun. She stood straight
up to the black-painted door and made the knocker bounce
on the broad chrome lips of its letter-box mouth. Her older
sister Lydia hadn't allowed her to call more than three times
in these intervening years, and then for nothing more
friendly than a cool Sunday afternoon visit to ask how
everyone was, can't grumble, been ages, empty teacups, bye.

She had taken the boy once only, aged four, and he played
with cigarette cards on the carpet, didn't trouble anyone. (*I'm
glad to see he's well-behaved. You wouldn't know he was here. Best
not to trouble Jack, though, he's resting.*) So Jack was hardly
troubled. Sitting, just sitting, since he couldn't read any more,
in the front parlour. Jack wasn't given a chance to shout
through more than a 'How are you, Cissie?' to her; she
wouldn't ask permission to speak to him directly, not since
the time he was in hospital, and as a result relations were
strained far beyond friendly speech. Three visits perhaps.
Her sister had cancelled so often Cissie had grown to expect
the cancellation before the journey. Lydia would phone her
message to the shop next door: a migraine with the worry,
or Jack's heart, she'd understand, resting, doctor's orders.
Most months, and most years, passed without first-hand

proof of the Captain's health; and she had no choice but to accept Lydia's version of doctor's orders.

But doctor's orders had changed greatly of late. Something must have improved to make Cissie feel optimistic, instead of sick in her stomach, standing on her elder sister's doorstep waiting for the door to open on a wary, accusing smile. It might simply be that Jack was failing and should take what enjoyment he could from his short time left. First the trip to the Isle of Man had been allowed, intended as a tonic; and now they had made this firm arrangement to go together, the three of them – it would be awkward – to brave the city show.

'You've arrived,' her sister welcomed her.

'And the weather's glorious. That's a good sign.' Cissie would need to work hard to sustain her optimism.

Lydia turned towards her kitchen, leaving Cissie to move through a gloomy hall and stand in a dining room that was dark on this bright day, both graced and cluttered with ornament. She walked in front of the black-leaded mantelpiece, peered at the pair of Dresden figurines, delicate and dust free, stopped to read the painted compartments of the old marble clock, its clouds and planets, as well as its fragile clock-face fingers. Eight years of bitterness hadn't altered her admiration for Lydia's 'nice things'.

Lydia pushed into the room with a teapot and tray. She began speaking as if she were continuing a friendly discussion. Cissie fiddled with the tassels on the green chenille tablecloth.

'Yes, this new doctor reckons the Isle of Man trip did him the world of good. Swears he's been brighter. News to me. The world's changing if new doctors know better than old doctors. "What was it on that island that did the trick?" he asked me. What could I say to him? I didn't know quite where to put my face. I said it was the deck of a ship that did it. I said it was the salt air. Old Jack piped up – "Bilge," he said, to me he said, "Bilge, it was company. Company. The closeness of people." I've heard that one before.'

'Yes, Jack did seem to perk up on the promenade, didn't he?'

'Most probably shock was the reason. *Your* performance.'

Cissie's eyes looked to the ceiling, found a rose, with cracks radiating from it; the lamp bowl suspended from chains was a fly trap.

'Lydia, I thought we said we'd try just for today to forget the past. It's no trouble for me to catch three buses home again, you know.'

Lydia poured strong tea into two large willow-pattern cups, then tried to blow the heat from the steam that kept threatening to rise. She offered a biscuit barrel with a newly sweet smile.

'So, anyway, I'm under orders to serve him people on a plate. And company that's stimulating, that was his word, but you know me, Cissie, I don't exactly approve of stimulating.'

Cissie crunched a ginger biscuit; crumbs caught in her throat as she manoeuvred to defend herself again. 'Lydia, what can I say? I'm here and I'll be only too pleased to help what way I can, for his sake. I won't be rocking your boat, Lydia. I'll behave myself.'

'For the first time in your life, yes. Understand though, I don't see eye to eye with that young doctor. I don't want Jack getting all excited again.'

Cissie mimed her best impression of calm: she placed her cup back on the tray, spread her hands flat on the cool fabric of the chenille cloth; she found some calm too, the peace she thought emanated from old things, from the pressure her palms exerted against the top of Lydia's oak table, gate leg, barley-sugar twist. She breathed deep, counted.

'Where is he now anyway?'

156

'If you mean Jack, he's in the parlour with his books as usual.'

Cissie thought she knew what her sister meant by usual. Before his total blindness Jack had the habit of reading in his chair – smokes to hand, whisky glass never quite dry. She talked to him there, it seemed ages ago, when she was a regular and welcome visitor – before she was married and newly settled, supposedly, in her own house. Even then the poor man had to resort to a magnifying glass. So she was only too happy to read to him out loud from his Conrad books. She remembered enjoying his childish pleasure at being read to. For all his dignity he had a winning weakness too. But their complicity in reading had particularly annoyed Lydia.

The strange thing now was that Captain Jack still sat in his chair, still pulled a book from the bookcase, still had the cigarettes and whisky glass to hand, as if he was reading his seafaring yarns, or waiting to be read to.

'Am I allowed to go and see him?'

'Who's stopping you?' Lydia shrugged. 'New doctor's orders. I've given up. Introduce yourself. He often mentions your name now. Ever since the Isle of Man. Naturally.'

She almost smiled. It was almost a joke, if Cissie would only keep patience, let her sister sting her a few more times, the words would no longer pierce skin.

Her sister trusted her at least to push the door open without permission. But the blaze of light that claimed possession of the room was a shock to Cissie; sunbeams had easily bypassed the plane foliage and travelled clean through the high bay window, without hindrance from net curtains, full force in the afternoon, danced on to the leaf-pattern carpet square, and concentrated their fire on the glass doors of the tall bookcase. The room was a furnace and a sightless old man dozed restlessly in his favourite rocking chair, baking inside an unbelted gabardine mackintosh. Cissie herself was overcome with warmth, but more from the thought of this man and his reading habit than the temperature of the room.

'Is that someone?' he muttered.

'Don't tell me you've been at those books again, Jack Argent?'

His face muscles took some time to compose the arrangement for a smile. 'It's Cissie, isn't it? Come over here.'

An arm was raised; it hung in her general direction. She had to refuse the touch for her sister's sake.

'You and your books, Jack. I'm just looking at them all again.' She pulled out a Conrad, felt its grey and blue dust cover on her fingers, skimmed a double spread of print, shut it, replaced it in its set.

'No dust behind those doors. No one else reads here. Do you still read yourself, girl?'

Cissie didn't want to be reminded of how she had read to a man in his prime but fast losing his sight. She did, she did, but not now, it was too dangerous. She might forfeit her afternoon.

'Not now, Jack. Just jigsaws if I'm bored.'

She made herself laugh, and there was nothing to laugh at, but she laughed and she made him laugh, which succeeded in wafting away her guilt, and she was able to change the subject.

'I was saying to Lyd: glorious day for us. Joining the crowd for the big show.'

'I'm game. This new doctor, he wants to try new things, and I want to give it a go.'

Cissie always thought of him as brave. Dignified, stoical – wasn't every blind man supposed to be? – but kind and open too. There were any number of points of comparison with her own husband. And the younger man was always somehow found wanting. She dabbed her face hastily when she heard Lydia reach the bottom of the stairs. The door creaked behind her. Her sister in her creamiest cotton raincoat.

'Well, are we all ready for the bus? I am now.'

Lydia pushed past Cissie and hoisted her husband up expertly from the chair, linked his arm firmly, and the Captain was on his feet, with help, and walking.

The showground gates were blocked with lorries and jeeps arriving late. The queue of pedestrians caterpillared down the cinder path into the high street, past two tiny corner pubs. The three stood outside, dumb with awkwardness and anticipation. A special edition of the newspaper previewed the show's afternoon highlights. Cissie obligingly passed on her summary to the others. The Lancashire Fusiliers would mount a daring display of manoeuvres, with the latest radio communications demonstrated from the cockpit of a Centurion tank, followed by unarmed combat and some simple self-defence drills. Naval cadets would be giving a vigorous gymnastic display with boxes and pommel horses, culminating in the formation of a sixteen-man human pyramid. Two teams of fire brigade officers would perform an authentic muster against the clock in competition. Police Alsatian dogs would negotiate an obstacle course in pursuit of a dangerous criminal – a police officer in disguise. Police riders would be contributing their usual mounted ride past; and motorized officers would show the speed and manoeuvrability of the latest police motorcycles. There would as usual be ample recruitment opportunities for those with a mind to a career in uniform, etc. . . . Cissie flapped the newspaper closed.

'Well, what do we start with?'

No response from the Captain.

'What happened to those aeroplanes we heard so much about?' was Lydia's complaint.

'I'm tired of hearing about them from my little Graham. Sick up to here with a certain Frenchman.'

'My feet are tired of standing here already.' Lydia could always add something to the subject of tiredness. 'What will I be like after walking round that lot? Dead on my feet.'

The sisters were in agreement at last, pleased to share complaints. The queue shuffled forward a paving slab at a time, the Captain needing a nudge to shift himself, unreachably quiet.

After the gate there were so many marquees, grubby circular tents grey, white and grey roped, grouped together as for a scout jamboree camp, and behind them, not quite encircling them like Wild West wagons, were huddled vehicles, lorries, tractors and carts, almost out of sight, positioned ready for the clearing up afterwards more than for the day itself. A fire engine, being red, could be on view, and bump across the grass in an emergency; the greyer, greener motors were kept half hidden; generators pumped and hummed.

'Too many people here,' Lydia complained. 'I could come over all panicky.'

'We can't get lost.' Cissie wanted to establish her confidence. 'Don't fuss, Lydia. We just have to stay together.' She linked her arm to Lydia's, joined the three together. 'What is it Jack's interested in?'

The sisters talked as if the man couldn't hear or answer.

'I humour him. All this new-fangled machinery he wants to know about. Jet planes. He's pretending an interest in things he never was before. He says it's the future. Why should he be bothered with all that?'

'You're just having a fling while you can. I understand, love.'

'Second childhood is what it is. I've no time for it.'

The man spoke up, suddenly, a natural response in the conversation proving that he followed every word. 'I'm making up for lost time, Cissie. Before I go.'

'You're not going yet awhile, are you? There's no hurry, you know.'

'Listen,' Lydia demanded. 'It's no enjoyment for me. It's all right for you, Cissie – you only have to see him on his days out. The poor man thinks he's a different person in company.'

'Ah, but whose company?' Cissie dared to ask.

Lydia looked shocked, betrayed by this new provocation. 'I *am* your sister. And wife, may I remind you, to the man for most of my life. I won't have your insinuations. I'm going to ignore them. Just for today.'

'Sorry, Lyd, I didn't mean anything by that.'

'Shut the cackle, both of you,' the Captain instructed. 'Just smell the air, the steam and the diesel fumes. All these people. I can feel them and I can hear them. But you have to describe for me, that's the catch, girl. That's what you're here for.' The Captain was giving out his orders, as if sibling disagreement were irrelevant to the enjoyment of his day. 'Lydia hasn't the patience – she can't help it. I don't blame her. Do an old man that service.'

But Cissie had to look to Lydia for permission to answer.

'The man's sick of being at home.' She'd given up most fights now; at least the ones with him and his doctor. 'It's his treat to be here. He's had one heart attack already. The old doctor said rest. This one says get out. They both say expect another one any time at all. That's cheerful, isn't it? Doctors. Take no notice of me, Ciss, you humour him.'

'Yes,' agreed the Captain, 'take no notice of her.'

Was it only because he was blind, or was there something about where he looked – nowhere in particular, not at the person addressed; back into himself and still troubled once he'd said his piece? Cissie was worried for him, she couldn't read his moods in the way she could her sister's. He trod forward, supported on each side by his two women. They steered him past officials, participants, exhibitors, drivers, spectators in their hundreds. She didn't recognize a single face and the Captain couldn't hope to. He was silent again and the sisters soon found it easy to ignore him, as if he was deaf too.

'He's aged quick, though, hasn't he?' Cissie was wanting her sister's support now. 'Who'd blame him if he wanted a day out?'

'That's why we decided on the Isle of Man. Following the doctor's suggestion. Jack enjoyed the trip and the Guinness on the boat over and the boat back. The doctor was pleased. All those people on the prom, they frightened me. Not him though. And it wasn't my idea to come here. But you can see, he's restless now. I can't remember him restless since he was in hospital for his eyes. I can't do right for doing wrong. He wants to be with new people. I'm not enough for him, apparently.'

Now she was the one to need her sister's comfort. It came with a patted shoulder, not begrudged.

The first noisy aeroplane of the afternoon trailed vapour high in the sky; its straight-line edges fluffed out imperceptibly. Something about its suddenness forced Lydia to a decision. 'I'm definitely not craning my neck all day for anyone,' she announced. 'He's all yours now.'

Cissie had her job to do, but choosing the tent to start her selective commentary for Jack was like a contestant plumping for animal, vegetable or mineral in a wireless quiz show. The smell of soiled sawdust gave the game away. She mentioned an assortment of rabbits flopped at the back of chicken-wire hutches, grey, black, brown. She enumerated the Bantams and Rhode Island Red bobbing inside a boarded pen. She distinguished racing pigeons from show pigeons, dusty grey, stony brown, all soft as smoke.

'That's the idea, girl. I can see them fine.' He was smiling.

She wasn't herself so interested in Jacob and Welsh Mountain and black-faced sheep, but he smelt them so he wanted to know their name and category. The dimness of light under

162

canvas depressed her, even trying to ignore the farmyard smell.

'Let's try the Produce tent, please,' she recommended. 'I can't breathe in here. I bet you can't either.'

He didn't answer, or complain.

Neat rows of jars had been set on white tablelinen, every one neatly labelled, each with its drumskin of greaseproof paper held taut by a thin elastic band. The judges must have unpeeled each top, dipped in to taste, and replaced carefully. Cards rested against fruit jams, plum and greengage, tomato chutneys, piccalilli and mint jelly. At right angles to that table were the baked cakes, cherry cake, fruit cake, scotch pancakes, and also home-made honey from local bees; on the edges, almost apologetically, beers in plain glass bottles; fruit wines of all colours except the too obvious red and white. But the central table, pride of place, displayed clean round potatoes, marrows, leeks, turnips, onions, parsnip, beetroot, rhubarb, fat cooking apples – all geometrical, as if in preparation for an art class to sit down in front of and sketch.

'Take me to the flowers, I want to smell them and you can tell me the colours.' His elbow nudged lightly at her ribs. 'Just like the old days in hospital, eh girl?'

'Less of that, Jack Argent. I'll just read the labels, thank you.'

Against the pressing canvas the flowers had insufficient light. She told him about the perfectly timed blooms of dahlias, chrysanths, gladioli, roses, fuchsia, even camellia, and a few fussy unnatural plants she didn't care for, cacti and bonsai. Those reds and oranges and yellows did shine through. She recited names for him, but couldn't hope to tell him how much she cherished these best-grown flowers; she touched them lightly with a feather of her fingers, she read their Braille; and it upset her to be this close to him and with flowers which he could not see the shape or colours of.

'You've gone quiet on me. I thought you were the expert with floral stuff.'

'It's too dark in here,' was her quick excuse. 'Let's get some light.'

He mumbled something about it being dark all the time for some people, but she pulled him to the tent's opening.

They stepped beyond ropes and cables through horse droppings and straw. Outside the tents, events were in strict progress. Horse jumping would have to follow the parading of Shetland ponies, shire horses, mares, cobs, geldings and foals of various ages. She could hardly report this parade to Jack, though she might find something to say about the magnificent mounted police, already tall on their large horses, taller again with plumed helmets. A reporter leaned against the Tannoy tower, scribbling shorthand notes on a programme sheet. The tinny voice reminded male spectators about a contest of shape and personality. 'Miss City Girl – our annual mixture of beauty, brains and sensible views about home life.'

'You're not interested in a beauty contest, are you, Jack?'

'Not any more.'

She moved them towards an ice-cream stall where cylinders of already dripping ice cream were unpeeled and plopped smartly on to cornet wafers. Two tents faced her: the tea stall where Lydia sat with her back to them; and a smokier, more enclosed refreshment tent, from which issued shouting and throaty laughter.

'I need a pint. I can smell the stuff and I'm parched, Cissie. So point me there and some kind man will see to me – you watch.'

She wasn't sure if she could leave him. But he seemed confident, bolder with the sour whiff of slopped beer somewhere near his nose.

'If you're sure you can manage. I'll be sitting with Lydia

on a hay bale. Tell your helper she's the one knitting in the cream poplin raincoat – by the arena ropes.'

She had to give him detailed directions. She knew where he was and he was safe, but she was realizing, as she spoke, how fragile their latest reunion was, how hard it was, now that she'd been allowed this closeness, to leave him in the care of others.

Cissie quickly found her sister, with a blithe pretence at confidence. 'He's fine, you know. In the drinks tent.'

Lydia knew better than her what Jack was capable of; blindness wasn't a hindrance to drinking, some willing arm would always lead him to the bar and another help him home. At this moment Lydia was much more interested in discussing the trials that wives suffer, deserved or undeserved.

'Things any better at home?'

The question was an ambush; her sister wanted to weaken her.

'What do you think? I have a life that is separate from his. And that's been my lot pretty well since we married.'

'I always felt sorry for your Joe. He's not a bad man.'

'Who said he was? I'm glad to get myself away from the house for a change. He's supposed to be doing the garden. But he's not really a success at that. Nor anything much else except tippling and talking. He'll be in his deckchair listening to the wireless. He's rigged up some extension wire. And keeping an eye on Graham, I hope.'

'Is he good with the boy? I wouldn't know, of course.'

'The boy's got his interests. Of course he wanted to be here, didn't he? I'm the wicked witch of the west for not letting him. But your Jack doesn't want him under his feet. The boy's in a world of his own. Aeroplanes and birds. He would have given his arm to be here today. He cried and I told him boys don't cry.'

'I'd have thought a boy would get bored with all these people walking round tents full of vegetables and flowers.'

'It's the fly-past. The air-show part. Some Frenchman is going to drop in on us. A space will be cleared in the crowd big enough to lay a tablecloth down and the Frenchman with the wings on will land on it as surely if it were a handkerchief at your feet. Graham knows all about the Birdman. Seems a daft thing to do in my opinion. And anyway with all these people we won't see a thing. We won't know which direction he's coming in.'

'Well, our Jack certainly won't be any the wiser.'

'We'll have to tell him, won't we?' Cissie thought about Jack again. 'Like those sports commentators on the wireless.'

'Oh, you can. He likes you to. I haven't got the patience, have I? I don't notice the things that will interest him. How can I do that? Who knows what another person wants to know? Even after all these years of married life.'

'Perhaps he's changed, Lydia, during that time.'

'He's become more difficult, I know that much. I used to know where I was with boats.'

'Maybe you don't understand him. He's a sensitive man.'

'Listen, Ciss. Don't you go telling me what he's like and what I'm like. I don't wish to know, thank you. We're all too old to change. I prefer knitting and sitting.'

Again Cissie chose to bite her lip. This was her sister and here was her husband soon safely back from the drinks tent.

A jockey-sized man in a cap presented the Captain safely back to his women. Lydia intended to knit with more determination. Jack was ready for a continuation of the commentary. They stood by the roped-round arena, where naval cadets were limbering up in a line.

'I wasn't long, was I? What's next on the programme, girl?'

'Gymnastics display.' Cissie couldn't suppress her laughter. 'They're jumping headlong over a vaulting horse and they're queuing up and running and tumbling in formation.'

166

'Go on, girl,' Jack encouraged her. 'Carry on. That's the spirit.'

But Lydia had to show her irritation: 'You sound like you're on the wireless. I could have stayed at home if I wanted that. I'm sweltered here. I'm splashing out on another Kia-Ora. Don't mind me.'

Cissie had made her promise to help Jack, so she stuck to the task. They moved closer to the performers. 'They're wearing navy shorts and white singlets; you can see their bulging white muscles.'

Jack, after his drink, seemed more than eager to play their game. They each held the ropes as if for stability.

'I used to be muscular like that, you know.' He squeezed her elbow tight, then released it.

'I know you did. I saw you in your vest. And you cut a fine figure, I remember.'

'Gone to fat now. It wasn't so long ago I had muscles.'

'Eight years as I know to. You were in your prime. Still in your fifties.'

'And look at me now. Snow-white and fat as a house.'

Jack tried to slip his arm across her back to hook her waist. But Cissie was uncomfortable about his attempted cuddle.

'Don't, Jack. How many did you drink in there? Anyway we can't, not here and not any more – you know that. I'm supposed to be relaying this show to you, that was the idea.'

'Cissie, no. Forget the gymnasts, they've been forced to do that, they're not enjoying it. Forget them. Lydia can't hear us. I've got my courage now – from the glass as usual, yes – and I have to ask you something. I've had a long time to think about this.'

Cissie looked back at Lydia to check the safety of their distance.

'You know when you visited me in hospital?'

She was wary of his questioning nonetheless. 'I do remember. Yes I do. I try not to but you just don't talk about it, do you? Lydia would die, you know. She wasn't happy at all about that little episode.'

'I have to ask you this question, Cissie, you'll have to excuse me but I have to ask it. It's been bothering me ever since the Isle of Man. But never seeing you for so long before that I didn't – it crossed my mind, but never seriously.'

She knew being close to him would have its risks for her as well as for him. Warmth might be generated. At the same time she had no wish to hurt her sister either. 'Go on, ask me. I don't mind. The Isle of Man was a shock to me too and I haven't been the same since.'

'Don't, Cissie. Just listen. When I shook hands with the boy. When I shook hands with the boy.'

'Yes. I don't think he knew who you were. He'd heard talk about you of course, but I don't think he knew you existed in real life. When I brought him to the house Lydia wouldn't let him see you.'

'Now what I want to know, Cissie, is is there any possibility the boy is the result – I mean you know what happened at the hospital years before, you brought me flowers – it was you as much as me – I may be the blind one and I did have difficulty seeing that day, but I didn't need to see, did I, not really, it was just feelings, wasn't it? It happened. Tell me it happened, because otherwise I might think my memory was playing tricks on me because I'm blind.'

'What are you babbling on about? My foolishness at the hospital? Any more than that?'

'Whatever you want to call it.' He seemed disappointed at her betrayal of the memory. 'But I'm asking you is it possible the boy—?'

'It's too long ago. It's all over with. It's possible – anything's possible, Frenchmen might fly. I'm not saying more than that. Just you think of the boy though. Everyone assumes the boy's father is Joe. Eight years ago he was a little more my husband than now, but only a little. But no

168

one's ever said he wasn't Joe's. And I don't want it questioned. Lydia mustn't have to think about it. And you can think what you like, Jack. As long as you don't broadcast it. I'll leave it up to you.'

'But just for me I'm talking now. Between you me and this noisy crowd. It's possible I might have a son.'

'You might, Jack. The timing is somewhere about then. But no one would believe you. Not in your state of health, they wouldn't. They'd take my word for it every time.'

'Don't be hard-faced, Cissie.'

'But you might be. There's no saying.'

'Don't tease an old man. I want to know what he's like, Cissie. I haven't got long.'

'Shut up. Long, who knows that one? My boy Graham is mad with his mother. Thoroughly narked. For not letting him see the flight of the French stunt-man at this show. He'll never forgive me. He'll never understand why I didn't want him to come. And how can I tell him? He's seven now. He wouldn't understand now. Or ever.'

'But what's he like?'

'I don't know. He's mad on planes and birds, I told you. He stares at me and Joe as if through binoculars. He watches us like we're in a film at the pictures. He's a watcher, that's what he is.'

'Of course he is. He's a boy with sharp eyes.'

'Don't talk like that. We none of us know. He's probably been hurt by Joe and me, and I'll have to make it up to him some day.'

'I'm asking you, Ciss.'

The gymnasts had completed their routine. There was precious little applause. The Tannoy was inaudible.

'You're responsible for my being here. It's your fault, you know.'

'Don't pin anything on me now. I was glad to keep you company, I am, you know I am, but it wasn't my idea, it was yours. Lydia didn't want me anywhere near you after what happened in the Isle of Man.'

'She changed her mind. She only wants to please me now.'

'Well, my sister is more than ever wary of me, I can tell you.'

'I wanted to be with people. Lots of people. It's been lonely over these last eight years. All I get is visits from the old mariners' lodge with their sea-dog talk. I can't read and no one will read to me. Not the way you did. But I get miserable at home with Lydia or without her. Not her fault. I think I probably married the wrong sister.'

'Maybe you did and maybe you didn't but we can't do a thing about it. And there's no point in mithering Lydia any more than she is already. She's worried enough as it is.'

'Well, then it'll be easier for her then. When I'm gone. She won't have her millstone.'

'Don't talk like that.' Cissie tried to calm his troubled talk. 'And what about the rest of us? How will we manage?'

'You've got your little family, you're all right.'

She looked across to the crowd. What made the fit of a family – a perfect fit, an awkward fit, unworkable?

'But I do want to help in some way, if I can. I want to see you right. I've been thinking about it. You've got a gift with flowers – everyone says so. And I've seen it for myself. Eight years ago at the hospital. I can still picture in my mind's eye those flowers you brought when you visited. When you stayed with me for a while at the hospital. You sat on my bed. I could reach out and—'

'Shut it. You don't know who's listening. You know very well you couldn't see them.'

'No, but I could sense. They were a great consolation to me in dark dark times, you've no idea. Flowers have always been a reminder to me of you.'

'Get off with you.'

170

'I'm only saying that I want to help. And if that helps this young boy who may well be—'

'That's all maybe. I'm grateful but I'd prefer it if you would consider my sister first and foremost.'

'Oh she's provided for. Lydia will survive. She's got the house. She'll take more boarders, more of the merchant navy boys. She doesn't need me.'

And he went quiet again. He'd spoken his speech and he turned slightly away from her. Cissie couldn't help thinking of the house and making comparisons with her own barely furnished modern brick shell. She'd rather have a flat above a shop. She tugged back on his arm and moved him slowly – he was heavy and awkward when walking – to where Lydia still sat outside the refreshment tent. She was sipping Orange Crush from a paper beaker. She was complaining about her corns.

'I don't know how you can bear to walk round. Aren't you uncomfortable? You know the doctor said to rest. You're not tiring him out, are you?'

'I'm having a fine time, Lydia. This girl can see everything. She tells me everything.'

'Lucky you then. Just be careful, you're not a well man, remember.'

'I feel well. I'm only sixty.'

'That's not what the doctor says. Older than your years.'

'Nonsense, Lydia,' offered Cissie with a reckless confidence. 'You're only as old as you feel.'

'Who do you think you are anyway, Cissie? Miss City Personality? There's a ribbon and crown for you later on – if you can talk rubbish, waggle your backside and smile at the same time.'

Another day she might have had a reply to that; if it hadn't been her sister talking she might have willingly laughed. But Cissie went quiet, feeling tiredness herself now. The Captain too.

There were planes going over, their noisy engines made necks stretch. The Tannoy announced who was flying at what speed and altitude. They were expecting the French aviator soon.

'I'm hot, Lydia. Cissie.'

'You look hot. Have you been walking him too far? And no need to look the innocent either. I know your games. And I've turned a blind eye – for my husband's sake.'

'That's a good one, Lyd,' Cissie hit back. 'Blind eye.'

'What do you mean? He jokes about it himself. So I think I'm allowed to, aren't I? He shouldn't be walking round here. It's dangerous for him. I said it would be.'

'No. He only wants to be among people.'

'How do you know what he wants? How could you? You've seen him three times these last eight years and caused trouble every time. The hospital, the prom and now here. Don't pretend. I only said yes as a favour to him – not to you.'

'I don't want your favours, thank you, Lydia. I've wanted to help him, and you too if only you realized.'

They turned back to where Jack was now standing closer to the refreshment tent, gripping the pole much too hard.

'What have you been doing to him? He's out of breath, can you hear him? And look at his colour.'

He was too still, and too quiet. And then his breathing became heavier. He was gulping in oxygen in thin breaths, chest heaving and nothing going in.

'Are you all right, Jack?'

He was too intent on the effort of breathing some air into his lungs, all too aware of this difficulty again, so that his concentration each time prevented him attempting speech.

'No, Jack, don't frighten us. I told you. You shouldn't have got him so excited. It wasn't the right place to come.'

'Shut up, Lydia. Can't you see he can't breathe?'

'Help him, someone. Give him some air.'

'There's a man fighting for his life here.'

They both knew the emergency had arrived, this was the test for life, and they were helpless what to do. Hold his shoulders or hope to break his fall with only their hands? The Captain keeled over like a toppling mast. Legs didn't support him. One ankle twisted under him. The weight of head and shoulders sought the hard ground. The limbs stuck at awkward angles.

'Someone . . .'

'He's a heavy weight. Can't.'

Then his large head was a rock on the ground that changed from purple to a pale blue-white even as they looked on.

Word spread through the crowd. Where were the St John's Ambulance people?

'Not even had the fly-past yet and somebody's already pegged it.'

The sisters looked over to the St John's Ambulance boy in a black beret too big, pulled too hard across his forehead.

'I'm sorry. I'll have to call Captain Cardew. He's having a cup of tea. He left me on my own.'

And the boy disappeared into the refreshment tent. A neat short man in gold-rimmed glasses appeared with a girl from behind the tent – just as the boy emerged from his search. One sister stood and twisted her hands together; the other knelt and listened to his chest.

'Here. Let me try. Watch me, Terence.'

He rolled up his sleeves, knelt at the body's side, turned the Captain all the way over on to his front and pulled his legs straight. His hands were his prayer. He ignored the sisters, ignored the girl he'd petted, and addressed his apprentice. 'Artificial resuscitation, Terence. Position the arms, so.' He briskly repositioned the old man's arms. 'Now press along the back and on to the lungs, there. Keep the massage going round and pull up the arms at the end of the cycle. And again: down, round and up. See.' His hands pushed on the body's back and pulled rhythmically at lifeless arms. The man from St John's pressed and breathed, demonstrated his routine for the instruction, it seemed, of the boy, more than the expectation of recovery. He knew it to be a body. His training was to persist beyond the reasoning of common sense.

'No response. His heart muscle's not responding at all to my rhythm. This fibrillation's not right at all.'

He persisted and his movements slowed until he stopped and he stood above the body to give one big conscientious pantomime shrug for any doubting spectators. They watched his performance even as they strained to hear the Tannoy's announcement of a delay in the Birdman's appearance. News was awaited.

'What do we do now?' asked Lydia.

'We stay with him,' assumed Cissie.

'We'll have to wait for our ambulance to get going,' the St John's man advised them. 'It's over the other side of the park. I've sent the boy to fetch the driver. And we take you all to the hospital.'

It was five minutes before a black and white ambulance van bounced over the grass and the pipes and the ropes, and the crowd cleared to let it through but pressed forward again to get their look at what death might be. A stretcher was pulled out. The Captain's dead weight was rolled on to the canvas.

'Terence, you can help.'

Lydia was the first to make a sentence. 'What can the hospital do? Nothing. He's gone. That's it. And it's not the place I would have wished.'

'Shut up, Lydia.' Cissie cried bursting tears over the space of dry grass he had filled.

'Go on, make an exhibition of yourself now. In front of all this crowd.'

Her head lifted itself from the hay bale. 'Yes I will. I bloody will.' A straw clung to her wet lips.

174

The crowd closed around the sisters again. Their collective curiosity was used up; backs pressed in on the women instead of inquisitive faces. Some other alarm, a rumour that the Frenchman was late with his landing. Something else had happened. What was the Tannoy saying? Noise. There was a new shock.

It was minutes later the older sister raised herself. 'Someone's brought this tea for us. Pull yourself together, can't you?' Then more agreeably: 'Come on, Ciss. We have to go with the ambulance. It's waiting.'

12

1990

It would have been hard to avoid the meeting itself, considering where he was staying. Hadn't he seen Sylvie bending down that morning in the hotel foyer? He'd stared at the taut spread of skirt her behind caused as she crouched to select the white plastic letters for the pegboard. He stayed long enough to read what her letters pieced together were announcing: MEETING ROOM A, 8PM: A FUTURE FOR THE RIVER – DR HARRY MILES (RAINBOW INITIATIVE). A proper talk and not a nest of accountants. A change from Time Share and Herbal Diet sales assemblies. A change from cloned Mormons. Could this be part of the manager's policy for quality? An experiment or merely an aberration? The man was to be encouraged, if in fact he knew what he was about. But it couldn't have slipped under his nose, because his nose was in everything. Everything required his approval and once he'd given it, Pete was guaranteed to be its most enthusiastic advocate. Gray knew that only too well from the convincing interest he showed in his special stir-fry baby sweetcorn, red pepper and tofu in a ginger and spring onion sauce. The man tasted them himself, pretended to be enchanted – or really was – and Graham hadn't for one moment doubted his intentions.

The talk might be part of some new cultural policy. Pete could be introducing yet more change and proud of it. Proud

to be provoking new responses from tired staff and customers with plateaued expectations. Both sides, Pete main-
tained, expected too little and got it. Which of course affected
morale in the hotel, which he dreamed could actually be
scintillating. Here he was offering them something new. On
the face of it, Gray reckoned, there seemed to be a generosity
about the gesture. Knowing some of the man's catch phrases
he tried to make guesses at the manager's rationale. A
consideration for the better interests of people. And an
opening out of the use of the rooms of the hotel. Making full
use of this extraordinary facility. Broadening the parameters
of what were deemed suitable uses. Bringing the community
right into the hotel. Offering the resource as a site of excellence, where excellence in all fields could be expected –
accommodation, service, cuisine – now it was to be music,
discussion too. Gray imagined the leader defending the
principle with his usual plausibility; had to chuckle at the
charming notion of hotel as community resource – soup
kitchen-cum-speakers' corner.

The manager took pride in being thought unpredictable;
his surprising ideas were a way of keeping his staff on their
toes and guessing. Pete had declared himself flatly against
canned music and successfully hired Myron on a three-
month contract. It was almost possible this talk feature could
be intended to replace the television. Gray suspected there
must have been times when the man with vision hadn't
actually done thoroughly enough the homework that pre-
ceded the evaluation that always led to his on-the-spot
decision and his inevitable actioning.

A worried-faced Sylvie on reception called Graham over
from the front of the lift doors. There was a message left for
him at the desk. Someone called Marvel – was that right? –
said there'd been a break-in at his mother's flat. She thought
you ought to know that she wasn't hurt, just shaken and if it
was possible to get over there. Did that mean anything to

him? Sylvie asked. He told her yes it did, but as she pulled a wide-eyed-with-worry face – she used to be a model, for lingerie, blouses and tops, she held her expressions a full second longer than most people – the lift arrived and disgorged two rock musicians, black-leathered from neck to toe, hair lank but new washed. She stared as they loped across towards the main door, then turned her attention back to Gray. 'Will you be coming to the talk later?'

'I have to make this call. Can you tell the boss where I am? I'm not needed in the kitchen till five.'

'So your mother's local, Graham. That means you're local too.' She gazed at him with surprise. 'Just like us. And we all thought you'd been shipped in specially.'

'Now you know, Sylvie. I tried to keep it secret,' Graham joked, because joking was always expected. 'Now can you get me a phone line?'

Graham tried the shop number. Oleanders' phone rang and rang and he had to wait.

Michelle breezed into the foyer, casual, dressed in big white T-shirt and jeans, turned Gray's head just as he was about to leave. 'Can we get you along to the talk tonight, Graham? For the lowdown on the river?'

He heard it like it was an invitation from her and her voice stoked some expectation he still had of getting closer to her. Gray had attended RSPB talks when he lived in the country, when slide shows came to the nearest market town. A well-spoken photographer in a wax jacket explained about the hides he had to set up, how long he had to wait and the measurements of his telephoto lens. It was hard to believe that Gray sat knees pressed together with Vivienne, hands touching, fingers playing, her long fingernails on his jeans denim, while an outdoors man with a reedy voice played tapes of woodland birdsong and identified the species with the appropriate slide. They each strained to listen as if at a chamber recital. With an effort to remember for future use.

Their minds went blank afterwards because it was night-time when they emerged, only owls flew; and they forgot everything on the drive home, other things in mind.

'I'd like to. But a few problems at the family home.'

'I never knew you had a family.'

'You should remember. I had to stop for it at the promenade. That was my mother. Now I've just heard she's been broken into. Anyway, what are you doing here?'

'Meeting someone. I'll have to see you later.'

Gray watched her race over to reception and flop athletically on to a waiting sofa, her bag landing in her lap neatly. He was wondering who, here; he had a jealous thought about Myron. But Gray had to press on outside to the bus stop.

'You heard, then. Marva got the message to you. They decided it was my turn.'

'Are you all right though?' Gray peered beyond her hunched shoulder. 'Is there much taken?'

'Not much. I haven't had the heart to tidy up. Besides, the police might need fingerprints for their files.'

She hobbled ahead into the living room. An upended drawer had spilled a heap of haberdashery on her carpet: cotton bobbins, single grey knitting needles, pins, combs, brushes, nail files, thimbles, grey wool on cards, Kirby grips, hair nets, powder puffs, lipstick canisters, compacts, mirrors, drawing pins, Sellotape, folded plastic rain-hoods, free gifts from magazines, tiny perfume bottles, an orange plastic tube of Tyrozets, a brown bottle of aspirin, cotton handkerchiefs, pocket address books, pencils, biros loose from their presentation packs, postcards from seaside promenades, old cigarette lighters, floristry wires.

'How much cash was taken?'

Mrs Connolly was sitting uncomfortably forward on the edge of her armchair, but pretending unconcern. '£120.

Pension day was yesterday. They seem to know. Do you think they're watching outside the post office?'

'You should keep it in the bank.'

'But I thought I'd let you know. In case you were interested in my welfare. Sorry to pull you away from your work. You must have had a lot of dinners to put out today.'

Graham fingered the mess and tried to scoop back into the drawer a handful held together with a tangle of darning wool. 'Who do they think it was? Kids?'

'Someone said it was youths. Youths who make a point of knowing who lives where and what time of night they go to bed as well.'

Another handful back into the drawer, pencil shavings, tacking pins slipping through his fingers.

'So why don't you move? Sheltered accommodation or something.'

Mrs Connolly gripped her stick. 'You haven't come back to put me in a home, I hope.'

'I've told you I've no idea why I came back, Mother. Except to work.'

'Your career, you said.'

'Where it's ended up anyway. Back here.'

'Good enough for most of us.'

Even now she could tussle.

'Are you OK though?' Graham tried to assess his mother's shock. She looked iller, thinner, more cramped and strained, more dependent on her walking stick. It had taken her time to walk back from the front door. But her words still bristled same as ever.

'You didn't catch them at it, did you?'

'I felt the cold draught first. I heard a window bang. And with my legs of course it took me an age to push open the bedroom door.'

'You must have disturbed them then. That's aggravated burglary. You *have* phoned the police, haven't you?'

180

'You're joking, aren't you? First I had to light a ciggie to bring me to my senses. Then I had a good long cough. That's when I began to see the mess around the place. A little later I phoned.'

'What's gone that's valuable?' Gray surveyed the small room in the hope of remembering objects from his last visit. The television set remained, it was black and white only. Some of the older things seemed to be still here, only not in their usual places.

'You see I don't have one of those videos, so maybe it wasn't kids after all. They only really took my precious ornaments, didn't they? And I wouldn't mind betting they'll turn up on *Crimewatch* in six months' time. There's a first: youths who know their onions.'

'The old clock would have been a weight.' Graham pictured its metal casing, and marble-column front, the patches of sky in miniature windows at each corner. From his last visit and from years ago when he had visited Lydia's house. He thought of the great clock being manhandled by black-gloved hands out of a door. And he wondered with how much care the little porcelain shepherdess was carried.

'Everything that poor Lydia left me. All her nice things.'

'Did you report them to the police?'

'Police wouldn't know what Dresden porcelain was, would they now?'

'You'll especially miss those,' Graham guessed. 'Your heirlooms.'

Mrs Connolly paused to guess his tone of voice. Pressed on. 'And this was the worst shock of all.' She motioned to the array of gilt- and chrome-plated self-standing frames that held her selection of family portraits.

'Well, your photos all seem to be there.' Graham didn't look closely at the frames, made an assumption from what he'd seen on his previous visit. Nothing of himself. Nothing of his father. He could well understand. 'As long as Uncle Jack and Auntie Lydia can be said to make up a family.'

Mrs Connolly was careful not to respond to his insinuation. When Graham peered closer, he could see small black felt-tip crosses, like Spot the Ball guesses roughly marked, on every face and staining their suits and dresses. The burglars had taken the trouble to spoil the studio wedding shots.

'What kind of mentality does that to people? That's just defacing, for the sake of it.'

'Felt-tip can be wiped off, surely. It can all be polished clean away, don't worry,' Graham tried to say. 'And were there any of my father, I wonder?'

'You mean Joe Connolly?'

'Who else?'

'You don't ask about him much, do you?' His question had distracted her from the break-in. 'I thought you would more. Aren't you interested at all?'

'What is there to ask?' Gray started. 'He went away. He didn't keep in touch, not really. The last time I saw him was in London. I was trying to be a student and he was pissed out of his brains. We bumped into each other in the Cruel Sea, Muswell Hill. No sooner do I try to get away from there myself than I hear he's died. I don't even like to think of it now.'

'So you haven't forgotten his funeral, son.'

He looked at her accusingly. 'No I haven't. Worst day of my life. Near enough.'

'You realize I'm next. And I'm hoping to get a few more mourners than poor Joe did.'

'It was just grim. And I had to put it out of my mind. And you know why, don't you, Mother? You and me at Euston Station.'

Mrs Connolly chose not to pick up the hint. 'I could tell you things. Don't you want to know? Your father. Your uncle. Dear Auntie Lydia. And me. The things I've done. Your hair would curl. What's left of it.'

'You don't have brandy, do you? I could swig one of those.'

'Listen, I'm the one that needs the brandy. I've had the shock.'

'Sorry. I was forgetting.'

They almost laughed together.

'Never mind the drinks. Just look at this mess, won't you?'

The three hardboard sheets that held her jigsaw puzzles separate had been tipped from the table. The green chenille tablecloth was intact, but the pieces from her three-on-the-go puzzles had slid and tumbled into mounds on the carpet. Gray bent down to gather them together, but could only find one empty box.

'Don't worry, they couldn't be more mixed up than they are now. Someone else will have to piece them together. One day when I'm gone.'

His mother dropped back fully into her armchair. Her legs were weak; most movements caused her discomfort. She couldn't possibly have joined him on the floor as a guide to the puzzle. Gray was grabbing handfuls of cardboard; some already connected pieces held weakly together. The backs were three different shades of brown, the fronts when they showed were simply orange, blue, white or more usually indeterminate. Graham would have needed three box tops to tell him what the finished pictures might be. He guessed: a stately home with formal garden; a large vase of cut flowers; sailing ships in modern setting. He had only seen one box top somewhere in the room.

'No. All I remember,' Graham spoke up from the floor, 'is before all that he was OK to me. He took me down to the river. And he pointed out all the funnels and named the shipping lines for me. Ellerman, Elder Dempster, Blue Funnel.'

'Yes and that's about all you got. There were some things that man just couldn't cope with.'

'You could say that about any of us.' Defence of his father, or of himself. An afterthought came: 'Seagulls make me think of him.' Then his head bowed seriously with the gathering of remaining jigsaw bits.

And when he'd collected all the pieces and funnelled them into one plastic bag in the one box he could find, Tall Ships on the River, he stood up and rubbed his hands free of cardboard dust. His mother had been silent in her chair for almost as long as he'd scrabbled on the floor. His face must have begun to show concern again. When she needled him it was easy for Gray to forget the lady's age and frailty. Now from her slumped body came a sigh that couldn't have been merely theatrical.

'I'm OK, you know. I can sit down here till the cows come home and wait for the lady from Victim Support. Marva said she'd be around soon. You go and see Marva. Why don't you? I've come over all tired now.'

Gray acceded to her will again, with reluctance. He closed her door quietly and walked round to the shop to report to Marva. She was serving a customer, friendly-talking to a man with a bouquet.

Gray explained: 'She threw me out again.'

'But she did ask for you, that's something I thought you ought to know. That's why I rang. How is she now?'

'She should be in shock, but she isn't. She looks terrible. But she's still wanting to rub my nose in something.'

'Just let her rest, if she can.'

Marva turned towards the customer. It was Beagan back again, calmer looking.

'Anyway, someone here wants to make it up to you. Could you mind the shop while I check on Mrs C again?'

'I can't be long though,' Gray offered noncommittally.

'It's all right because Mr Beagan's got something he wants to say.'

Beagan's face wasn't so certain. Marva laughed as she tried to arrange an awkward reunion.

'Can I buy you a drink over the way?'

Marva was encouraged. 'So I can just lock the shop up. And you two can do your catching up.'

'Fair enough,' offered Graham guardedly. 'I've got half an hour or so.'

The two men walked gingerly to the pub opposite, walked in the door with the saxophone above. They stood at the curve of the bar, ordered pints.

'Sorry about before. I do remember you. The same schools, OK, yeah. Fair cop.' He passed a pint glass across to Gray. 'So what have you been doing with yourself all these years?'

'All these years. Not much,' demurred Gray.

'With me it's been too much. Did she tell you?' He let out a laugh. 'I try to block it out, it helps.'

Gray felt awkward at what sounded like an apology. 'I know what you mean, anyway. But I tried it myself, except since I landed back here – my mother, you know, keeps dredging things up. And I spend hours now thinking about them. Days in short pants.'

'Nothing special about school. Good to get it over with.'

'You must remember Prof though?'

'What was so great about him?'

'Didn't you find him inspiring? You were there.'

'I might have been. But I can't say I remember a blind thing.' Beagan smiled at his pun. 'Blocked it out. What is it I should be remembering, anyway?'

Gray had a picture of a narrow room, two aisles of desks. A blind man in a teacher's cloak reciting and overgrown kids in black blazers hunching over desks, listening or not listening, all looking in different directions. The sun coming through the windows and the teacher unable to see how the shadows fell, and every dust mote dancing in the light. One pupil, Graham himself, standing slyly next to him, watching the man for clues, but not daring to breathe; another by the windowsill, another bravely reading a comic, feet gently balanced on a desk top. Something peculiar about the room's dynamics. With most people you looked and talked and looked away. With this man you could look with a different scrutiny. And somehow you could talk more completely because he wasn't watching you either. And there was the anxiety of wondering what he was thinking. Whether he could see more. Knew more. Knew everything. His judgement, Gray thought, must have had more weight than other people's.

'Don't tell me, I know, you wanted to be a friggin poet.'

'Not necessarily.'

It was true Gray had read what poetry books he could find in the public library and tried to shape some gloomy lyrics to impress the girls. Thought about writing a whole notebook full; filled not very many pages.

'Prof encouraged me. You must remember that he singled me out in the class. He said I'd go far. He believed in me. He said that I had some promise.'

'You didn't go very far, did you? Was that your promise?'

'But now it's important to me to know – I mean, if things had been different. Pathetic, I know.'

'Oh, grow up. Another might have been. Regrets I've had a few. I've had a few of these too. I'm ahead of you. Drink up. Another pint?'

'I blame it on the family mess.'

'You heard what you wanted to hear. A friggin dreamer. Always fancied yourself something special. Prof wasn't God, was he? Anyway he was blind so he couldn't see what was in front of him. For a kick-off, Gray, he couldn't see what a berk you were.'

They laughed. Gray almost agreed with that estimate.

186

'Let me buy one.' Gray pulled out his wallet. 'He died, you know.'

'Course he did. But younger than him have gone and who makes a fuss about them?'

Gray had to wait at the bar for the landlord to emerge from a cellar trap door. When he'd finished the business of buying drinks, Gray added: 'You won't remember that he held you up as a shining example. "Beagan wants to go to sea. He knows exactly what he wants to do. He's going straight on the pilot boats. Beagan's somebody that knows his own mind." He admired that.'

'Yes. I went on them. And then I went off them. Here I am fifteen jobs later. No better off.'

'But deciding what to do wasn't a problem for you. It was easy. Whereas some of us . . . we were in a mist.'

'Old Prof was completely in the dark. Making his pronouncements on people and their futures.'

'You're saying he didn't care?'

'I really don't remember him. It's gone. I don't see how you can draw any lessons from all that.' Then Beagan stopped drinking from his glass. 'But listen. One thing I do remember – you had an uncle that was blind. In the merchant. I do remember that.'

'What's that got to do with it?' Gray flushed at the thought of that. The surprise flustered him to make immediate excuses. 'He was blind. Yes. And he was my uncle and he was my mother's hero for years, but I can't remember him myself. Anyway that was way before I ever clapped eyes on Prof.'

'I just thought that might have been why you were so taken with the teacher who was blind. Just a thought. There you are, that's surprised you.' He was already halfway down his second pint, pleased with his perceptiveness. 'Nobody else gave a toss. Just accepted it. You made this big deal that he was blind.'

187

Beagan was capable of some sense after all. Not denying all memory. Just a front he put on to protect himself. But that caught Gray off guard. He decided to try something else on Beagan. If no one else remembered it, he began to wonder, did he, or had he dreamed it?

'And I suppose you have no recollection of the Birdman that fell from his plane and died. French, he was.'

'Why should I?'

'The big air show. Years back. I was seven, and you must have been too.'

'I don't believe I was there. I don't believe *you* was there either. I don't think you're quite here now, if you ask me.'

They laughed, drank down.

'No, I wasn't actually there in person, well, not far off, but I still have a strong memory of it. It's ancient childhood. It hangs there and it just seems important now.'

'Just because you're back here everything in your life has to be important.'

'No, there *was* a Birdman.'

'So what?'

Gray dropped the subject. Perhaps Beagan only made intermittent sense. Then threw his usual cloak of negativity across everything else. Entertained the occasional notion, then closed up again. Gray was irritated enough to press. 'But if I asked you about football?'

'Don't ask me about football.'

'You were the one spotted from the touchline and given a trial. The man in the camel duffle coat.'

'I don't talk about football now. Blocked it out.'

'Another thing blocked out.'

'Another thing, yes. Which I don't talk about to strangers. There's already been more than enough in the papers. I'm not sure I can take any more of it. I have to block it out. Advise you to do the same if you're grieving about something.'

'I don't think that's what I'm doing. Not grieving. No.' And then he wasn't sure. A little fearful of the piercing of Beagan's intermittent sense.

'I used to think I could block it all out. I did for years. I lived in the country all that time. Never gave all this a thought. Now I've even started to write some of it down.'

'Poetry at your age?'

'No, more like memoirs.'

'At your age. I thought you'd grown up to be a cook.'

'I am. I have time to kill in my room. And I think about things. The old lady's gone old. Terribly old. I hadn't realized. Bit of a shock really. And I haven't been in touch with her for years. Now this break-in.'

'Guilt?'

'Loads, yeah. But she isn't easy.'

They each supped a mouthful.

'Women aren't, though, are they? My wife went off on me. Just like that. Said I'd gone off my head. Divorce after fifteen years. It was the boy. She said it changed me. I was a different person. Of course it bloody did.'

Gray shuffled in his seat, ready to escape. He had work to do before he could hope to look in on the talk at the hotel.

'But if I'm asked to go to Basingstoke tomorrow' – Beagan was in full flow – 'I'll go. I'll start again. It's easy. They'll have flower shops there I'm sure. I'd have to come up for the cemetery visits, of course. But I can watch all the football I need on TV. No, this place is full of old people coughing their way to their grave. Hospital city I call it. And this Waterfront garbage is lies about the old boats. The city's finished. For me it has.'

'I think I know what you mean about hospitals.'

Gray stood up to go. Beagan looked up from his beer glass. The conversation had ended by lowering him.

'Yeah. Sorry I can't help you with your memoirs.'

*

Graham had missed the first half of the talk. Michelle was sitting at the front next to the speaker. She lifted a hand to acknowledge him from the stage. Peculiarly friendly, he thought. Suddenly friendly, suddenly not. The last time he'd been with her she'd been running, he'd been trapped by family. She'd flown, he hadn't been able to. Since then fleetingly. He found himself a seat at the back. Spotted Grant three rows away, next to a crew-cut head.

At the front the spry, lizard-necked Dr Miles was drawing his talk to its close: 'There seems some baleful irony, however, that these spillages should be happening in the year when the world's whitest-painted sailing ships should be scheduled to grace our wharves and docks' – he swept an arm across the air grandly – 'for the planned extravaganza of Waterfront 90.' Graham studied the man's bony face for signs of humour. 'What an extraordinary vision that is. When all that seems most picturesque and I might add, saleable, in the word "maritime" – and our tourist office will know what I mean here –' he turned to Michelle, who smiled a quick smirk to dissociate herself '– is being showcased for our cameras, when we know our river is not well. No; I can tell you *they* won't be keeping us informed about the latest oil spill only last week.' He paused, scratched at his scrawny neck. 'Suffice it to say, in conclusion, that Waterfront 90 contrives to be only backward looking if it refuses to consider the future of our river.'

Michelle started the clapping, her broad smile a recognition of the speaker's last barbs. She had to point to a suited man standing mid-row. The clapping faltered.

'I'd just like to come back on the speaker's worries about the tourist facility potential. Basically we all want to see people enjoying themselves on the river. Don't we? Be it on the ferry or watching the magnificent sailing ships. I mean we're all interested in history, that's all very fine. Especially where it enhances our wonderful waterfront, internationally known and loved. But I can assure you we're doing what we can in the development corporation. And may I say we're quite open about the occasional hiccup. I'm only glad of the opportunity to point this out this evening. You may not know that there's a musical initiative too.'

A younger man, brawny, close-cropped head, the one next to Grant, interrupted the official rejoinder. 'Listen here. I served on the tankers and the doctor's right, that was what we did as a rule. We discharged the ballast tanks out at sea, of course. Right out. No harm done there. But I'm not so sure now. No, I'm not so sure now. Erm, that's all I want to say.'

Grant was proud of his friend's contribution. Quite brave and unlikely. Michelle thanked the speaker eloquently, professionally. She invited new membership – leaflets and badges available from the Rainbow stall at the back of the room.

'If anyone wants to stay for a drink – not in the hotel, it's too expensive – but if anyone would like to get more actively involved some of us will be in the pub around the corner.'

The space around the chairs cleared. Grant had slipped away with his friend. Interested bodies gathered round the book stall. Michelle was by the stage amongst the friends, fellow members, admirers and questioners surrounding the speaker.

Gray took himself outside down the street to the high-windowed pub: generous expanses of bevelled glass, some frosted, some clear; ornate lettering on every aperture. He nursed his drink and waited. Then, when he saw her brought in by her Rainbow crowd and seated while they fetched drinks, he moved seats to ask some questions about Myron.

'How do you expect me to help you if you won't see me properly?'

'If what? I didn't know this was a strings-attached friendship. Friends. That's all.'

'Why Myron? What do you see in him?'

191

'Graham, how can I say this? You're not my physical type actually.'

'I'm sorry to hear that.' He tried to conceal a shrug of disappointment.

'It's not your age, don't take offence. He's different. He believes in himself. He might be crazy, he might be, and I can tell you he isn't a gentleman.'

'You mean you don't actually like him.'

'No, you're way off there. And if you really want to know, my own father was a musician too, in a show band. They said he was an informer, but I don't believe he was. He was pretty-faced and angry too, just like Myron. He'll be in one of the English cities. With another woman and another identity entirely. Never mind my mother and me. Who would blame him?' Michelle would keep searching. She would try other cities too.

The thought of her search silenced him. It explained the postcard message she'd scribbled at the museum.

Now her campaign colleagues were approaching their table, escorting the evening's speaker with drinks to sit with Michelle.

'Don't worry. I won't hold it against you.' Trying to be mature, whatever that might be. Needing quickly to be less personal. 'No, I support the cause. I don't like what's happening, same as you. I just thought, friends, you know. Anyway, I'll still help with the Waterfront campaign. When's the next meeting?' He was already trying to retrieve his link with her by being businesslike.

She was explaining to him about an idea someone had for using planes, actually microlites. Did he know anyone who could fly?

Gray would have been excited at the idea in other circumstances, if he had stood a ghost of a chance with her. 'Maybe *I* could. I've done a little bit myself. When I was in the country. I've always been interested in flying.'

'Wow, that's great, Graham.' Her eyes beamed personally directed joy, a knack she had; no wonder he'd been misled.

'You're booked then.' Michelle closed the sale. 'Your name's down, great. I'll pass you details via the hotel. There's plenty of time.'

She turned to give some time now to Dr Miles.

Gray thought he saw Myron's plump face and mop head appear, pressed close against the frosted glass of the pub door; they receded. Gray wanted to disappear back to his room to sift and sort things in his mind. He felt queasy at the way events were accelerating; excused himself; waved to anyone that would notice.

13

1957

The darkness in the room was unexpected. No light from any window. No breeze of fresh marine air through slatted shutters. No Francine either, taking her cough down the stairs to sound a spluttering start to the day, the automatic preparation of two bowls of blackcurrant tea, four croissants. Blaise missed his wife on these trips abroad, but Francine had no wish to budge from the Landes.

It was a narrow bed in a narrow room. At the top floor of the hotel, back room, no windows, he remembered as he woke. And the interpreter, Marie-Sainte was her name, she had slipped out of the room and out of the hotel without waking Blaise. She knew he needed the sleep to be alert for his big day – and he'd have further preparations before the flight itself: transport to plan, wings to fit on, parachute pack to check. He hoped the girl would return soon to help him bluster past any further British obstructions. She might even be useful to him on the plane, deal with foolish questions from reporters. He could even ask her, as she had done last night, to strap his wings on straight – provided she agreed to go up with him in the Dakota.

He thought it unlikely the knock on the door was Marie-Sainte returning. The knock was too confident and official-sounding.

'Monsieur.' A shiny-pated man, soaped and scraped so

clean around the face he shone, tall in a morning suit, black tails, grey-stripe trousers, walked his apologies into the room. 'Monsieur, monsieur. Whatever can I say? My sincere apologies once more.' For the Frenchman's sake the hotel manager employed his arms for emphasis. 'For the room. My apologies. But the show, you see. We are always full for the city show. But this year is a special show indeed. And I can have a more suitable suite ready for you presently. I have made such a room vacant.' The manager looked across at the walls, at the space where a window might be expected, then pressed a palm to his forehead, at the ceiling. 'This room of course could only have been for one night. I was not told. What would your compatriots think of us? When in point of fact the Corinthian knows how to treat special guests. I will escort you to your new room immediately, a maid is preparing it even now.'

'No, not necessary,' Blaise was telling him. 'I am very happy. I do not wish to be moved. Not now. This is my room and I am comfortable. Thank you.' He was hardly awake and he was having to speak English.

'But you are too gracious,' the manager said with relief. 'Surely. An honoured guest such as yourself. I should explain that last night we were completely, completely full. The officers from the army and the air force and the police force, they all decided to stay in great numbers. And the farmers from all over the north of our country. More people than ever this year. So you see . . .' The manager pulled a grey-printed pamphlet from his pocket. 'You can see for yourself in this year's programme. The list is just so much longer.'

'Monsieur.' Blaise wished to encourage him from the door. 'The little room is exactly correct for me and for my equipment.' Blaise nodded towards his wings on the floor, against the wall.

'Ah yes, I see.' The manager gave his understanding nod. 'I've heard about the wings. You wouldn't like me to find a special room for them? Under lock and key. The hotel safe, alas, is a little too small for such a magnificent span.'

'This is the special room. This room.' Blaise was sounding his impatience.

The manager held the door open. A maid stepped under his arm with a tray of fresh coffee, brioche and confiture. He smiled at the Frenchman with his own quiet pride, then as he stepped out into a corridor, casually handed him the limp programme as proof of his own crowded weekend. 'Your name's in there. And there's even a map.'

Blaise snatched it from the manager's hand, hurled himself on to his bed and started on a cigarette as if he might chew it to shreds. He forced himself to scrutinize the many lists of attractions, difficult in English, but he was searching for something in his own field, something to do with aeroplanes, even just his own name in print. He could at least make sense of a sketch map of the showground, where childish tent shapes formed a circle round a target area – this he took to be his landing area as well as a ring for the parading of horses and other livestock. The edges of the map had city buildings to the north-west, a line of trees to the south-east, and towards that line of lollipop trees headed an arrow with a crudely drawn aeroplane attached. Blaise could infer which way he was due to enter the showground area. He took some comfort from this printed evidence that the flight would take place.

A lighter knock on his door was not the manager returning, but Marie-Sainte offering an excited smile to him. She looked fresh and less flustered than the previous day, dressed carefully in more official dress, a suit, lightweight and shiny sky blue. She was more determined to help; and Blaise more willing to accept her help. He handed the programme on to her.

'I haven't time to read this. Please, I ask you. I must begin my morning training. That stupid maître d'hôtel.'

196

He was pushing himself through his stretching exercises, touching toes alternately left and right, and Marie-Sainte understood she was expected to translate for him the parts which referred to his own daring feat. But first she had to satisfy herself by reading through the whole document. Marie-Sainte struggled with the sentences – they floated somewhat free of her understanding – and hearing Blaise puffing through his press-ups now she knew she had to skip most of the lists that followed a sentence proclaiming: 'The tents will again be full of the usual animal, vegetable and mineral treats with keen competition for trophies and prizes.' It was the conscientious student in her which made her scan the complete contents before selecting (and reading aloud in French for him) the only small part that would interest Blaise.

'. . . the noted French aviator, Blaise Desain, the so-called Birdman' – Marie-Sainte looked across to see if he would stop his physical jerks – 'will take off from the airport three miles upriver and when an altitude of around 8000 ft has been reached, he will exit and be carried by his own wood-constructed wings and glide slowly towards the showground area, where he will land safely by releasing his parachute at the appropriate time.'

His press-ups had stopped by now; he changed position for sit-ups. It made him angry that the programme made his danger sound such an everyday stunt, only needing a simple set of instructions to follow. Not something never before attempted in this country – and in France only in front of a handful of people and never in a such a built up area before. As usual they were underestimating his danger. He breathed in through clenched teeth as he fell backwards and out noisily when his head was levered back to his knees. Marie-Sainte thought he was angry with her. She added that they did use the phrase 'death-defying', which she translated for him.

She read the full list of all the aviators and their planes

197

from the programme. That made him even more irritated. A lunatic from Yugoslavia; a jet from the local American air-base; two young English fools with Spitfire and Hurricane, of course they were the highlight, the true reminder of the Battle of Britain. Left-over heroism from the war as usual, not one man's valiant new heroism. The past, always the past for the English. Ten more sit-ups, then he picked up his tunic.

'Time for the airport now. I'm ready to inspect my plane. What about you?'

Marie-Sainte remarked that he was ready for anything, and that she was too. Blaise insisted he did not wish to talk to the organizer, again, ever. He did wish to get his wings safely on board, make some vital measurements and discuss his flight plan with the pilot.

'We'll need to get these wings safely on to a truck.' He reached an arm across the middle of her back. 'And I have a favour to ask you, Marie-Sainte. You have flown before, haven't you?'

On the road to the airport, Marie-Sainte was pressed close to Blaise in the lorry-driver's cab. The driver concentrated on the road and Blaise stared hard at his own knees: he was thinking through his plans, and she didn't want to break into his concentration.

He'd parachuted from smaller planes than this. A Dakota was large enough by parachuting standards. But he wasn't sure about the width of the door. He'd noted the measurements and from previous experience that might present a problem. He'd asked for a larger Dakota, even a cargo plane, something with broad enough doors. He would not only have to launch himself out of the doors, he would need to have clearance for his wings. They'd be folded back on him, like a bluebottle's, or they'd rest down diagonally and awkwardly like a creature in a children's play, a disgruntled angel. He had to think of the movement required. He

198

couldn't simply spread his wings out. From the back of a transport plane, yes, that would be possible. Plenty of clearance. But from the fuselage hatch of a medium-size Dakota, the movement would be more restricted. Folded close then door open (immediate wind rush); wings first then chest out; wings back to catch the updraught (stronger wind rush); then out and hold wings forward on the fighting air. He rehearsed how the sequence of movements would have to go. He would only be able spread the wings when he was out in the air, no retreat, one chance only. The width of the door opening had to be cleared. If the wing ends caught the door, his balance would go, or the wings blown back so suddenly would splinter, hitting the steel of the fuselage structure. Blaise considered all these possibilities from the front seat of a lorry driving through the city.

Marie-Sainte was much more aware of the bombed out church they passed, the street-corner pubs and the half-built cathedral, some high terrace mansions and thousands of tiny terrace houses hugging close in narrow streets, always sloping down to the river.

Eventually the houses visible from the main road thinned out and plane trees lined all the adjoining roads and the wide fields started and the airport approach was signalled by lines of peculiarly squat upturned lamp posts. Marie-Sainte turned for a look of relief on the airman's face. Nothing but concentration, and perhaps a touch of anxiety. Blaise had planned how he would get himself and wings level out of the opening – as if he didn't need to think further than that. When he would also have the job of maintaining his balance and breathing too against the blasts of wind. Would he then have the arm strength to steer the wings, and hold his flight pattern for a gradual descent? He'd been able to before. No; his experience and physical fitness would take care of those worries. He just needed to talk it through with some of the flight staff in the hangar.

So Marie-Sainte left him to take his wings to the hangar and argue with the pilot and engineer about hatch sizes and flight altitudes. She couldn't help him any further with technical matters. He could make himself understood. She sat with a cigarette in the brown-painted cafeteria and waited. She was pestered for over an hour by a reporter, who it so happened was also going up in the plane. She found him unattractive, with thin slicked back hair and a loose dark green suit; he kept offering her cups of tea and chocolate bars.

The Dakota at last appeared in front of the viewing lounge. Steps were fitted to the hatch and the two passengers walked straight to the plane and boarded. The Frenchman, the pilot and an aeronautic engineer were the only ones already on board. The plane moved immediately. Take-off after only a little taxiing.

Blaise didn't speak of his anticipation of flight problems to the journalist. Marie-Sainte would have spoken to him already. She would have told him enough for an informative article: where he came from, his previous record, what he thought about before a jump. Blaise wasn't talking. The man was too concerned anyway with his own flight. The reporter got talking to the engineer all about his wartime flying; and the engineer reciprocated with interest. They became immediate friends. They shared the aerial view of the city's outskirts spread out more and more like a map, the higher they rose. The airport was lost behind, the river shimmered, woods squatted. And up higher it was possible to make out Welsh mountains and coastline. They pointed like boys out of the tiny porthole windows. Flight was always wonderful, they agreed. They let Marie-Sainte help the Frenchman with his wings. She was careful and quiet; he was irritable and silent. But Blaise was soon strapped up tight, confident enough to offer a broad smile. A hug was physically impossible; she was content to pat his chest and tiptoe up to peck each cheek. She straightened his parachute pack, pressed the marvel of his balsa wings. Then: waiting.

When the moment came for the door to be opened the men stopped talking rather suddenly. It was the pilot who judged the park was one mile ahead of them, just as the Birdman had requested. One mile for descent, 8000 altitude and he could control his descent with comfort and steer a careful course at lower altitude and out of the wind and then he'd just have to float with parachute right down to the showground. He'd done that part in practice. He'd done it all before. Blaise crossed himself, took a deep breath, no look back, and jumped.

His wing, or something, slapped the door and the figure disappeared at dizzying speed somewhere down behind the tail and right out of their view. They looked to each other for an explanation. It happened so quickly and they couldn't see. The wind noise made it difficult to be sure of the sound. The reporter and the airport engineer started to whisper about his chances, discussed the thwack they were sure they'd heard. But they each had enough confidence in the Frenchman's experience to right any imbalance in take-off. They made their guesses as to how long his descent would take and how close he would get to the targeted patch of showground below. It was intended to boost confidence. Marie-Sainte was fearful; badly needed a cigarette, knew she wasn't allowed. In a plane without her Birdman. The men looked over at her with something like pity, continued their conversation like passengers on a train.

'He'll be fine though, won't he?' the reporter said more directly to Marie-Sainte. 'He's done it all before, so you were saying, miss.'

'You look very worried, love,' the engineer probed. 'It's understandable. He's a fine man.'

'No, Mr Blades. We're embarrassing mademoiselle,' the reporter tried.

'She's blushing, look.' The engineer had become excited by their talk. 'I think the young lady is sweet on our Birdman friend. Did you see her help him with his wings? Am I right, love?'

'Our photographer on the paper took them for man and wife last night. Did you see the shot, drinking a toast, a charming couple, *n'est-ce pas*?'

More braying laughter, more redness in her face. Handkerchief needed. Laughter silenced.

'Don't worry, love,' the reporter said more seriously. 'Only a joke. Sorry.'

'Nothing meant.' The engineer tried to pat her knee. 'No harm done. Take no notice. Your hero'll be safe.'

The Dakota rumbled high above the dog-leg of the river. Above the long line of docks. Above the railway line that serviced all the riverside activities.

'What else is on the show? Anything interesting?' the engineer asked.

'The usual – sheep and bulls, ponies and dray mares – hundreds of them. Like a giant farmyard.'

'Bet it stinks down there.'

The plane would circle shortly then return to the airport. There were no plans to fly over the showground, since airspace was too busy that day. They'd have to wait for news of the jump when they landed. The organizers would be in close touch with the main showground.

Their take-off had been announced earlier by the Tannoy at the showground; and an estimated time of appearance given. The crowd was told in which direction; they didn't need to be told which way their airport was – upriver. But they didn't know whether to expect a plane or a Birdman – how big a speck in the sky. But it couldn't take a plane more than five minutes to cover that distance. Nothing but a few square miles of fields and scattered trees and houses. The plane was reported to have taken off. Since then the show organizers had heard nothing. The telephone call from the airport and then nothing.

At the city's boundary Joseph and Graham Connolly scrambled over the garden palings and into the fields. Joe set his sights on the cricket pavilion, where they might serve him a beer, the boy some Orange Crush. Sporty people, smell of wood and hops, scoreboards, something there to distract the boy. Certainly Graham wasn't keen on walking, but had learnt to turn most tiresome walks-with-a-parent into an I-spy game. At least he didn't dawdle, but pressed on ahead, on the lookout for skylarks and aeroplanes, anything. Joe tramped along the border of fields, trees overhead, flies from the manure heaps; no, the countryside wasn't his element.

Out of the last field they slipped through the gateway of a broken plank in the perimeter fence on the least public side of the cricket ground. Next to the sight screen, to one side though, not in front, and nobody would notice them, they could sit quietly on the grass. The boy could gaze into the sky or watch the ball if he wanted. There was plenty for him to I-spy. Joseph would settle him and then wander over to the pavilion for the welcoming smell any drinking room gave him.

'Hot after that long walk. I'll just go and get us a drink. You can see the scoreboard from there, can't you? And when I come back . . .'

Graham played with an ice-lolly stick in the grass, content to amuse himself as ever. Joe walked quickly round to where the chairs were grouped, and where the wide wooden hut that was the pavilion had its doors wedged open. When Joe reached the cinder path apron, he turned to mime a big wave for Graham. Men spectators walked towards him balancing pint glasses on small trays. The boy finally acknowledged his signal by holding high his ice-lolly stick, then sinking back to the grass. Joe had the boy's permission to explore the grown-up dark.

And didn't emerge with his tray of beer and orange until half an hour later. He scanned the boundary for his boy, next to the sight screen he expected. He must be hiding, mucking about somewhere. Joe walked as fast as he could with a tray. Peripheral sight of parachutist falling fast. Something was dropping down behind the sight screen. His first thought was for the boy. He tried to hurry with the tray, without spilling good drink.

Graham had watched the plummeting descent and knew near which clump of trees the clattering fall would be. There couldn't have been much of a parachute. Nothing opened. He was the only one seeing it, or thought he was. Fortunately, he hadn't moved far from the sight screen.

'Are you all right? Some pop for you.'

'Something's happened. I saw it.'

Joseph's eyesight wasn't a patch on the boy's. But he'd seen something dropping too. 'I think I might have too.'

'I saw it. He fell. In the field just over there.'

'I'd better tell someone at the pavilion. You wait here. Stand behind the sight screen and don't you move.'

'What about my man who fell?' He claimed the sight, and wanted the reporting of it. The boy started to run.

'No, don't you go over there. You stay behind the sight screen, I told you.'

His father's strides overtook him. He sent the boy back like an eager but disobedient dog. 'I mean it.'

Then Joe Connolly stepped more bravely than he really felt in that direction. Almost ran to the place he expected to see a crumpled mechanical contraption, flapping with shreds of parachute silk; but when he got closer to a lump which distance diminished to a fallen scarecrow's rags, he could soon make out the awkward wooden attachments wrapped round, ripped from a slumped body. His running slowed; he couldn't walk there alone; he'd read and seen enough action, and action films too, to know not to look; and he did the sensible thing, turned around to find help first.

The boy was collapsed next to the sight screen, in tears, and all Joe was able to say to the cricket officials, players and spectators who met him at the pavilion door was: 'Have you got a telephone? Something's really happened. An emergency. Beyond the far boundary. It has.'

They didn't welcome the intruder who'd drunk in their pavilion not five minutes before, and already brought trouble with him.

A barrel-chested cricket player, ginger moustached, pushed through to where Joseph was. 'Who the devil are you? What's all the kerfuffle? You realize, of course, there's a game going on.'

This was the team captain, already out, stumped. When he heard, he quickly agreed to release the doctor from batting duty. The doctor had been padded up for eighth man in, a half-hearted cricketer, couldn't wait for the rugger season to begin. He preferred rugby because it was on the move all the time, not grounded by boredom, watching from a boundary, where the only thing happening was elsewhere, and to someone else.

'I don't suppose, Doc, you've got all your implements with you?' his captain asked. 'Something of an emergency, I hear.'

'In the car.'

'Right.'

The doctor broke into his first run of the afternoon, and his dull cream whites flapped excitedly as he crunched across the cinders of the pavilion car park to his Hillman Minx. Not a Gladstone bag, but a small brown leather document case, stitched at the corners, was enough to hold all his medical essentials. He ran across the grass and into the field, following panted directions from Joe Connolly. Squinting from the sun, he thought he could make out a shape on the ground; then he lost it; he looked for some confirmation from the man puffing uncomfortably behind him, but that man wasn't capable of running and looking at the same time. So much exertion this afternoon. And then the doctor was almost upon a body so entwined with straps and wood it was more mechanical assemblage than human body. Connolly had stopped for breath.

No blood to be seen. But bones and limbs all pointed somehow wrongly in the airman's tunic. Face losing colour already. The doctor felt for the pulse at the throat. He felt where the Frenchman's neck should have joined smoothly to his spine. He even lifted the weight of his head, held the goggles either side of his skull, tried it back a little: no resistance. He let it fall gently back. He had to reach behind a piece of splintered balsa wood and undo a strap to feel where his vertebrae should have been a straight line but now formed a double bend. He felt where a hip pressed awkwardly upwards into tunic material; he took his fingers along the thigh to the tangled bunch of his knee, then too short a distance to the crunch of small bones that should have been his solid ankles. There would be blood inside the boots.

He of course saw that the parachute rip-cord hadn't for some reason been pulled. He couldn't help noticing that one wooden wing was barely damaged, the other a stump, it must have broken off and left him in flight. The doctor noticed these things with far less interest than what he thought of as the spectacular positioning of the bones. The coroner would have to consider those matters in his own way.

'Poor blighter. Poor soul. It's like the war again. I can't. And I can't let the boy either,' the father was heard to say behind him.

'No.' He turned round on this interference. He had felt alone and at peace during his examination. This was an

206

interruption to his train of thought. 'No: multiple fractures to neck, collarbone, back, pelvis, legs, ankles, arms too. Although cause of death may well be simply lack of oxygen. Taking into account the speed he must have fallen and the altitude, of course he'd have had the greatest difficulty breathing. That's more than likely the cause.' The doctor could almost hear himself called upon to give his evidence at the inquest. He would have his judgement ready. But he wouldn't have to speak it with the same impatience as now. The doctor picked up his unopened bag and started on the path their feet had made back to the pavilion. His exhilaration was leaving him, his training controlling his mood more comfortably.

'I'll telephone for an ambulance to collect him from here. No doubt we'll be getting all the background in tonight's papers.'

Joseph Connolly and the boy trudged back along the fields. The boy's face was dirty, sleeve-wiped, swollen. Joseph tried a fatherly arm around his shoulder.

'It's a mystery, honestly. They don't know who he is. Not yet.'

'I know who it was. I saw him come down. I did. And you wouldn't let me see him properly either. Standing behind the sight screen away from it.'

The boy was so persistent, it wasn't right.

'To be quite truthful I feel a bit queasy myself, just thinking about it.' Then he thought about it and it made him angry. 'God almighty, Graham, child, if it hadn't been for me, you'd just see terrible pictures before your eyes all the time, I should know, shouldn't I, from the war. You don't want to be seeing sights like that at your age. You don't, believe me. Son. It would have lasting damage throughout your life. And I know what that means.'

'All day I wanted to see him. And it wasn't fair.'

'Well anyway, it may not have been who you're thinking of. They don't know. Not for definite. Nobody's identified anyone, so we don't really know, you see.'

The crowd was only told a technical hitch had arisen with the Frenchman's flight, some slight flight problems had occurred and would be rectified as soon as practicable. If anything untoward, God forbid, an accident had taken place, the organizers hoped that no one would panic, but there were plenty of other flying feats and if one mishap had indeed taken place this should not spoil the afternoon's enjoyment for everyone.

The Battle of Britain fly-past was distraction enough for most people. The low-flying friendliness of one perky Hawker Hunter, one cheeky Supermarine Spitfire in easy formation cheered the audience. A small prototype jet plane from the local American airbase then buzzed extravagant loops and figures of eight at dangerous and noisy speed. Most people were able to put the Frenchman safely out of mind. And those who were standing by the tent where an old blind man in gabardine raincoat was ministered to with increasing desperation by two women in their thirties, they were able to witness St John's Ambulance put to the test, as in a demonstration; and there were those who were convinced the noisy, choking heart-attack victim was an enthusiastic actor in a very realistic resuscitation and stretcher exercise. But the old man didn't come back, nor the women who looked like sisters, and there were no smiles on the black-uniformed ambulance volunteers, as the hospital ambulance bumped him over the showground. Another Tannoyed announcement promised the organizers would pass on news about the whereabouts of the Frenchman just as soon as it was confirmed.

Some stories had already appeared in the early editions. The compositors had all the names ready typeset in running order and it had seemed safe for the editor to let the story go unchanged under the headline: Birdman Wings in on Show. 'Blaise Desain, the French aviator extraordinaire, successfully accomplished a daring leap from the sky. This afternoon at 3 he safely parachuted the last 1000 feet, after floating the greater part of his descent on home-made balsa-wood wings, and landed perfectly on target in the showground to the delight of thousands of visitors at the biggest City Show since the war.' What followed was an expanded selection of information culled from the official programme: a list of fliers; a list of major sponsors and exhibitors; a list of livestock and vegetable competitions. This official version of the story went out in the first two editions. The type was set; the presses rolled out the first afternoon editions. Nobody in the newspaper office knew any different until over an hour after the Frenchman ended his life in a quiet field equidistant from airport and showground. When the reporter who'd travelled with him in the Dakota had checked at the airport in person, had telephoned the show organizers, had checked with his own desk editor, had rung the nearest hospitals, the search became urgent, and he had finally to enlist the help of the interpreter Marie-Sainte. The presses had to be held, even though it wasn't front-page material, until a confirmed story of the tragedy could be filed for the last edition, and no further damage done to what he thought of as his own personal by-line: Staff Reporter.

Marie-Sainte was the one who had to identify the corpse – they only needed give her a glimpse of his head, spruced up a little, and spared her the crushed, unrecognizable limbs. She took it upon herself to inform the French Consul in person. It was a taxi and ferry-boat ride to the sailing club where he was a member. He explained he'd been himself to the airport and wished Blaise safe flight, bon voyage on behalf of the government. Now he sported life jacket and shorts, puffed a pipe with the unofficial insouciance of a

209

mail-order catalogue male model. He sat her down suavely at his table, brought her brandy. She explained what had happened. She made it clear she'd been interpreter for all his short visit and she'd helped him with his wings and she'd flown in the Dakota, but she'd not known of the tragedy until after she'd landed. The Englishmen in the plane had been beasts. She'd been closer to Blaise than anybody, yes, perhaps, but most definitely Marie-Sainte didn't wish to be the one to ring Francine and tell her her husband wasn't going to return. The Consul could make that telephone call, that was his job; it would be upsetting to her, she felt guilt for the affection she'd given the man, but only after he'd offered the same to her freely too – it was equal; she'd surely blush and make too many excuses if she spoke to the wife. The Consul might only decide to send a telegram, but that was up to him. He would in any case make all arrangements for the return of the body and offer any assistance with shipment and funeral expenses as a mark of respect. He comforted her as she emptied herself of tears at the sailing club, touched her arm a great deal and asked her to be sure to contact him soon because he had many connections who might be generous to her as a lone young Frenchwoman overseas.

On the breeze-blown ferry boat back to the city Marie-Sainte came to a decision about continuing her education in Paris, and trying to stay in the same apartment as her mother. She might be able to save up for London another year. She had the reason she needed to get away from this city.

When he returned to the garden with his father, the boy had tried to resume his game in the dirt of the potato patch. The shadow cast by the early evening sun against the house almost obscured his play area. He crouched, head bowed, with his model airman, dropped from his model plane, crashed in the soil. He kicked at them, raising grey dust. He

210

turned and threw stones, twigs, anything to hand, over the fence into the wheatfield in the general direction of the cricket pavilion. And he didn't understand any of it, except he knew he felt upset about it.

He went to tell his father at the other end of the garden again: 'I feel sick in my stomach.'

His father had soon returned to dozing in the deckchair, not listening properly to the radio broadcast, a talk about London.

'Do you want some Andrews, son? That usually does the trick for me.'

'It's not going to go away. I can feel it, Dad.'

'What have you had to eat today, I wonder?'

'No, Dad, you saw what happened. You nearly went up to it.'

'Put it out of your mind. Best thing. I have already.' Which wasn't quite true, he knew even as he said it, because this wasn't so far away from a torpedo death, still terrible, still the thing for nightmares. The drink might be the best for covering all that up.

The boy went back again to the end of the garden, looked across the fields. His father didn't understand. He couldn't play the plane game now, so he threw stones into the fields, stone after stone from the collection he'd made to clear this patch of earth for his airport.

Now his father had folded up his deckchair and taken his empty beer bottles inside. He had unplugged the wires from his wireless set and he was sitting waiting for the evening newspaper to be delivered. There'd be reports of the show. He could keep the boy quiet by showing him the true story in the paper. Some reassurance from the real world.

But Graham still wanted to know why his mother was so late, why she wasn't home yet. Even though she had gone to the show without him, and he was annoyed enough about that, he was still worried that something might have

211

happened to her. Since terrible things do happen. Would the newspaper tell them? She ought to be home by now. He had to tell her what he'd seen. And his father had nearly been right up close to the corpse.

Joseph felt protective of the boy, but also inadequate to the protection of him. This afternoon in its pieces had left the family somehow in its own fragments. Not just the boy. His wife would return to what? Bringing with her the foolishness of this whole Captain Argent business. The boy's fallen Birdman. And now he didn't really know what could happen for them all after this. After the Isle of Man. For himself it was feeling that something was certainly finishing. Too messily. A drink at the Coronation would help matters temporarily. But London next, probably, and separate from the boy.

14

1990

Graham pushed the wheelchair gingerly up towards the reception desk. Nurses, visitors overtook them. He pressed a nose flat at the Perspex.

'My mother here, she's had a fall. We think she might be suffering shock.'

'Patient's name, please, and GP?' The question floated from below a crown of curls.

Gray gave his mother's surname, his own, but failed to answer the second part. Marva stepped past Gray to supply the local information. The woman looked up with more interest at a female speaker.

'Don't I know you from somewhere? Do you work here?'

'You might have seen me popping over with flowers,' Marva admitted. 'We're from Oleanders, over the road. This lady is too, sort of. We think it's her shoulder this time.'

'Is that how you say it? I never did know. That's where I've seen you, then. Olly-anders. How's business, love? Quiet like everywhere?'

Marva was beginning to lose patience. The old lady in the chair was worryingly silent. 'Mrs Cecilia Connolly is her name. Her GP is Sedgewick. She's already bad on her pins, she was broken into last week and now she's done something to her shoulder. She said she heard the crack.'

The woman typed the details on to her keyboard, and in

response a printer at another desk stuttered to push a curling label out.

'It's busy tonight – I'll try and get you through as quick as I can, seeing as I know you.'

Gray leaned over to hurry her. 'She is in pain.'

The receptionist knew how to deal with male impatience, had daily experience of what men knew for certain. 'Take a butcher's, sunshine, they all are, otherwise they wouldn't be here.'

Gray peered round the desk to the waiting area, where seats overflowed untidily, as at a holiday coach station. A child of two screamed and screamed, bunched fist in his eye, clutching a wet snowball of cotton wool.

'I couldn't help it,' his mother addressed the room. 'It was an accident. A cup of tea. I'm not having another social worker in my house. No fear.'

Gray and Marva tried to sit next to a grim-faced man in work clothes, sleeve ripped as far as the elbow, holding his wrist rigid. He moved along the leather-look bench a few inches. Enough room for Marva to sit next to the old lady's wheelchair. Gray had to stand awkwardly, as if on a bus, exposed to the collective stare of all the stunned outpatients, nothing else to look at except posters about a gigantic exploding eye in full colour, one about dirty syringes, one, without illustration, about blood donors. Gray shifted and surveyed the dramatic edges of the room. A trolley was the sedan for a young man in nothing except jeans and a serene alcoholic smile, his cropped hair blood-dampened from a long gash above one ear. And propped on the next trolley sat bald-headed twins, same sports jackets, same trousers, huddled against a wall, wearing identical camel bedroom slippers dangling loose, one ankle between them bandaged, it was difficult to tell whose.

Gray said, unnecessarily, 'Are you all right, Mother?' His voice sounded like a shout, the accent wrong for the city,

214

'Mother' unnatural, but he hadn't, after all, said Mum easily in recent years.

Tired themselves from trying to be stoical, the heads turned because it was a less talkative meeting place than any bus station. Gray resorted to his watch. His mother wasn't answering. Her jaw had stiffened in sympathy with her shoulder. She held everything tight to herself in case it all collapsed into her, skin, bone, gristle all together, in a delocalizing of pain, just there, in her and all through her.

'We'll have to wait, Mrs C. We'll listen out for your name.'

No response from the patient. A suggestion of a nod.

'Do you want to read a women's magazine?'

Marva turned to quieten his stupidity.

Two nurses danced from behind a cubicle curtain, cards in hand, shouted the names across each other – Davies, Mc-Killop. And again crosswise, as if this was one double-barrelled name they were both attempting.

Eight names before a call included Connolly. And then all that the shuffling into a cubicle resulted in was cardigan and blouse unbuttoned and half off. Her loose bare arm hung somehow free from her clothing and seemed to hover in her lap. And then what? The old lady looked from Marva to the nurse and then to him: registering her sense of absurdity, waiting all this time just to sit with a nurse and look at a wall.

'What are we waiting for?' Mrs Connolly spoke at last, with a new wince.

The nurse answered: 'Waiting for the consultant. He's Iranian, Dr Haji. But very good.'

He nodded as he processed in. 'What happened to this lady to make her so distressed?'

'She fell awkwardly, doctor. We wondered if she was in shock.'

'And she's unusually quiet – for her.'

'No I'm not.' A voice of defiance.

215

They laughed, but not altogether convinced.

'You see,' the doctor encouraged her, 'she has an indefatigable spirit. Haven't you?' He pronounced this so carefully, as if to dispel, with one word alone, all their worries about foreign doctors. His hand stroked her arm, probed her shoulder blade gently, fingered her spine, pressed on her knee, rested at her back. Mrs Connolly stiffened with every touch.

'We'll send you to X-ray, then you'll need the arm dressed and plastered by another nurse and she'll issue you with a sling. And then' – he breathed deep – 'we'll have to see.'

The nurse led them away to X-ray. Marva pushed the wheelchair down the corridor. Gray pressed the buttons for the lift doors. Before they opened the nurse explained, 'You'll have to wait for X-ray now. Are you family?'

'Yes.' Marva nodded.

'We both are,' said Gray with a pleased confidence. He was establishing his right to wait. He wouldn't escape, he wouldn't stay away this time.

'We could admit her on our emergency ward but she won't get any sleep. She might also be better off at home. I'm afraid there's no guarantee there's a bed free for her.'

'I think I'd like to see her settled in safely,' Marva said firmly. 'Put my mind at rest.'

'I'll second that.' Gray allowed Marva the lead in these delicate negotiations.

'Once Dr Haji has seen the X-rays you'll know if it's necessary. I think he is a little worried about her.' The nurse was hinting at her own concern. 'Her bones are very brittle.'

They waited with Mrs Connolly in the wheelchair in a corridor outside X-ray. A trolley, bearing the head-wound youth singing and clutching his skull, rolled past and smoothly through the danger-marked doors.

'I might have to ring the hotel. Depends how long we have to be. What about the shop?'

'The shop's closed. I'll have to work late tonight, won't I? You don't have to stay if you don't want.'

'I do though,' Gray assured her.

'She's very quiet, isn't she?'

'Are you OK, yourself?' It was a pointless question. His hand dared a pat on to her sleeve as an explanation of sorts: sympathy for worry that had to be greater than his.

Then the old voice broke through the moment: 'Where am I? I can smell chrysanths.'

'You're in hospital.' Marva stood forward. 'It's your flower girl that smells.' She coughed a little as she said that.

'All I can hear is you two babbling. Don't start getting ideas, will you? Hospitals can do that to people, you know.'

'We thought you were asleep.' Marva pulled herself back to everyday smiling toughness.

'What was she talking about?' Gray whispered.

Cissie Connolly sat up suddenly. 'I've been here before, you know,' the voice confided to them.

A bright porter appeared that moment to bend down and undo the brake on her wheelchair, wheeled her smartly away. 'Me too, love. Every day of the week, and some of the hours are unsociable, I can tell you.'

She was pushed niftily into X-ray by the porter, a red light flashed above the doors, and then she was delivered as quickly back to the corridor waiting place. Marva and Gray sat silently on the nearest corridor seats, separated.

'Are you still here?'

'Course we are, Mrs C.'

'Is Jack here? They used to let me visit him.'

'What are you talking about, Mother?' Gray was irritated by her loss of awareness. 'You're not the one visiting. We're visiting. Me and Marva. And you're not well.'

'The nurses left us alone. Jack was a lovely man.'

Marva and Gray could look puzzled above her wheelchair without arousing her suspicion.

'You two. You're not up to any funny business, are you? Don't think I don't know about all that. I'll have to tell you one day. Graham. Before I go.'

'You ought to rest, Mother.'

'Yes, Mother,' said Marva, half joking, worried.

Gray got the wheelchair in motion again.

'You have to go for your sling, now. They may decide to keep you in for observation.'

'Everywhere hurts, Marv.' Her bony hand raised itself awkwardly backwards on to Marva's knuckle. They waited. The lift doors opened like curtains for them.

15

1949

Mrs Bulstrode, Cissie's employer at that time, kept a flower stall going at the central market, and one at visiting times at the hospital, in case trade was slack at the shop. But trade wasn't so very different then: people still mostly bought flowers for weddings, funerals and hospital visits. There were plenty of graves to visit, war graves and memorial cenotaphs for military parades to march past and salute every year without fail. And men still convalescing in hospital unlikely to work again, men who were fit and strong before the war. And the walking wounded weren't ashamed to unbutton their army surplus khaki shirts to show off their pale resilient torsos, as if they sported terrible gashes or rashly bought tattoos. So many lucky men because the women were in a majority. They were the lucky men who returned from active service with their stories. Lucky men too had been in reserved occupations, able to be draughtsmen and farmers, seamen and dock workers without interruption. And some were fortunate in their postings – Canada, Scotland, the home front – just as their relatives were unlucky to be in Egypt, Normandy, Burma.

Cissie had heard of the resentments of women and the secret shames of men, when someone had an easy war and their neighbours far from it. Her brother-in-law's poor sight had disqualified him from full service. He'd assisted with the protection of the river, his knowledge had been useful. She knew war widows who had to appear proud and not in too much of a hurry to marry even if they had the unlikely opportunity, to fight off the too public memories that relatives claimed. And relatives would insist on visiting, sitting in the front parlour and nodding once with a Cyprus sherry to a forces photograph on a sideboard.

And the man Cissie made a mistake in marrying, at a time of weakness, the man who had seemed a lively soul at the VE Day celebrations, who could dance proper steps, quickstep and valeta, charmed her the next time they stepped out on the town together, he was drinking more than ever, though never in her company. He was trotting out his tales of a torpedoing to a settled audience at his local, who still pretended to listen and agree he was a card, a character, a gentleman. The man was scarcely ever at home. And Cissie made herself busier than ever at the shop because there was more to do. Mrs Bulstrode might be going into retirement soon, her husband's fortune was made importing sugar, and she could concentrate on her precious cocker spaniels.

Cissie still felt herself tied somehow to the fortunes of her sister and her husband, the Captain. She looked up to these people. They were her standards. She'd admired their house and its tasteful contents unhealthily. It angered her so much she wanted to be brave enough to set up on her own, show them; prove herself equal, need Lydia's approval less, even if it meant trying to score off her sister in order to prove her mettle to her brother-in-law. Was it fair that the man so dignified and upright, with a gentle chuckle of humour in his voice, who responded to the youth in her voice, could be so chopped down by misfortune, eye problems, in his prime? He was a fit nearly fifty. Her own husband was still in his thirties but not half so vigorous. None of this seemed fair, but resentment only partly accounted for Cissie's more than proper sympathy for the patient.

220

Because of Mrs Bulstrode's arrangement with the hospital, visiting times only, Cissie was a familiar face on the wards. She could shut up the shop and service the hospital, without suspicion. Matron allowed her to collect up all the old stalks, empty the vases from the wards, pour the water foul with soft rotted foliage down bleach-drenched sinks, and replenish them with new blooms. Cissie skipped down the long quiet corridors. Nurses she half knew called out to her.

'It's the flower girl.'

'Have to keep the place cheerful. It's virtually spring.'

Cissie was regarded by all the nurses as a fresh and friendly face, even by matron who kept a stern eye on all who passed. They all liked to see Cissie busy by in her long maroon coat and floral blouse, tossing her fly-away hair behind her, thin arms cradling bunches of cut flowers.

'It's harvest festival all the year round with you. Am I imagining it or are there more than usual at the moment?'

'Yes, I am quite busy. These wards are inclined to look grim without my splash of colour.'

The wards were tall and pillared, mushroom walls, dark-stained woodwork; small table by each pillar, high table and squat cabinet by every bed the same. Each vacant surface on the ward and every window still to be checked for vases, twigs and stalks in a jam jar, as for a church's nave. Cissie walked the gauntlet of the men's ward beds, flowers clutched to her bosom. They whistled.

'Petal. You shouldn't have.'

'I haven't. Not for you.'

Cissie had no difficulty putting men in their place if need be. She responded more to kindness in men than to cockiness. She pressed on ahead for a curtained bed at the far end, where it was quiet.

'Here I am again, Jack. Are you decent?'

She dived through the curtain, bumped hard into a tall

heavy woman, ginger bun under her cap, changing pillow cases.

'I thought you'd have gone by now, Mrs Connolly.' Which flustered Cissie momentarily.

'I stayed a bit longer.'

'And weren't those vases only changed yesterday?'

'I like to keep everything fresh.'

The nurse cast a suspicious eye across to the bed where Captain Jack was propped, dozing against a new buffer of pillows, bare hands and forearms, pink as a butcher's, on top of the counterpane.

'Got a special patient here, have you? Is that what it is? Someone you're specially fond of?' She chuckled to herself, as she gave the mattress five heavy blows with the heel of her hand. 'Well, don't we all have favourites?'

Cissie decided to elaborate the excuse, instead of blushing. 'The funeral homes are still sending us all their left-over floral tributes. Nothing goes to waste.'

'I think you do us all a great service. To sweeten the atmosphere.' She sniffed the air warily. 'Especially men's wards.'

'They have to be tended,' Cissie told her with conviction, 'otherwise they pong. I'm talking about the flowers, you understand.'

The nurse sniggered at Cissie's sleight of hand. The women had a complicity already, an understanding of hospital feelings, different from the outside world of compromise.

Cissie stepped up to the bed, reached up to kiss the man's bandaged eyes. 'This one's my favourite. Aren't you?' She addressed him in his sleep.

'Hmm. I see how it is. You won't be needing me now.'

As the nurse passed through the curtain folds, Cissie dropped into the bedside chair, as if it were her own rocker in front of her own coals and this was comfort. She lifted down from the table the book with the linen bookmark dangling, eased it open to where she'd last been reading when he fell asleep.

'Is that Cissie? Carry on, angel. I didn't drop off, did I?'

She rubbed a hand on his arm and pulled it back for page turning. She had already read to him about Youth and someone called Lord Jim. He knew his books so well he could ask her to read extracts, even without sight he could direct her. This afternoon she read about a certain ageing Captain Whalley who needed to keep working on his boat for his daughter's sake, ignoring the problem of his failing sight long past the point of safety. Terrible loss of dignity in the end.

'Are you sure this is the story you want to hear?'

'These tales make sense to me. Don't ask why. You will keep reading them for me, say you will, child.'

Lydia, his wife, wouldn't ever read for him. So, naturally, Cissie was agreeable. She read through descriptions of ships and their cargo, landscapes, rivers, the foreign names, she took them in her stride, she'd always been good at English. The words soothed her ear by a kind of rhythm that the sentences developed, they pressed on in a winding way, leading somewhere she wasn't always sure about. The stories were not always interesting to her – no happy marriages, no love tangles. But he was nodding attentively as if there was a clinch or a murder every single page. He was smiling like a child. He might even be weeping underneath that cotton lint taped to his eyes. She imagined, as she read, she could happily cosset this child as if it were her own lost father. That would be a heaven of right feelings compared with the recriminations of her life with Joe Connolly. She would lavish care on him and his bravery – this bravery now, not wartime risks. She'd sink into his big pink arms and sniff his sweet breath. And he wouldn't ignore her, because he'd be dependent on her, and she wouldn't mind at all, unlike her bossy sister, who was not a patient woman and had a new interest in lodgers and no time at all now for invalid ex-sailors.

Cissie heard doors flapping and soon felt the cool afternoon's draught. She could hear sounds from outside, the approach of hard footsteps, click-heeled. The longer they took to approach the more certain she was they were not nurses on duty, but Lydia's.

The curtain was tugged open hard and wide: 'What a charming tableau! I must say!' Lydia tugged at the outsize top button of her winter coat, pulled at the soft wool scarf at her throat. When she breathed out, her chest heaved in the attempt to stay calm.

'I'm reading to him. Jack likes these books.'

'The girl's doing no harm at all, Lydia,' the voice from the bed bleated. 'Don't go getting the wrong impression.'

Lydia pushed a shoulder between the chair and the bed. Jack leaned back on the pillows, was soon quiet enough to seem to be asleep again.

'Except it's not your husband, is it? Where is your own husband anyway?'

'Where do you think, Lydia? In the pub, being charming.'

Lydia was peeling her gloves off, pulling things from a black leather shopping bag. 'Do you mind? I've got his personal things here.' She pushed past the chair to place her neat pile of coal-tar soap, flannels, hand towels on the shelf of the bedside cabinet. 'Thank you.' In her not amused voice.

Cissie had closed the book and pushed the chair back, ready to leave. Lydia was pulling out a Thermos flask of tea.

'Well then, it's up to you to keep him at home, isn't it, Ciss? You've got a nice new council house, haven't you? There's a garden. In need of digging no doubt. You're lucky to get that. There's many are happy enough with flats, but you're not satisfied, are you?'

224

Cissie hated her sister most of the time. She hated the way she was spoken to by her. She hated her presumption. She hated her possessiveness. She hated that she was married to a kind-hearted man. She hated especially when she talked about husbands.

'When are you going to surprise us all and start a family?'

'When I'm good and ready. And maybe I won't, I'll be a shopkeeper instead.'

'You've got a nice enough house.'

She hated that Lydia's house was full of nice old things. She hated that Lydia complimented her too much on her new but empty-roomed austerity council house.

'Since when have bricks and mortar helped a woman start a family? It didn't work in your case.'

'I couldn't. You know very well I couldn't. It wasn't Jack, he was capable, so far as we know. It was my side, the doctors said I couldn't, something not quite right with my insides which I don't wish to go into even though we are standing in a hospital and there's doctors and nurses know all about that kind of thing.'

Lydia walked them down past the end of the bed, out of her husband's earshot, but still within the curtained tent.

'So how was Jack about kids?'

'He was disappointed, if you must know. I don't say he was disappointed in me. Like any man, like your Joe too I don't doubt, he wanted a son. Of course he did spend long times away. And on shore leave he didn't stay in the house very long.'

Cissie didn't sympathize with her sister. She hadn't treated her man kindly. She had been proud of him and far too proud through him. But she hadn't cherished him. And she wasn't the right person in any case to bear his child.

'He'll be housebound from now on.'

'He will,' Lydia admitted in a disappointed voice. 'And I'm not looking forward to that.'

She turned back towards the bed head, away from her sister's impertinent questions. 'I'd better see my husband alone now, if you don't mind. If he'll have me. You've probably tired him out with your attentions.'

Lydia enjoyed the verbal tussle with her sister, but still didn't trust her. She patted the bedclothes hard to rouse him. 'I'm here to see you, Jack. I had to catch two trams to get here. And, believe me, it's not warm out there. I've left the lodgers to fend for themselves.'

Cissie broke in again: 'Don't worry. I've only been reading to him. They've got lots of books in the common room and I know he likes this one Conrad chap.'

'How ridiculous. He should be resting. And you should be at home.'

'Should.'

'What's keeping you here?'

'I've got more vases to clean out. And I might need to nip over the road to Mrs Bulstrode's for a fresh supply of early daffs for the corridors.'

Lydia seemed relieved that she was busy with her work, but suspicious of her closeness: 'You're a sight too handy nipping back and forth, for my liking. But I can't stay myself more than a few minutes. Like I said to him I've got my lodgers to feed. Thought I'd call over though.'

'They're like your children, aren't they?'

'What if they are? I'm going to have it hard from now on, him the way he is.'

'I'll pop in on him from time to time – as I'm in the vicinity.'

'Not too often, though,' warned Lydia. 'I just have to explain to him about these toiletries, then I have to be off.'

Cissie wandered as far as the women's ward. She busied herself at a windowsill, cleaned out a few more vases. She was mistaken for a cleaner. She was asked to help move a bed across the ward. She kept herself close to the doors which gave on to the same corridor as the men's. Her ears were attuned to pick out a pair of hard heels clacking through to the front entrance and away to the tram stop and the night.

Cissie took herself back stealthily after official visiting time was over. The lights had been dimmed to give the few patients the chance to attempt sleep. So it was too dark to read. She slipped inside the curtains again. His big white head nodded above the high pillows.

'How are you Jack, really?'

'A bit confused, to tell the truth, love.' Jack shifted in the sheets to demonstrate his wakefulness. Eye opening wasn't possible. 'The rest of me's in better shape, you have to believe me. It's only my eyes that hurt.'

'I can see that, can't I? I've always known that about you.' She rested a hand on the sleeve of his grey winceyette pyjama jacket.

Curling white hair rose out from his broad pink chest, his veins visible. Jack pulled Cissie's hand into his jacket. She felt the belt of flesh round his middle, pressed her fingers comfortably into it.

'Your fingers are chilly, child. Let me warm them for you.' He folded them in his two soft fists.

Cissie relaxed. She rested her head sideways on his stomach, looked up with amazement at his bandaged face. She felt a warmth she'd never quite felt on a bed with Joe. And beyond any guilt she felt, there was pity for the man, regret for lives lived otherwise.

'You know how I've always felt about you.'

'I've felt similar, Jack, when I've been allowed.'

'Not everything's allowed – is it?'

'My being here isn't either.'

'I'm very glad you are, child. I need you to be here. I have to feel, because I can't see. Come and sit on the bed properly.'

Cissie peeped out of the curtain before hitching her wool

skirt to her knees to raise her legs on to the mattress. The Captain's fingers pushed into the strands of her hair, massaged her waves, pressed all round her tingling head. If Cissie hadn't pulled the weight of her body full on to the bed she would have slid off. She pulled at his arms, she reached for his shoulders. She kissed his chest because she dare not kiss his bandaged face. He calmly lifted up his blanket to let her in on top. Cissie moved to loosen her clothes, free herself from their buttons to give herself fully to him.

Cissie had to stifle the convulsions her whole body made. She bit the coarse woollen blanket to prevent the cries that would otherwise have issued full-throated from her mouth. And when he was still and her body calmed, she lay trembling with worry about his sweat and high colour, would the doctor notice, would it do him harm? She worried about any tell-tale smells. Their breathing was still audible. She buttoned her skirt back and her blouse. She straightened his pyjamas. She eased her new heaviness back into the bedside chair and marvelled at what she'd just done.

The clatter of shoes running on the wooden floor sounded especially loud to her enlivened senses. She pulled herself to sit straight in the chair, straightened her waves, grabbed a book as if she'd been reading to herself in the dark.

The feared voice shouted through the curtains: 'I had to come back, Jack. The trams are running late and besides, I think I must have left my purse here.'

Until she saw Cissie in the chair.

'What in hell's name are you doing still here? My sister. And halfway on the bed.'

'I already told you I've been reading for him. He's resting now.'

'You've been on his bed, haven't you?' She glanced at the crumpled blankets. 'You've been slobbering over him, while he's stricken.'

Cissie was standing now, edged against the wall. Lydia

228

stared hard, reached for a bedside vase as if to strike her sister. Her hand roughly pulled out five daffodils and their dangling, closed up heads, hurled them in the direction of her sister's face, showering her husband's bedclothes with vase water and Cissie's front with broken leaves.

'What kind of twisted person are you?'

The flowers flopped into the pull-around curtain and dropped to the floor. A tiny grey-haired nurse, the sister, was standing arms folded.

'What on earth's going on here?'

The Captain's confused voice was roused. 'Hang on there. I can't see, you know, girls. What's the matter now?' He sat up, moaned with the pain from his eyes and face.

'Precisely what I'm wanting to know,' shouted the ward sister sternly. 'I've got patients here seriously ill. I can't be having them disturbed like this.'

Cissie tried to shift behind the nurse's back.

Lydia looked to the woman for support. 'What do you think, matron? I'm this man's wife. And that woman there—'

'No need. I was just going anyway.'

'My sister. Could you believe that? Go now, Cecilia, and don't come back.'

It wasn't possible to claim pride, but defiance came quite naturally. 'You've never understood, have you? The man needs cherishing,' she cried. 'Not all this.'

'Don't tell me what he needs. Don't you come back, just don't come near him, ever, and don't even think about visiting our house either. You won't be welcome to me or to Jack.'

'What a disgrace, the pair of you!' The sister claimed control of the situation. 'I'm afraid I'll have to get the porters to eject the both of you.'

Lydia quietened after the upset of Cissie's departure. She began for the first time to cry, dry, difficult sobs. Cissie could hear them following behind her as she slipped away.

'That woman has her own husband. That woman. My sister. Who would credit that?'

If Cissie had been a drinking woman she'd have slopped a full bottle of Cyprus sherry down her throat to make her forget. If she hadn't been a strong swimmer she'd have taken herself to the promenade and leapt in the dangerous river. Instead Cissie walked right through the park, stomped round all its paths, bruised by her banishment and filled with his sperm. She wandered in the chilly night until the pubs had shut and all the regulars had been ushered home. Then she headed for her council house. She marched straight upstairs. She climbed into her wide marriage bed and pulled her husband to her.

'What's got into you?' Joe Connolly was surprised to say. 'You're friendly all of a sudden.'

He was tired, sleepy otherwise. But he didn't mind straightening his drink-softened cock since he was so unusually welcome this night of all. He rammed blindly into the surprisingly warm wet flesh of his wife, was relieved to soon ejaculate inside her, fell sideways into his pillow bolster, stared at the brown on grey flower-pattern curtains.

'Do you think we'll ever have a family?'

'I hadn't thought so.'

'Me neither.'

They lay silent, not used to easy pillow talk together. Daily information was all he could approach her with: 'How was the Captain anyway? How's Lydia taking it?'

'She was mad with me for visiting. I'm banned, Joe.'

Her husband laughed. 'Thank goodness for that.'

'You don't understand, do you? I mean totally banned from the house.'

'I can't say I'm sorry.'

Cissie knew she would have to be hard from now on – towards him because he didn't understand anything and didn't even try. And towards the couple who'd excluded her so implacably from their lives. Joe's exertions mixed with his alcohol dragged him soon into his sleep.

'Completely.'

She wept most of the night. It was particularly difficult for her because she had an inkling then, as she'd heard women say with such certainty, that she was pregnant from that night.

16

1990

In the weeks since his mother's fall it hadn't been easy for Graham to get away from work to visit her in hospital. Staff cuts at the hotel had meant Grant wasn't able to cover for him in the kitchen. Gray still had that nervous stomach reluctance about going because he hadn't found being with his mother at all comfortable. He didn't expect ever to get close to her, or for forgiveness to fall between them. But each time he saw his mother – and he didn't feel proud of this, she was an old woman, he was her only son – something new was set off by something she said, some reminder, something past and forgotten, by him. And he resented that. But it had him awake every night late in his little room scribbling in his notebooks. He followed her hints. And the clues and his own guesses multiplied as he gave them his attention. He had been tracking down some of the old mysteries he had all but forgotten, when he was a child of seven and his world changed. His compulsion was only to connect the darkness of childhood with this life restarted.

Graham hadn't actually missed visits he'd promised his mother. But he hadn't been able to go whenever he had free time, no one could expect that of him. On the bus ride to the hospital there was always hope the visit might be better than dutiful, awkward. There was the possibility, there was, that in her weakness she might let him be of help. Always supposing he could know what to offer – talk to doctors, reassure with the usual bland alleviations. In any case each time he announced himself at the ward station, the nurse said: 'Her other visitor's here already.'

Marva always occupied the chair beside the bed. And at first he was embarrassed how she monopolized his mother and was able to talk to her about the shop and flowers in the market and reminisce about their more fanciful customers, and the ones who tried to treat Marva with insufficient respect. Marva possessed this knowledge Gray had no access to.

But as Mrs Connolly's condition had deteriorated, and not slowly, the patient talked less. It was uncomfortable for her, she was more heavily drugged, she slept more. And so when their visits coincided, they talked more with each other. Their concern for the old lady's condition was mixed with an interest in each other that bordered on flirtation.

'What's happened to your girlfriend? Run away again?'

'She's a friend. Not more.'

'Not for want of trying, eh, Graham?'

'She's involved in a campaign I have some sympathy with. It's all about the river.'

'Superwoman strikes again.'

'Michelle's full of energy and enthusiasm, if that's what you mean.'

'And with a conscience. My my.'

'I said I might help with their campaign. They want to do something at this Waterfront 90 festival. If I can help I will. They think they'll get attention because rock music people will be there, apparently.'

'Yes, I read the leaflet and I chucked it.'

Marva's lack of interest wasn't spite directed at him. Her own energy was being directed into most of the responsibilities of Mrs Connolly's illness. She'd been the one to speak to the nurses, bring in the flowers and the fruit, the soap and fresh facecloth, hand towel, 4711, Vaseline skin cream. She'd filled the bedside cabinet to bursting with linen, under-clothes, and fragrances to ward off the stinks of morbidity.

'How's my mother been today?'

'There's no doubt,' Marva whispered low. 'She's fading.'

Graham nodded, because he sensed too that an end was approaching. He hadn't had time to register any nervousness about how it would be. It was now, and no preparation.

'It just doesn't seem right to see her like this.' His hand pointed to the bed and completed its arc close to his cheek. 'I mean, nothing to say for herself.'

'It's late in the day, Graham.' Marva laughed. 'But you're trying.' Gray didn't feel laughed at. The teasing was not unkindly meant.

'But don't you think she seems to shrink further into the sheets?'

'Graham. She's still conscious. She might hear you.'

Two nurses strode up to grip her, elbows linked inside elbows, to lift the body up and turn 30 degrees to cheat the onset of bedsores. It seemed unnecessary, unkind to disturb her from whatever rest she'd got left. Pillows were plumped on the hour, bedpans regularly brought. Mrs Connolly's eyes opened and looked gratefully on the girls determined to disturb her peace.

'I don't mind.' Mrs Connolly smiled as she piped up with conviction, 'You're getting me ready, aren't you?'

'We have to keep you clean and tidy and sweet-smelling for your visitors, don't we now? Your son's here, did you know that?'

Mrs Connolly didn't reply to that information, but gazed at the nurse, as if about to say something more, then closed her eyes to sink back into her rest again. Pungent ammoniac whiff from the sheets, and the swiftest linen change by the nurse team. Mrs Connolly slept through the four hands fiddling underneath her bones. Marva and Graham pondered 'ready'.

'We'll fit a catheter, if you like.' The nurse was addressing Marva. 'Don't want her getting in a flap about wet sheets.'

'Nothing seems to bother her much,' offered Marva in admiration. She wanted to be asking if signs of strength were signs of hope.

'Well that's how we want it – no need for pain at her stage.'

The nurse checked the morphine drive and the pipework into the veins on her hand, walked calmly away, apparently satisfied.

'She seems calm enough.'

'Not suffering.'

It was as if Marva and Graham patted each other on the backs with such anodyne phrases of comfort. A complacent game between them, when they knew what she felt ready for.

'Just a relief. Who wants her to be suffering?'

'At least she can sleep.'

They let Mrs Connolly sleep deeply. And once the immediate anxiety about the old lady's condition had passed with another peaceful interim, they turned away from her and looked across the bed to each other. They talked across her bed as if she wasn't there, or wasn't alive; or if they insisted she was alive then they were sure she approved and blessed their curiosity in one another. They had to talk about something else, to assert against evidence the still strong magnetic forces that pulled people's lives out of expected shape.

The hospital was quiet now. Marva was curious about him because it might help her to know. 'Your postcards always intrigued me. And the phone calls to make sure your mother was OK. What you were doing must have been interesting. And I bet the country was calm compared with here.'

'I spent a long time in the country and now I don't know why. Somebody helped me a lot.'

'She was older, wasn't she? Did you like her very much?'

'Yes, she was. It was my adult education. She pushed me to get more professional training and I didn't mind at the time.'

'But you think she was getting rid of you?'

'I blame it on her business partner – I found out he was actually her husband – he was pulling his money out of the guest house. He advised her to sell up quick and get a property in France.'

'OK for some.'

'Thing was: I didn't figure in this plan. So I started applying for jobs – anywhere, but not the country. I needed new people.'

'And what did you get? Old people. And hangers on like me.'

'But I think of you as independent.'

'I've your mother to thank for that. She taught me the trade, and she helped me stick up for myself with the customers, the awkward customers, the snooty ones and the racists. I'd been in care, and foster parents, so I could be as tough as anyone, had to be. But she supported me. Your mother was like my own mother to me.' She added, 'Like my own mother would have been.'

Gray didn't ask about her family, it didn't seem pertinent. 'Didn't you ever want to move on? Or go to some other city, somewhere more exciting?'

'Sometimes I did. Dreams though.'

Gray had raised his voice now with excitement. 'Didn't you ever feel it was a complete waste? You were in the wrong place. You'd been in someone else's life, instead of your own. And a decade and more could just go by and where had you been? In the wrong life for too long.'

'Not as much as you, obviously.'

'Or have a child with someone?'

Marva shook her head. Gray was beaming. Across his mother's bed it felt like they were able to consider the things they didn't do, but without deciding it. The things they hadn't done yet. And Mrs Connolly asleep was what allowed them.

Then it seemed to happen in slow motion. Mrs Connolly sat herself upright, turned herself slowly, pointedly towards Graham, looked hard into him.

'Sorry I couldn't take you to the air show.' Her voice was clear, slower than normal, and deliberate. The message she'd pulled herself awake for had to be spoken. 'You know I was only trying to protect you.'

Mrs Connolly lowered her trunk with an impossible grace and resumed the position it had occupied so comfortably before.

'Did you hear that?'

'Yes. Wait, there might be more.'

'What did she say?'

'She's gone back down again.'

'About the air show. She was talking to me. What did she mean by protecting me?'

'Somebody just gave you an apology from another world. Do you understand, soft lad?'

'She means the Birdman and my uncle and I do remember being all cold and frightened. I do. I was with my father in the garden.'

Marva wasn't sure Gray had taken in the proper force of what had been gifted him. She might have to interpret for him later. The protection was a secret he might not fully know, or be ready to accept yet.

'We'll have to tell the doctor. That's incredible. I thought she was nearly gone.'

They watched her in hope of another dramatic movement. And her breathing did change as they watched her more closely. Breaths came faster, and more laboured, then, reassuringly, at a more regular speed. They listened. Gray checked the sweep of the second hand on his wristwatch, for the intervals of intake and exhalation.

'It's OK. They're not getting any faster anyway.'

'I don't like the sound of that. I'm going to call for a nurse.'

The two nurses marched back to her bed, turned her slightly, checked her medication, smoothed her sheets. The shifting had the effect of slowing her breathing, as if a sleeper had been temporarily cured of snoring with a nudge in the back.

'That's better,' Graham thanked them. 'And if the doctor's on duty tonight, then could I have a word?'

'Yes, of course. She said she'll be popping round to see you specially.'

The nurses walked back up the room to their ward station. Little and large.

'Aren't they great, those two?'

He nodded. Protecting him from what, though? Something his uncle might have said? Or an imminent death?

The vigil went on. There was no question of further talking of selfish matters, that inappropriate chat between strangers brought close. On the alert again. Her nostrils didn't move, her chest had all the heaving movement, and her mouth now loosened and quivered in sympathy. Regular enough in pace, except that somehow it had acquired a rasp along her throat. And as soon as they became attuned to that defect they were immediately alarmed to detect a bubbling in her lungs. The sounds seemed to multiply as the bodily changes accelerated.

'What's happening now? I don't like the sound of this at all.' Marva was the one distressed.

The doctor appeared, young, fringed, cheerful, placed a hand softly first on his shoulder, then on Marva's.

'She's just settling to it. Her systems are closing down slowly. Maybe even quite quickly. And she's letting them. It

238

shouldn't alarm you. You have to understand some people do. She probably knows herself that she's ready. And they sometimes make one last effort to let you know. May take time, but I think she's nearly ready.'

'That was what she said just before – she said she was ready. And she spoke again just then. She was making sense too.'

'That will be the morphine,' the doctor explained, without surprise. 'She'll have some sporadic lucidity in the midst of her last dream state.'

A regular flow of morphine was driven automatically into her blood stream.

'No, doctor, she spoke clear as day.'

'She obviously needed to. Was it an important message? This sometimes happens.'

'It seemed like she was apologizing to me.' He was almost shouting, in danger of crying at the irony. 'After all this time. Imagine.'

'Don't take it to heart, Gray.' Marva spoke more calmly, picking up the doctor's acceptance. 'Something from a dream, the doctor said.'

'No, hang on, Marva, you heard it. She looked at me and she said sorry she didn't take me to the air show. As if it was yesterday, for fuck's sake. Sorry, doctor, you know, my language – shock. I was seven, that's when it was.'

'Don't, Graham. It was only amazing.' Marva talked through her own slow tears. 'She always was amazing.'

'Protecting me from what? The French flier I actually wanted to see? Or being there at the death, Marva? Which was I being protected from? I'd have to think about that one.'

'They both died, didn't they? Your uncle and the Birdman – Mrs C told me all about that. It upset her for years.'

'Upset her? Upset her? I knew the moment it happened. I did, Marva, because I went all cold.'

239

Marva hugged Gray's shoulders. They shook silently against the wall.

The doctor allowed a minute then her hand patted firmly on Marva's upper arm. 'You should go home now. We'll give you a telephone call when we think the time is coming. Come back tomorrow morning. You're tired yourselves.'

'Can't we wait?' Gray insisted, too bravely.

'You might distress yourselves further.'

'Well then, do you mind if we do go?' Marva had been shaken by the sight of Mrs Connolly in her last distress.

'Go home and come back tomorrow. She's comfortable, there's nothing more any of us can do, not even me. We're just waiting for when she decides in herself to let go.'

The permission was actually welcomed.

'Thank you, doctor.'

'Yes.'

And they walked awkwardly out into the autumn wind.

'What was it she said? I have to get it right in my mind.'

'Something to do with your Uncle Jack probably. She was very fond of him. You did know all that, didn't you?'

Marva was never sure how much of the whole story he knew, or if like her he only had a few pieces. There were times she wished to break through his stupidity and make him understand his mother more fairly.

'You know how she said she visited Jack in hospital. Some time around 1950, that was. About the time you were born – well, some months before actually. Had it occurred to you she might have been protecting you from—'

'But Marva, I *know* what she was protecting me from.'

Graham wasn't listening. Wouldn't. He shivered again, turned the movement into the beginning of a run, twirled back to ask her: 'Why don't I cook you a meal, a treat? The least I can do for you. You've been here all hours. I've got away from the hotel when I could. And, to be honest, I'm glad I have now.'

240

He was high, almost hysterical.

'Listen, Graham, I've got wreaths to weave.' She tried to bring him down to earth.

'You won't sleep, will you though, now? I'm starving, Marva. I want to cook you a special meal. A thank you.'

'Are you sure that's why?'

But his mind was on food. Marva gave up on the probing of history. 'No need, you know.'

'I'll come back to the shop with you first, to check your kitchen arrangements.'

They didn't talk much in the van because the engine was so noisy and because Marva was preoccupied – she had an order to make up. They had only just finished talking across his mother's hospital bed. More than chatted. The old lady couldn't hear, or she wasn't letting on. They talked. They talked like they were leaning across a pub table, introducing little hints of interest about each other. Smiled right across her bed, and each of them offered up admissions to this one stranger close in a dim curtained room. Marva mentioned scrawled felt-tip letters pushed through her low letter box. 'Go back'. But go back where? She had to laugh. Gray traded her something of his previous, stunted, life in the border country – before the hotel and this back home suddenly business.

In the shop Gray watched Marva's skilful hands quickly set to the weaving of a tribute. Carnations and tight roses, red and white, she poked into the firm green sponge of Oasis. She built a structure from the gathering of stalks, she threaded wires along the stems up to the chins of each head; she distanced red rose, red carnation evenly, tugged heads sideways so no gaps showed; and pushed gypsophila where the suggestion of a space broke the outline, until the arrangement became one whole thing in its own right, and no longer a clashing of details. He hadn't realized what work florists' fingers did. His own mother's fingers had no doubt been as

241

nimble, except he hadn't noticed at the time. Now he didn't even recognize the shop space as familiar.

He had to crouch on his haunches to concentrate; nowhere to sit except the florist's chair, and Marva herself was standing there, not sitting. The only other chair was hidden altogether by unravelled ribbon spools and long cardboard boxes half filled with flowers. But Gray stayed crouched; his legs ached; and she was concentrating on her work. He watched, as he hadn't watched his mother. His mother. He couldn't really say he knew what his mother used to do all day in the shop. Marva would. He'd probably seen from the workroom, like now, her paisley-cotton-wrapped figure busy behind the counter when he was younger, but, no, he hadn't taken an interest. More intent on following his father in escaping. And now all there was was hospital.

'How long is that lot going to take you?'

'I've got a funeral tomorrow. This goes on top of the casket – three more wreaths after this. One in the shape of MAM. I'll be here till late tonight.'

'You don't mind if I watch?'

'Watch away. I can do this in my sleep and often do.'

Her fingers twisted at wires and stalks. Senecio, laurel, hosta, variegated ivy leaves all helped to vary the texture and colour.

'You stay here into the night? What do you do for eats?'

'I make a sandwich out of the fridge. Too tired to be hungry.'

She reached up to a cassette recorder precariously balanced on a shelf carrying otherwise only dust and plastic vases. Pressed play: someone with very fast fingers on piano, blues, from a long time ago.

'Why don't I come back later? I can easy sort you some quick dinner. I owe you, anyway.'

Marva's fingers worked more flowers into spaces there

242

didn't seem to be. They moved if anything quicker since the music started, in time.

'I mean – also I feel guilty about my mother. Of course I do. In that hospital now. I don't know. We were talking, weren't we? I haven't had much of a chance before. Not with hardly anyone.'

'You don't need me, do you, to make you feel guilty? I just work here, remember.'

'But you've been so—'

'Shut up with you. I can get myself something. Or I can ring for a Chinese. You don't have to put yourself out.'

The bluff note, but not unfriendly, was an echo too haunting of his mother's voice.

By the shop window was a pattern of shadows. All the fresh flower stock had been moved to the cool and dark of the back. No shoppers paraded for the terrace of closed shops, no passers by, except for the furtive cars that pulled up outside the off-licence-cum-video shop, home supplies running out. From the workroom now could only be seen the solid low counter and the empty till drawer open like a dry tongue. Early evening lamplight pressed through the grille across each front window and through the closer weave of the door so that the shadow was a wide open chicken-wire mesh that seemed to soften a bare concrete floor.

'I'd like to though, Marva,' he pressed. 'If you don't mind eating at ten. I can get away and down here again by then.'

'Does that mean I'll be getting all your hotel's leftovers?' She looked up from her delicate construction. 'I don't mind that, honest. Got to be better than my sandwich.'

'You'll let me be grateful then? This once?'

She was too busy tidying straggling stalks to answer. She sprayed the heads softly all over with water, placed the tribute down behind her chair.

'I'll be back ten. OK?'

Marva didn't want his gratitude, but she wouldn't now refuse his company; because they'd shared a vigil at his mother's bedside, they had talked at the hospital. A hospital bed could create a peculiar intimacy for visitors, even enclosed by curtains, even at the expense of the patient.

When he returned, he rattled the front-door grille to awaken her attention and she had two more wreaths finished. Two smaller mixed bouquets still to be made up. He was carrying two bulging carrier bags. Aluminium pots and plastic containers stretched the plastic. Leaves flopped between the straps.

'Just needs some finishing off. And warming up.'

'I'll need some warming up myself. It's bloody freezing down here.'

Her brown fingers were grey. And rust from wires, sap from foliage dirtied them more. Her black leather jacket, epauletted, draped on her shoulders, freed her hands to work the arrangements; green ribbed-wool turtle-neck insulated any body heat; working jeans.

'You've got a microwave or a cooker, I take it?'

'You'll find all that upstairs.'

Next time she looked up, Graham was standing ridiculously white-tunicked at the foot of the staircase.

'Right, you can stop work right now.'

Marva spluttered a laugh, then moved just in time to save her last bouquet from damage.

'That'll have to do. Freesias look fine with almost anything. But who even notices at funerals?'

She had to brush scrunched up paper and all the snippings from stalks down on to the floor. He waited for her, then threw a stiff white tablecloth across her work table. He borrowed from the shop shelves a cast-iron candlestick, a three-branch candelabra, and wedged a scented purple candle in one holder, with two stray rose heads balanced in the

244

other branches. That was table decoration; he wasn't trying to turn it into the hotel.

When he next appeared from the staircase, he was pouring a smooth Rioja for her, urging her to nose the trickle in the glass. This game of hotel service amused her, but she needed to swallow a proper mouthful to relax. Men who had tried to cook for her before, mostly white, had always made such a display of kitchen activity, and gone on to spoil their efforts with explanations. She did feel more comfortable with this man's approach, and not only for his mother's sake. Tiredness counted too. He was holding two white plates high, then floating Marva's down. It was a painting called terrine, a flat rectangular slab, a flag, three bands of colour: gold, white, green and something in the centre; plus strong salad-leaf garnish, watercress, rocket, two cherry tomatoes and a small pool of glistening red wine vinaigrette. Marva gazed: this on her workroom table.

'Hope you enjoy. No meat, no fish, naturally.'

'Too beautiful to eat. I've never eaten a flag before.' Marva stared at it.

'You have to eat it.' He darted a fork at his own mousse, scooped, broke across the clean stripes. He tried to taste the layers of carrot, artichoke, spinach, and test them for himself.

'Which country though?' Gray asked. 'That's the question.'

'Let's take a guess at Ghana.' She laughed across at him, lightly, giving no real clues to him.

'Or Jamaica, I thought. Even possibly Ethiopia. Apparently not, though. I hadn't got my stamp album with me when I made it. Sorry.'

'A good, noble flag, wherever. I'm told my mother came from Jamaica, my dad from Ghana. Who knows what to believe?' She gulped some red. 'Thanks for the thought.'

'But it melts, I hope.'

It melted; Marva melted. She ate slowly, she smiled. He pushed his plate away, his flag ragged, half-eaten; sipped his glass nervously, watched her finish. Then Gray disappeared upstairs again.

His next plates were piled with steaming rice, pitted with red beans and *petits pois*, criss-crossed with strips of red, yellow and green peppers savagely grilled; the mountain was snowed upon.

'I can smell coconut, can't I?'

She leaned forward to sniff the dish and steam misted her gold-rimmed spectacles and she had to remove them. She looked up at Gray. 'It is, isn't it? Rice and peas. Graham.' She used his full name.

'With additions, yes. Too bland for you? I wasn't sure.'

'No: love the colours. You're good. Where did you learn?'

'Not from my mother.'

'Mrs C was good at some things,' Marva agreed. 'Not cooking though.' She tried to ask him how he came to his job at the hotel.

'I told you I spent some years in Shropshire. Someone taught me, well, took me in hand and trained me; and encouraged me.'

'The lady you were telling me about.'

'It's not important now. Closed book, really.' He stuffed rice into his mouth, made further elaboration impossible. 'Another one of those?'

But then she sensed his discomfort, filled her own mouth with colours too, tried also to taste everything separately.

'This is what I can do. And I wanted to do for you.' His prepared speech came out awkward.

'And I couldn't be more grateful.' She noted his touchiness. 'You're filling me up.'

She shifted her chair a few inches, sighed hard, straightened herself. Her arms were now free to adjust jumper sleeves higher up her forearm all the way to her elbow.

'I'm not finished yet.' He was out of his seat again.

246

Gray now brought small plates from the fridge upstairs. He'd arranged mango slices in crescents, swirled a kiwi-fruit couli on a pond of yoghurt, and for further decoration two mint leaves floating, ruby blood drops of pomegranate seeds glinting. Two glasses of sweet yellowy white wine.

'Fresh fruit and pictures too.' She laughed. 'Punishment.'

She tried to savour it with the delicacy she thought it deserved. He gobbled his own peremptorily. Hurried her plate away.

'Coffee and brandy now?'

'You're a good man, Gray.' And to herself as he was out of the room for the drinks, she muttered: 'I'm tired. And I need to take my mind off your mother.'

He was pouring coffee at her shoulder and touched her arm with his free palm. She nuzzled lightly into his sleeve. He placed the coffee pot on the floor quickly, there was no room on the tablecloth. He raised her to standing full height; nose against nose. Kind introductory kissing, then some sudden pulling together, while his feet searched for a more comfortable landing for their legs. She held him, the moment too, chin on his shoulder, and spotted below them the litter of flower stalks and tissue paper. Her foot could kick them away if need be. Then she consented to the lowering. Together they sat, positioned themselves, lay back on the cardboard. And when her head tipped back for him to kiss her throat, and work again at her jumper, she read the word MAM in floral red, upside down; and she saw her tribute arrangements were in their neat line, and their water droplets had formed their own pool.

'Sorry, it can't be here.' Marva straightened herself to stand. 'Upstairs, I think.'

Gray stopped. There must have been silence, before they were ready to stand, until they began to hear the motor cars outside. And they thought they heard noises at the door.

247

And shouting somewhere. Was that a window smashing across the street? The expanse of glass in the shop window seemed vulnerable.

They lay across the bed in her smartly furnished flat. He kissed her high forehead up to the join of her scraped black hair. She licked the brandy from his teeth and gums. He stroked every line of her, every dark round of her. They had both missed months of the shaking thrill and smell and juice and body warmth of bed.

Later, when Gray had to stumble to her small toilet, he'd stood peeing and the smell of her was there and the smell of him too rising to his nostrils. One tiny frosted window. Same layout as his mother's. This was the same flat in the same block above the shops, same porthole window on the stairs. He'd lived here from when he was seven. He'd truly returned now.

'I can't help myself feeling a bit guilty – about us?' he regretted saying to Marva in bed.

'Why, because she might be there downstairs, when we know she can't be?' Marva was laughing, she might have been affected by drink. 'And it's only her ghost doing another jigsaw – can't you hear the pieces being stirred, smell the ciggie?'

He was surprised at something like hysteria. 'I can't be having ghosts tonight. Please.'

'Don't tell me you're spooked, Gray? We both saw her tonight and we know, we know – don't we?'

'I just have a feeling she wouldn't have approved.'

Marva was irritated by this sudden worrying about his mother. So many years had gone by, what did it matter now? 'What do you expect? Her blessing?'

'I'm thinking it feels a bit like incest. Sort of. Her in the hospital.'

'Well, thank you, mister. What does that make me – your

248

sister? You've got eyes?' She pinched a wodge of purple-brown around her knee.

'I mean because of your closeness to her, like a daughter – that's all I mean.'

'Sure I'm your sister, bro'.' Her voice was an exaggeration of a voice heard in a movie. She was laughing now, if uneasily.

Gray was hoping everything would be fine, after all.

Marva's wall phone jumped into a ringing.

'We mustn't answer that.' She was adamant, it was after one o'clock. 'We mustn't.'

'It might be the hospital though.' Gray's guilt still rankled. 'What if it is?'

'We've just come from there. And neither of us wants it to be the hospital, do we? I'm not expecting a call. Not at this time. No friends I want to speak to.'

The rings were pressing rings. She reached for him, handled him; then she straddled him playfully. She was guying the act they'd enjoyed earlier, like a play acting of thank you and shut up. The phone was forgotten; it stopped anyway.

'Does sex make you feel young again?' She felt stronger from what had happened.

'Younger,' Gray was prepared to admit. 'There has been lost time with me.'

'I can go months.' Marva was almost boasting. 'But then I need – this. Puts me back on track. And it doesn't always matter who it's with.' She was confident and conclusive.

'I'm just anyone, am I?' Gray was questioning her motives now.

'No, but we needed to be close tonight, didn't we? It was important.' Marva didn't say 'for her sake'; her strong smiles were all to pretend the closeness was only for his sake. Gray was nodding too hard.

She switched on a TV set with a remote control, sound down. A football tackle, she switched; an orchestra silent, she switched; a high vantage of New York roofs and office tops, she chose that with some pleasure, left the picture mute.

Gray resumed his puzzlement. 'But she kept mentioning my uncle, didn't she?'

'Mrs C always did.'

'And never mentioned my father.'

'You'll have to work that one out for yourself, won't you?' Marva was careful to point out. 'But, Graham, she has talked about *you* sometimes. You just weren't around to hear it.'

He stroked her arm, as if in thanks, up to her shoulder, on to her shoulder, her collarbone, where a few locks hung, then back down her arm to her fingers. She turned her hand and squeezed his fingers, then released them. She was concentrating on some puzzle of her own now.

'See that place. That city. I dream of that.'

The film must have been taken from a helicopter – Empire State, Chrysler, Sears, World Trade Centre, Statue of Liberty, Ellis Island.

'And I'm there flying in and I'm so excited. There's someone to meet me at the airport.'

Gray looked at her and realized he didn't know much about her, except in connection with his mother. He stared at the screen. 'I have that dream too, sort of. Don't know where it comes from.' Now her fantasy, or that circling camera, had started something off for Gray too.

He half turned to his half of her pillow. Marva hadn't heard his offering anyway.

'And it's my real mother,' she continued. 'There she is coming out of the crowd, and I've never seen her before but I recognize her, no problem. I'm sure I do.'

And Gray hadn't heard her not hearing. He addressed her cassette collection instead: 'But you see, with me, Marva, I'm up there flying, actually airborne, and, this is interesting, it doesn't have to be that city, it could be anywhere. My wings are outspread and I can see everything. Everything. It's great.'

When he turns back to see her reaction, Marva is hugging herself obliviously. 'We hug as soon as we meet. We both have to take our glasses off – too many tears on our winter coats. New York City – four below. She knew me straight away though – of course.'

Marva's face dived straight down into the pillow. She butted the thought out of her head again. Woke herself from that nightmare quickly. She would need to listen to Gray still talking.

'So exhilarating. But then something's gone wrong. My wings. And I'm just falling.'

Marva's eyes are damp, still appalled for herself, and now aware she ought to feel something similar for him. But she has had to guess at the drift of his story, and decides to laugh it all off quickly for both of them: 'Dreams are bloody frightening, aren't they?'

Their distance was opening up again, as the weight of their tiredness fell. His last drowsy contribution before sleep: 'And we're in the dark, aren't we?'

17

1990

Because the phone rang for so long, Marva had time to pull a T-shirt on and pop her specs in place before answering. It was as early as one of her market mornings, but she knew it was the call.

'We tried to contact her son at the Corinthian, but he wasn't there. You've been her main visitor, haven't you? We're ringing to say Mrs Connolly passed away peacefully in the night.'

'What time?' Marva meant what time was it now. She'd taken her watch off in the night, left it on the bedside table. The catch might have scratched her man's back.

'Around one o'clock. I tried this number then. I'd not long been on duty.'

'I might even have heard it. I was asleep, sort of, at that time.'

'We prefer to ring at an earthly hour. If we can.'

'Thank you. For ringing.'

'Sorry. It has to be. Yes.'

'Do I come up and collect her things?'

'Are you next of kin?'

'I bloody looked after her, if that counts.'

'Come anyway. You're from the flower shop, they said.'

'Yes, I'm fucking Oleanders.'

'I understand you're upset. Will you be OK, though?'

Marva hung up the wall phone. She'd surprised herself with her language. She'd let herself down at a moment which wasn't in itself unexpected, but reckoned you couldn't know how you would react when the time came. And the time had come and she wasn't there at Mrs C's bedside. The time had come and she was poking sleep out of the corner of her eye under the lenses of her specs. She was regretting the night before. She was irritated that she wasn't prepared, but you can't be prepared, she reasoned. She needed to make coffee before her bed partner got up and claimed the news for himself simply because they'd spent the night in her bed above the shop. A mistake, she realized. A mistake to weaken.

She could be angry with him. She was. But as the kettle clicked its boiling off, she examined her swearing to the nurse on the phone. Next of kin was what grated. She felt closer to the woman who'd died than that lady's last remaining family, the son who, by chance almost, had slept in her bed.

Mrs C had saved her life. When she'd done spells in children's homes and worked her sulky way through various well-meaning foster mothers, getting a name in her records as a problem child who stole and got into fights. Grown-up for her age, yes, bright, the social workers said, but full of anger. Or spirit, they sometimes phrased it. Which meant she was bound to get into trouble, ending up pregnant, mixed up with drugs or worse. And Mrs C had taken her on at the shop. The YOPS scheme had been extended. Marva had grown up in her ten years with Mrs C. She hadn't got into trouble or pregnant. She happened to like flowers. She'd been keen to learn. She'd grown close to the tough lady. Like a daughter. They'd laughed about customers. Had a joke. And when she'd fallen ill, Marva had helped her. Willingly. She loved her. And felt closer than this grown-up son who'd materialized these last months. She felt more bereaved than the tubby white-skinned man slumped on her bed could possibly. That might be why she now felt anger towards Graham.

'The phone call's got you up and you're not coming back to bed then?'

'*The* phone call, Graham. The one we were dreading.'

Graham said, 'Well, we can't pretend we didn't know it was coming.'

'How can you say it like that?'

'At least we know for sure. It's over.'

And the way he said that annoyed Marva. He was relieved, more than he was upset or stunned or devastated – which was part of her mixture of emotional states. And he was feeling this relief, because he felt so cosy, with Marva, there in that flat, as if this was still his home and here he was at last. But Marva felt he was taking a few things for granted, as if time stopped the night before, and this was a new day, a new life and he was going to embrace it. He wanted to make this great thing about the two of them getting together. The solution to his problems going back years. He thought he'd made his peace with his mother. He thought a fortnight of vigils made a reconciliation.

'It's not over for me. The hard work starts today.'

'You know what I mean. All I mean is some of the tension goes. A weight lifts – that's how I feel, anyway, I'm trying to be honest here.'

'You may think you have it all sorted. Everything simpler now without your mum?'

'But I thought we'd come to a special understanding between us.'

'We went to bed. It was your food seduced me. A weak spot, OK? Is that the same thing?'

'It was more than that – wasn't it?'

She couldn't deny he was kind and he was charming and he was persistent and he went to a lot of trouble. She couldn't pretend she didn't enjoy some of all that. That in bed it was easier to reach some release after being physically strained, all tense for weeks. Hospital visiting was nothing like relaxing, even if you couldn't help dozing in your chair, and then you felt guilty about that too. You don't eat properly, you hold yourself tight for the next awful development and then the next and the next. Added to which she was probably lonely. No man since when? Since before Mrs C's health had started going downhill. Since Graham had come back. The timing of the two coincided. She had devoted herself to the woman's welfare. It wasn't duty. The lady deserved it. She'd done the right thing right up to when the hospital took over. And it was tempting to feel relief and be distracted when you didn't have the responsibility there in your home. She was tired. Off-guard. Excuses. Excuses.

So she'd drunk his wine. Marva had dined on his expertly warmed up hotel dishes. His colourful terrine. His own version of rice and peas. His fruit something. And she'd enjoyed it.

'OK, so it was good. Weird too.'

'So why the regret, Marva? You weren't saying that last night, were you?'

'Just the timing. Thinking where she was and where we were.'

'She didn't know. She was out on morphine. She wasn't in this world, was she? You saw. She was gone last night really. The doctor said as much. Don't you remember?'

'To me she wasn't gone until this phone call. This one now.'

'We both know one o'clock was the real phone call.'

'She died in the night. What we were doing – I don't know what she would have thought.'

'Coincidence. Why wouldn't it have had her blessing? She was happy for us to be visiting together.'

'She was doped out.'

'She certainly didn't object to our friendship. Now you're the one making a problem of it.'

'I kept no secrets from your mother. She was like my mother. She knew everything. And I didn't get a chance to talk to her properly. And say my thank you. And that's nothing to do with you.'

'Oh, thank you very much, I must say.'

Marva stood up from behind the small table, walked edgily across to the bathroom to take a shower. For some reason she didn't want to touch him, she just wanted to leave him to coffee and his own idea of breakfast.

'I'm getting ready now because I have to go down there and make the arrangements.'

'I know. After last night too,' he said, hoping a reminder would reactivate some warmth in her.

'Especially after last night.'

But he didn't understand her guilt, which hadn't affected her last night. He was puzzled and offended by it. It threw confusion over his relief.

In the shower, Marva almost regretted her sharpness towards him. This was going to be one of those big days when directions in life become clear, or at least clearer. Not clear yet though, because she did have to wonder herself, if she was saying some perverse thank you to his mother by going to bed with him. Gratitude. Or then again, was she, in effect, giving him some warmth that his mother hadn't been able to give him, and which he probably couldn't have taken from her in any case? By helping him she had helped Mrs C. Out of charity? Pity? Was it pity for him or for her? Round in circles. The possible reasons for things. She couldn't know. She tried to wash away the smell of him and imagine a new life without responsibility for his family. She took her time doing her hair in braids.

Gray banged on the bathroom door. 'Marva, I've been

thinking. Let's just go along together. I'll help. I'm family, remember.'

He was and she wasn't. She'd had the last ten years with his mother. Did it make any difference that he had been missing for twenty years? Was everything forgotten for the Prodigal Son? And she wondered if he knew as much as she did about his real father. Mrs C had told her all about the two men in her life. It was just that he brought these complications she didn't need just then. Marva would have preferred to do it all without him.

'I can sort out time off from work, don't worry.'

'I want to see her on my own, Graham.'

'Why's that?'

She rested her head against the bathroom door and let the first rush of tears since the news push through, just one lot, and clenched the rest back for later. There would be times, plenty.

'For all she's done for me, she's my responsibility.'

'Not only yours now. Think of the time I've had off for visiting.'

She was angry then. Angry that the lady had died and left her on her own. Angry for him being so nice for one night, one night, and her falling for it. Angry that he messed his life up arriving too late. Angry that he didn't take the trouble to get to know his mother. And for not talking to her before. For wasting his time in the country, when he could have been useful in the city. For not understanding about his real father, for not taking the trouble to find out. Marva had helped him and now she wished she hadn't helped him. Because all this didn't help her one bit.

On the other hand she had been comfortable with him at the hospital. He had showed some pity and some loyalty. He had talked to her. The two of them had talked about him and about Mrs C. It was almost fitting. The two of them. And maybe Graham was right that Mrs C wouldn't have disapproved of what they were doing the night she died. It was understandable in a way, natural, if a bit desperate. Maybe the warmth between them had all been for her benefit. Something like a tribute to her well-meant hold on people.

So, by the time she was dressed and ready, Marva had decided to concentrate on the practical, to support Graham. Maybe the anger she felt shouldn't have been directed at him. There was selfishness about these feelings which wanted to say, what about me? My life. She wanted to tell her side of the story. No one had asked before. There hadn't been a chance. Was that something to be angry about? No. For the time being, Mrs C had to come first.

'Yes, you help, Graham. You get yourself shaved and we'll go to the hospital together.'

The short distance could easily be walked, so the shop delivery van was left behind. Marva was keen to talk.

'I grew up where the so-called riots were. I saw all that. Nearly ten years ago; nine. And I learnt that Mrs C grew up there. She was born, her and her sister, Lydia, in rooms above a pawn shop.'

'She never talked about it to me. Too painful. Lydia married out of all that. And Mum wanted to too.'

'You see: that was something we had in common. Same district. Toxteth.'

'She shared that with you. I am surprised about that.'

'My father was a lawyer, according to my birth certificate. Law student more likely, vanished back to Ghana. My mother was Jamaican, she gave me up for adoption, she caught a Cunard to New York, didn't ever write. She's probably still there.'

'New York. I didn't realize all that. You've been on your own all this time then?'

'I was on a youth scheme and Mrs C took me on full time, no question. Because we got on and I was good with the

258

flowers. She sorted me out the flat above the shop. And she protected me when ignorant customers made what they thought were jokes. She taught me to love the flowers. Taught me the names, how to spot the dried out ones and the forced ones from the blooms just right and fresh from market. She gave me all her tips on arranging them. And she said I looked a picture holding the flowers, their colours came out true. She called me her flower girl.'

'You were what she wanted. I never took the slightest interest in the flowers myself. I think I might have been a disappointment.'

They walked away from the shops and towards the main road. Litter in the underpass, rain in the slate-grey sky.

'She helped make me adult. And whether she did for me what she would have done for her own son if things had been different, I can't say. I was glad of it.'

'By the way, I wasn't jealous, you know.'

Marva ignored this and went on with what she needed to say: 'She didn't tell me not to live. I had black boyfriends. I had white boyfriends and, OK, they were always older men. I brought them to meet her. She said how polite they all were. And we had a laugh about them when they'd gone back to where they lived. And I stayed and I didn't ask her about her husband that died in London, or her son who disappeared to the country somewhere. I knew not to ask stupid questions. Of course I got more inquisitive when you came back to the city, all of a sudden.'

They crossed the zebra crossing on the main road and entered the gates of the hospital, started the walk up the long drive.

'Yes, when I came back. That set the cat among the pigeons, didn't it?'

'A bit of a shock to everyone.'

'To me too, Marva. I didn't want to get involved at first. But, well, you and Beagan, and her getting burgled and her fall, and getting ill, well, I thought I ought to help things along, you know.'

'Oh, I think it might have helped her. In her funny way.'

'It certainly helped me connect things up a bit. Still working on that though.'

'Yes, it helped you, didn't it?' Marva found her sharpness again. 'I'm not sure what it's done for me.'

Inside the hospital, someone, not the nurse who'd phoned, she was off shift now, passed on the doctor's letter, loose in an envelope, addressed to Mr Connolly. They both read to the scrawly explanatory part, which they deciphered as: pneumonia, carcinosomething. And with the envelope was a leaflet about Death: What to do. And Marva was given a blue plastic bag of clothes, plus an envelope of rings and spectacles. They asked what next and were told next of kin had to take the envelope to the registry office for a death certificate. Marva agreed to catch a bus halfway across town – not out of pity at all, but because she was involved, blood relative or not – she had to see it through. So she set off again with her sort of half brother, half lover, her friend for someone else more important's sake.

Marva sat with Graham in a leather-benched anteroom. The waiting room wasn't full of grief and tears, but chattering and newspaper reading, no different from a doctor's waiting room. Once they were inside the room, the registrar turned out to be a woman in a black suit, who pleasant-talked her way down the length of the paper, all for the sake of Graham's signature. Copies for all eventualities, a cheque paid. Sometimes Marva and Gray talked cheerfully. And sometimes they were silent. This was something practical to do, the headache of nearly tears and not enough sleep dispelled any anger towards him.

Another bus into the city centre and then the probate officer had to lead them down the length of his form, explain about tax. Time waiting, time travelling, the grey day was

260

emptying. After all that business it was back to the flat: ring the solicitor, for copies of the will. Ring the council. And ring about the electric, TV, her newspapers. It would take days. Marva was the one who knew all the details. She would be the one to cancel everything, inform everyone.

Graham had to get back to the hotel, explain. Marva arranged the funeral by presenting herself in a cramped room to make all the choices about cremation, caskets, service and number of cars. A blonde, very white woman with curly-framed spectacles sat at the desk of the funeral director's; and directed her in croaky whispers to a suitable hymn and reading.

'You know best. I'm no good at all this.'

'Are you next of kin?'

'No, in fact.'

'Who is?'

'Her son. I'm helping him out.'

'Men are useless at this, aren't they? I understand, love.'

And she advised on the two short obituary notices to be placed in the classified ads, following proper form, family first. Main entry would be: 'Peacefully after short illness. Greatly missed by her loving son. Cremation service. Flowers family only, please. Donations to the Royal National Institute for the Blind.'

Mrs Connolly, an expert in these matters, had had plenty of time to inform Marva of her funereal preferences. Insisted on the charity for the blind, because of a certain someone. The blonde lady advised Marva to place a separate notice herself, if she so wished. She slipped from the room to allow Marva time to pencil something on the back of her Death leaflet which approximated to how she felt: 'My boss, my loss. Mrs C, like a mother to me. Desperately missed, Marva.'

When the funeral director ghosted back into the room, she asked: 'Are you sure about no flowers?'

'I'll do a wreath. I'm Oleanders, by the hospital.'

261

'Yes, I think we've dealt with you before.'

No one else could have done the flowers and Marva thought hard about her pair of bouquets, one for her, one for Graham, as soon as she left the funeral parlour. It would be: simple tight roses, white lilies, cheerful gerbera and good old autumn chrysanths. As for wreaths: not Mam, she'd done too many of them; not Mum, it wasn't accurate. But Mrs C was just right, though Marva would have to make the template herself. There'd be plenty of time at the shop before the funeral. There'd be no repeats of him staying over. He had his work to do. She would be too busy.

One hearse starting from outside the shop. Shoppers, people she knew, all dumb on the pavement, staring as the tyres pulled slowly away. Two bouquets and a wreath spelling *Mrs C* on top of the coffin. At the crematorium chapel, two rows of mourners, neighbours from the flats, from the shops, and hardly a distant relative among them. Mrs Bulstrode's son in a long tailored navy overcoat. A minister for hire had been given the bare information by Graham to come up with a eulogy. Marva had given him certain jobs to do. In the brief service before the coffin went through the mechanical curtains, the oration came out something like: 'Shop was her life; career woman before her time; tragic loss of dear sister and then dear husband both in 1970. One loyal son. She was ... brave. Independent. Lonely ...' Marva stopped listening to his words. All wrong, all completely wrong. No mention of Marva, no understanding of their closeness, or the little spats and chats they had between them, but anyway over with quick. She kept her mouth shut.

After the funeral Marva only spoke to Graham on the telephone about paperwork arrangements, but they were both busy and it wasn't easy to meet. She wondered if he was becoming more withdrawn, and should she be worried? An appointment was made to visit the solicitor, a pretty spiky-haired woman, thin and smart, green eyes. There was money enough in insurance policies to cover funeral expenses. The estate was divided equally between Gray and Marva. Which was agreed to be a fair division. The lease on the shop was paid up, so Marva could carry on with Oleanders, if she wished. The solicitor and Mrs C assumed she did. The will stated that Marva could have anything she wanted from the flat, her 'nice things', the clock, the shepherdess, chenille tablecloth, etc.

Gray was first to explain to the solicitor: 'She must have made the will before the flat was turned over.'

'Yes, those things were all taken.'

The solicitor was determined to be unruffled. 'But presumably covered by insurance.'

'Going down so fast after that, there wouldn't have been time to change it with you.'

The solicitor continued: 'Does that apply equally to the boxed remains of a Captain Jack Argent's library, English classics, Conrad, Dickens and such?'

'No, they weren't taken when the place was broken into. No taste, burglars.'

She sniffed a discreet laugh before allotting them to Mr Connolly. 'And also to Mr Connolly, a sum set aside to pay for flying lessons to be bought at the airport. An unusual item, but presumably one that you'll appreciate better than I.'

'Her little joke,' Marva said. 'A special bequest.'

'More like an apology. A long time after the event.'

The two could have argued about the sly intent of the lady's gesture. But Marva was ready to return to the flat and the shop and decide on what next. And Graham was happy to disappear back to the Corinthian and plot something in his room.

18

1990

After nearly three weeks of not hearing a word – not even how are you? – Marva decided to check how Graham was coping since the funeral. She closed the shop again, took a bus into town. She waltzed through the Corinthian's revolving door and asked at Reception.

'He does still have a room here, doesn't he?'

'Yes, I think he must still be up there.' The receptionist struggled to locate him in her guest and room memory bank. 'On the top floor, I'm pretty sure. Do you need directions?'

'I'll find my own way.'

'We don't see so much of Graham out of hours these days.'

When Marva knocked, Graham didn't show surprise. The room had no windows. Daytime or night-time it was dark, except for a bedside lamp. On top of two wardrobes were crammed hotel stores, plastic-wrapped toilet rolls, packs of paper towels and roller towels. This was the dark room she'd heard speak of. In the field of light from the bedside lamp he had spread a wide map of the river estuary across the floor at the side of his bed. Pencils and rulers were scattered across the paper. He had been studying it closely, plotting something with care. And stacked unevenly on the bedside table were a pile of notebooks, red and blue mixed; one spread open, recently scribbled in.

'Busy making plans?' Marva tried.

And he reached over to pull the open notebook closed. 'I just do this scribbling to try and piece it all together. Have to. But there's just so much, I mean, *stuff.*' He waved vaguely towards a pile of cardboard boxes, books and papers, jigsaws, more books from his legacy.

Marva nodded as if she understood.

'It's been hard.' He looked about to explain. 'But you should have the jigsaws, not me. When am I going to have the time for jigsaws? Have that one. A thousand pieces. Flowers and stuff. You'll have more time for all that.'

'Your mother loved jigsaws. Such patience with them.'

He pulled himself awkwardly from the floor, reached for the top box on the pile.

Marva saw a spread of green canvas material, like a tent or a sail, folded on the floor, but she didn't ask directly.

He handed the box to Marva. 'You piece that together. It's beyond me.'

'I'll see what I can do.'

Marva accepted the second-hand gift without enthusiasm. She sat at the bottom end of his rumpled bed, started peering at his map on the floor, thinking of this kite-like cloth by his bed.

'Have you taken up the flying lessons yet?'

'I have. Just got to build up my hours, before I can go solo. Did I tell you I did some gliding when I was in the country, strangely enough? Wonderful sensation. Everything spread out underneath you. So, yes, I'm keen to do more.'

'It was very thoughtful of your mother.'

'The lessons will be useful. You knew I'd been helping with the Rainbow group, didn't you?'

'Still chasing Michelle, then?'

'No, it's not that. Helping, I said. There are all sorts of things happening at Waterfront 90. We'll play our part in it like anyone. Some environmental issues need airing. You ought to be there. There'll be a big crowd. High-profile publicity. Boats and planes, and the great Michael Mc-Michael.' Then he looked up at her. 'Why don't you come? You might see some unexpected stunts.'

Marva was doubtful about a note of mischief in his voice. 'You're not planning to make trouble, are you?'

'You'll have to be there. By the Seafaring Museum.'

'I've never been there myself, but my friend, Gloria, says they've got fine displays of merchant ships that sailed the globe for the sake of the home port, taking arms and shiny goods to sell to Africans, but no mention, no mention of the return cargo taken to the Americas and exchanged for cotton and tobacco. She heard about a black protest to set the record straight, because something terrible was missing from the story of their history – isn't that always the way? – and she wanted me to join too. I would, but I've been too busy.'

'I didn't realize that. It's a place I've got a lot of time for. As I might have told you before. Especially the dredgers.'

When they'd both visited the hospital, at his mother's bedside, Graham had already expounded at length on the scale-model dredgers in glass cases, the way they cleaned out the river's natural silting, with their buckets and suction pipes, and dumped the mud out to sea. He seemed pleased that some was saved for landfill.

Marva needed quickly to discourage him on this topic. 'No, I'm probably going away soon. That's what I came to say. I'm planning a trip to America. New York.'

Gray didn't seem disappointed. 'You said you would. Best of luck then. What about Oleanders though?'

'I might not keep it on. But I wanted to wish *you* luck, Graham, honest.'

It was true, she wanted to repair any ill will that might have arisen between them following his mother's death. She didn't want a relationship, but she wanted him to know she appreciated the time he'd spent with her in the last days.

'I might not be here long myself. Manager's moved on.

The vegetarian meals aren't as popular as they were supposed to be. I've tried my best though. Now I'm reduced to cooking steaks. Me and Grant. What a joke. But I keep myself busy – with my research and planning, as you can see.'

'You will be careful, won't you?'

'You sound like my mother.'

Marva smiled to herself at the compliment.

Graham turned towards her. She was worried by his new expression, a little more than keen.

'Do you want to know, really, Marva, what was behind the flying lessons? Because I've been doing my research. The library's round the corner from here. I've checked the cuttings files and the dates. And it all connects up. Pretty well.'

'If I must.'

'Way back in 1957 there was a Frenchman called Blaise who was known as the Birdman because he had these balsawood wings which he used to launch himself from a plane at the height of eight thousand feet.'

'I've heard you speak about him.'

'That brave man came to this city and he flew at the air show. And he stayed in this very hotel. Maybe in this very room. Just think. In this room. He flew high above the city in a Dakota, launched himself from that plane and saw it all spread out below him, and you can just imagine how he felt to be floating down, if you've ever flown yourself.'

'Didn't he die, though?'

'But the point is I was meant to see him at the show. My mother took her sister, Lydia, and my Uncle Jack to see all the aeroplanes and everything. But instead of that I was stuck with my father in the back garden and, it so happened, I saw him falling. It was by a cricket field.'

'So you did see him?'

'I didn't see him close up. My dad stopped me. But the Birdman died. And Uncle Jack died on the same day. And if I'd gone there instead of Jack, maybe it would have all been different. No one would have died and my father needn't have gone off to London.'

'Come off it. You know very well their situation was impossible.'

'I'm saying that the reason my mother bought me the lessons was an admission that *I* should have gone to the air show, not him, on that day. She was saying sorry for all that. I mean thirty-three years on.'

'Do you really think so? Surely she said her sorry in the hospital. That was just a generous gesture. She was capable of that. I should know.'

But Graham wasn't listening to the possibility of inconsistencies in his argument. 'I mean even today I still feel brushed by his magnificent ambition. Such vision.'

'You're what?' Although Marva was worried by the strangeness of some of his remarks, she didn't wish to get any more involved.

'Yes, he changed my life. I mean this was when my mum and dad split up. This was when my dad went to London. He was drinking too much already anyway. It's all too much of a coincidence. It's like fate. It's starting to make sense. I'm writing it down, you know.'

'Good for you,' Marva offered, not very convincingly. 'It might help.'

There was, however, one question Marva had to ask him before she escaped that claustrophobic room.

'I wanted to ask you before, Graham, but it's all been so ... I mean, did you know about your real father? You can tell me now. You must have.'

He pulled his brandy bottle towards him. Poured an inch into a small well-used glass. 'Listen, Marva. I was in London for a while trying to be a student. My dad was thirteen years downhill: ever smaller offices in the city and pubs right across Kensal Rise, Kilburn, Archway. Poor bastard didn't deserve that. A laughing stock in the day and loved for his

268

rounds by a pack of cheery deadheads at night. I saw his room in Kensal Rise and it smelt of piss. I can smell that smell now. The toilet he used was blocked up and flies were tracing parallelograms above. I can't see one of them slow diagonal flies without thinking of my father dead. But if I try to think of him alive, it's always a herring gull. He used to take me to the docks, they flew everywhere – it was magical to see all the boats, the colour of their funnels.'

'Yes, I heard he wasn't such a bad old stick.' Marva tried to humour him a little. 'Just had a few problems combining the bottle and family life.'

'Imagine, will you, I'm all screwed up about being a student and wanting to do something useful in the world, find myself, lose myself, fuck knows. A girl I was living with persuaded me to contact him and I met him in a pub in Muswell Hill. And he had a blazer on and he looked smartish, maybe a bit sweat-smelly, with glasses on now. Took the piss out of my long hair. But he was older, stouter, I could hardly remember him except for stubble and whisky breath and the hairs creeping on to the back of his hand. He introduced me very grandly to this lady friend with round cheeks and a green miniskirt, Kathleen. She stands up, walks to the front and sings "Sailor" in the sweetest brogue, making eyes at him. Stop your roving. Come home safe to me. All that. I tried to keep up with their drinks. Later on we went back to his room. She helped him along. I loped behind, completely fuddled. A week later, before my end of year exams, I get the call he's dead, a message through the university. So I'm thinking, what a way to finish up. Kensal Green Cemetery, a mere three drinking cronies, one of his work colleagues, Kathleen, me and my mother.'

'Your mother didn't speak about him much. Except about them getting married in the war when everybody did. And how she tried to make a home, but really she wanted to do the shop. Basically, let's face it, she wasn't happy with him.'

269

'Too right she wasn't. And what does unhappiness breed?'

'No, but I meant about your real father? She told me and I didn't know if you knew all about that?'

'I'm coming to that, Marva. Anyway, on the evening of the funeral, at Euston Station as I'm walking my mother down the platform, trying to stay polite because it's all gone off to order, all of a sudden she takes her case out of my hand and says: "I've been meaning to tell you. Now's as good as any time. I wasn't sure if you'd guessed. Thought you had though, with your intelligence." (I thought this was a dig at my being a student and not staying in the home city.) "He wasn't your father. Your uncle was." Just like that. Straight out. No preparation.'

'So you did know all along?' Marva asked.

'Listen, I couldn't take that. I was young. I was having my own problems settling in London. I didn't want to be there. I didn't know what I wanted to do. I dropped out of my studies. Dropped out, that's what it was called. I wanted to get well away – for a long time. My mother stepped on to her train. My father had just died. She'd come down, dropped that little bit of news and then gone back to her shop. It was her way. Unforgivable, in my book, the way she did it. Hadn't given me any time to respond. I'm on the platform. Just gobsmacked. And I just didn't feel I could talk to her. I decided. Not ever again.'

'You were in shock and you couldn't deal with it?'

'I managed to put it out of my mind completely. For decades, I mean. All the time I was miles away, in the country odd jobbing and cooking, all those years. It's possible, you know, to block it all out for years on end. I was a mystery man there. For decades. Until I came back here. Which was also a test of my determination. And as things turned out, by accident, really – and mainly with your help, Marva – I came, just about, to think of my mother as a person, not just the bearer of my bad news and the cause of all my difficulties. I mean I'm glad in some ways. It's cleared a few things up for me.'

'Well, you can't fling blame at this distance. You don't want to get obsessive either. That would be no good for you.'

His head went down and he reached for more brandy to go into his glass. 'Uncle Jack's a blank to me. I try to picture him. A big red blob on a holiday promenade. I shook hands with him. If you listen to my mother, my father couldn't hold a candle to the Captain. But he just seemed like some old blind man, pitiable, pathetic. What did my father have to worry about? He just didn't compare and I suppose he didn't have the confidence either. But it wasn't a fair comparison, was it? It never is. It's all an accident, this family business.'

'And you have to live with it.' Marva tried to calm him. 'It's the same for everyone, remember.'

'So, you see, I don't think of myself as the Captain's son. And I resent being so long entangled in my mother and father's problems.'

'We're all in that boat, Graham, and we have to move on.' She wanted to move on herself.

Graham lifted his head in a kind of relief. 'You've been a great support, Marva. You're not hungry are you?'

Marva had heard this line before. His offer of food was always the offer of seduction. 'No, I don't want you to feed me. Not again.'

'Shame. Only I've got some interesting soup downstairs. Vegetable consommé. You make this brown stock with all your vegetables and you get your egg whites and you pass it all through a muslin bag, and like magic it clarifies everything. Clear brown see-through. Beautiful.' He gulped his drink again. 'I mean it clarifies everything. Brilliant.'

She wanted to get out of there, see some daylight. Graham had a curious glow of excitement. Marva wondered if he was deep in the second stages of bereavement, cracking up, or else on drugs. Not her problem now.

'See, I've been trying to write in these notebooks. I thought it would help if I could make sense of all that stuff from ages ago. It goes on – it doesn't stop.'

'Are you sure you're OK? Will you be OK, now?' She was by the door. She didn't want to hear.

'I know what I've got to do. Oh, but what about you, Marva? I'm on about myself all the time.'

'I have to close up the shop and then I'm off. Who knows, I could be in search of my roots.'

'Roots. This is it.' Graham was laughing now. 'Kunta Kinte. Good on you, Marva.'

All the time she'd given to his origins, and now he was laughing at her attempts.

'But, hey, don't you forget about Waterfront. Might be interesting.'

She'd got the door open now and was more than ever convinced of his instability. But, no, not her problem. So she was about to go, duty done, leave him to whatever he was going to do next. Oil pollution on the river, wildlife at risk, write his life story, or his mother's or his father's or some mad Frenchman's, whatever. She would wish him well.

As she stepped out of that room, Graham looked up again from the notebooks and called after her: 'Are cataracts hereditary?'

'They operate on them now, don't they, no trouble,' Marva assured him.

'Because I always need to be able to see things clearly.'

'Do you think that's so important? Do you?'

He was inside his own head again. She needed fresh air.

19

1990

Marva was surprised to receive a parcel in the post from Gray. She recognized his squarish handwriting on the giant padded envelope. When she untaped and unstapled the bag the first thing she pulled out was a jigsaw box Sellotaped shut, and the second was a batch of notebooks elastic-banded together.

She worried that this might be some melodramatic farewell Gray had planned. The way he'd been in that hotel room had concerned her. Surely he wouldn't do anything stupid. She just wanted to get on with her preparations. She'd had to throw out the last of Mrs C's stuff – the last bits of non-perishable stock – silk flowers, vases, buckets – and close up the shop for good. Now she was getting her clothes ready for her trip so she could make a new start. And she didn't want to be worrying about Graham any further. She had herself to think of. But she did peek inside the notebooks eventually. A part of her was annoyed that he wanted her to read them. The parcel felt like a pressure from Gray to read his version of his story. Nonetheless she was intrigued. She saw enough to guess, from the date of 1957, that these were his reconstructions. Then she decided she didn't want to read about them. One day, perhaps, when she was away from him. Then she'd find out what exactly happened to the boy to set him so against his mother. Right now she resented the sly intrusion. She'd take the jigsaw, no question, but in fond memory of Mrs Connolly. She'd save that for a time she had the leisure to piece together one of Mrs C's puzzles. She might even take it to America with her.

But the cunning thing was the tickets Gray had included in the parcel. Waterfront 90, two tickets: Michael McMichael plus support. Now she wasn't especially interested in the star himself, but she knew enough to know it was a ticket worth having and something of a privilege to see the man in person. The great songwriter from the sixties who hadn't forgotten the city he came from. And there was just so much publicity about his visit on the regional TV news, in the newspapers, on the local radio, Marva couldn't help but know.

Michael McMichael, one of the city's music heroes, came specially to the city for Waterfront 90 and there was a reception at the airport when his private jet touched down. Fans of his, mothers now, waved and squealed at the still cute fifty-year-old boy, waving back at them with such winsome modesty. Then a limousine drove him into the city so he could speak on morning television. The interviewers asked where he was born and where he went to school. They laughed loyally at his meagre memories. A young woman reporter shepherded him out of the studio – a fitness item always occupied the next spot – and her camera crew followed him out of the converted dock area down the streets where the lovable lad was bought his first guitar. First he was helped to visit the school he attended when he was young and unknown. He joked with a tongue-tied headmaster even more youthful in the fullness of his ruddy cheeks than the hero himself. And the cameras went with him to the corner of a dual carriageway, a feeder road to a motorway, a grass verge, not a house within sight, and he clowned by the roadside. The crew insisted he stand in front of the legendary football ground and he was to hold a bunch of flowers while his latest composition, a tribute, 'Have to Remember', played. The last violins soared and a helicopter camera pulled away down the hillside to the river and the last lingering shot to music was the waterfront where the ferry boats pushed a few bewildered tourists across the river for their best view of the city buildings. Fade to the breakfast TV presenters previewing the first live performance of the year's hit song – that night only at the Waterfront festival.

Marva knew all she needed to know because every soul in the city had been mailed or handed publicity leaflets about Waterfront 90. McMichael was top of the bill, the two supports, also home-grown, were thinner, paler, stubblier, and their bands had wacky names suggestive of drugs. It was a special day for the city and cameras would click. But Marva didn't know whether she would go at all. Or who to invite, if she did. She'd ask Gloria, though she knew her friend wouldn't care for white-boy soft rock music. Instead Gloria would be sounding off about the Seafaring Museum and the slave trade again. When actually she could make it her goodbye to her friend before going off to the US.

She thought about it and decided she *would* go to Waterfront. Did she owe it to Gray? Not at all. But then again she had dipped into his notebooks and read a little about his fixation with the Frenchman. She was beginning to think more kindly of his gesture – the jigsaw, the notebooks, the tickets – a thoughtful bundle. And she knew Gray would be there at the concert somewhere, doing some stunt for the environmental people. He told her as much when she'd been to his room. Well, he was going to carry something through that meant a lot to him and she was curious what it would entail.

The affair was being staged for a television channel somewhere. A custom-built stage had been constructed for that evening. The day before, the waterfront area had been cordoned off, security guards in navy-blue uniform with officers' peaked caps policed the entrance, daring to frisk the heavy men with black T-shirts, hard hats and lapel badges claiming their roving crew status. Preparations by sound crews and scaffolders and seating erectors occupied the space most of that day. The large projection screen with the sponsor's name like a foreign film subtitle across the bottom. Two separate stages were set up, at angles suitable for two batteries of American Music TV cameras. These would be for fixed shots, there would also be a daredevil video cameraman crawling over the stage, when the performance got started. The local paper made a full-page article out of the preparations: media news. And even if there was a scatter of people instead of a crowd, the camera could easily make the space appear full.

The City Corporation tried to make a big show of it. Tourists were expected in numbers during the day. Hotels could hold special 'events' and promotions. A parade of tall ships, on a cross-Atlantic marathon to Cork and Dublin, had been persuaded to sail into the river estuary and past the waterfront. That was a splendid photo opportunity for all the assembled nostalgics. Old sailing sloops and schooners, similar to the ones that decorated Mrs C's jigsaw covers. From Sydney, Boston, Nassau, Cannes, Lisbon, they would be sailing past the Seafaring Museum. Outside the concert cordon, there'd be other crowds waving: day trippers, ex-seamen, middle-aged locals with an underused car and nothing better to do; grandparents with irritable grandchildren in fashion outfits; those who'd lost relatives at sea and only had the ship paintings on their walls; the kind of people who came to stare at the models and moving parts inside the museum building; the sort who just strolled by the quayside where the pilot boats and tug boats tied up, and added their dream contribution to collective memory.

Marva got there early, waited for Gloria just inside the main entrance as arranged. However much she bobbed around to catch her eye, over shoulders, between heads, Gloria didn't materialize. People of more than twenty years were starting to fill these standing areas; the well-heeled were filling the seats. And no sign of Gloria. She listened for the public address system just in case. She read her programme. She watched seagulls wheeling over the gathering heads. The spaces between people had shrunk. There weren't groups any more, separate from other groups. There were only strangers right next to each other, but quite comfortably waiting for a performance. And more likely than not standing talking, hoping to recognize another face and wave hello; while those alone were thinking seriously about their own day. Marva's transatlantic flight was booked. Two hours before she had been in her flat packing. Apart from the parcel, Graham hadn't been in touch. She looked around the crowd for a sign of him.

The first band sidled on, without introduction, picked up their guitars from the stage floor. Backs to audience they thrashed straight into the start of a shouted number. The heads around Marva went immediately from gormless torpor to vigorous mechanical shaking. The show had started. The band galloped through their short set without a word of chat to their audience. Dropped their guitars when time was up and loped off stage to hospitality. Second support, slower, slightly catchier and people began to dance where they stood. Which was when the campaigners, strategically seated at the edge of the stage, lobbed oil-choked seagulls, dead ones, one at a time, in all directions like grenades into the Waterfront crowd. A girl with a shiny black fringe handed them out to her team out of two rucksacks along with instructions. Each dead bird created a hole in the crowd as people spread to avoid it. And the squeamish audience dressed in their finest casual T-shirts ducked and dodged the missiles. Oil everywhere, splashed on to the stages, on to the floor and across into the seats, while the carefully scruffy band on stage tried to strut their ten minutes regardless of the interruption. It didn't look as though the protest was connected to the bands.

Of course, the short, pretty-faced girl was at the centre of the commotion. Marva recognized her as the one Graham had been chasing at the promenade – when she'd first met him – different clothes, same jumpy presence. It was Michelle still leading Graham a dance, and he didn't seem to mind. Disjointed chants from the gallery: Corporation policy. Disgrace. Wildlife. Poisoned water. Then shouting and jostling, as if drunks were arguing, and it was all over quickly, only to be replaced by rumbling. Arrests were attempted. Security couldn't easily get through the bodies to the perpetrators. There was confusion down there, in front of Marva, but it was a chaos that most in the audience found amusing. It gave them something to talk about and agree about. The cameras would roll and make sure the unacceptable creeping into view could curl away in strips inside the editing suite. Marva wondered where Graham fitted into this and why he hadn't made his appearance.

A rumour started that the Rainbow environmental group had something else unexpected planned. Recent oil spills posed an increased danger to the wildlife. So they had hired a microlite to let all the crowds – the tall ships' watchers and the gathering music crowd – know about the serious situation. And, as Marva knew, Graham was the only one with enough flying time to handle one of those little flimsy planes. So she started looking up to check the sky. She started to listen for something resembling an aeroplane drone. There was time because the stage was being cleared of instruments, checked again and once again for sound, a microphone adjusted better to the height of the big man McMichael. The crowd waited especially irritably – because of the messy distraction – for the main act.

Appearing first from the north, the microlite flew over the

278

edge of the city area, not at 8000 but at 3000 feet. He wanted to feel the air underneath, the chill round his ears, feet on the wheel axle and his flapping green canvas like wings above him. He only wanted to be the Frenchman up there and watch impassively the crowds below. Because seeing everything was still important to him. He steered the machine over a boating marina, then the wide container base with its giant gantry of cranes and collection of tiny-seeming rectangular boxes. Then he could make out the main dockland road and the first tunnel entrance, and the line of empty docks and flattened dockland warehouses. At the river mouth he saw a line of tall ships, white hulled, white sailed, inappropriately clean on the dirty river. The deafening engine noise only increased his exhilaration. He was approaching closer to the waterfront, moving over the Irish ferry terminal and becoming more aware of the possibility of crowds.

Marva was ready for the loud insect buzz in the sky. It pleased her. Something was right about his involvement. Gray finally got up there in his microlite, and he was happy. He was flying. Marva was excited about the flying, never mind the protest. Whereas the crowds weren't there to watch any environmental demonstration of his. He was just some distraction while the technicians took their ages to get sound checks right for Michael McMichael. Boredom in the audience, no particular anticipation, backs of heads, backs of T-shirts. Anything could distract a spectator. They needed entertainment as well as their entertainment. Something daft that someone else was doing. They watched in the hope something terrible would happen.

Then of a sudden McMichael ran on to stage and waved at the audience, Hello Waterfront. He flicked his head back, plugged his guitar in, checked back on his backing band, shouted, 'Are you all right, Waterfront? I can't hear you,' before starting the first chords of a medley of rocking numbers from the old days. This entrance stole completely the audience's first view of a microlite trailing its sails and tail-banner above the stage area.

Marva might have been the only one to keep her eyes fixed on the plane. Michelle's environmental agitators would no doubt have been expectant too. All part of the orchestrated demonstration. But this was Gray's individual moment of magnificence, not to be eclipsed by McMichael. Because he was able to soar above the river, the docks, the ships, the streets, the high sea-facing office buildings, the brand-new hotels, the old public houses, and swing directly above the refurbished tourist area, the grand old dock, the art gallery and the Seafaring Museum. Above it all. Embracing it all within his view was so satisfying. He could see below him the crowds settled for the sail-past and the rock music. They might look up to his protest and connect him to the group's issues. They might ask who he was. And what it was all in aid of.

Only Marva knew he wasn't a crank. She was just glad he got up there. However late in life he took his mystery on and rose above it all. It was something he'd desperately wanted in his own mind to do. From the moment he'd first heard tell of the French airman. All his life from seven the air show had been his mystery, and it had taken him time, difficult time, to piece his way to a mostly completed puzzle. He'd been distracted when she last saw him and now Marva could almost envy him the solution to his mystery. He was lucky after all.

That was why he was up there in the green buzzing microlite. The pollution problem was being completely ignored by the municipal celebrations. His kite-winged machine trailed a green-lettered banner which furled back at an angle behind him, with only the word 'Protect' legible. He was enjoying making an exhibition of himself. It felt right, whatever the crowds were doing down below. The concert crowd laughed because they were sure it was all part of the show, something else for their amusement, another wacky stunt to stop them getting angry about having waited in one place so long. The ships' crowd merely raised their binoculars for a puzzled few seconds.

He flew above the stage area. McMichael, good sport and a man with opinions himself, enjoyed what he thought was a welcome specially for him, and gave a wave and a thumbs up at the banner. Right on, he seemed to be saying. Neat. He pointed up to the sky generously and his crowd looked too.

Now Gray was the bravest of fliers, Blaise Desain, stranger in a close city. He knew what preparations had been made. He had protected his wings for the flight in his poky little hotel room. He had argued with the authorities. He had expected such press coverage. Gray was just happy to be sailing so high. It was a perfect flight, in memory of the Frenchman, and he was able to rise above everything unsatisfactory in his life. He pushed the crossbar to turn the craft southwards over the cathedral towers in the direction of the airport. Other people seemed to wave up at him. He had to smile, and waved down to them, wobbling the craft a little. And as he swooped and buzzed away he was a man fulfilled. He flew off into the distance, point made. Marva watched him disappearing, thought only of Mrs Connolly. That was goodbye.

Towards the end of McMichael's act when the star was having a talk to the audience from the microphone and he made a special point of waving and smiling his hello again to his home town, a man pushed forward and shouted, 'McMichael, what about me?' He aimed a shot from a hand gun. The crack came a split second after, but the bullet must have hit a drum then a spotlight. The star hardly had time to flinch. The man who shouted ran straight back into the crowd. And everyone blamed the environmental lot and their madcap displays. Surely the police were on to them straight away. Michael McMichael, true performer, resumed his act with the climactic song, 'Have to Remember'. All smiles to the end.

But some people recognized the man, said that it was a local guitarist with an unhealthy obsession for McMichael. A grudge, they said. He used to sing at the Corinthian. Myron something. Not from here at all. He just vanished from the city. The police had to ask the public for help, with the co-operation of the press. There were photos of McMichael in the newspapers – shaken, not injured. His words were forgiving, because stars these days had to expect such attention. A grim mugshot of Myron and a sad tale attached. The man who tried to shoot McMichael went to ground. The newspapers dug up a drugs connection. The police issued descriptions and said he was dangerous. McMichael disappeared to his country retreat without further comment. Myron was the name. The police didn't track him down in England. He was only arrested at Kennedy Airport on the same flight as Marva. When she had tried to get clean away.

No, she'd never bothered with drugs since the time she first became a working florist. Why did they ask? Because of her colour? And why should she have any connection with this Myron character who used to sing in the city? All because someone talked to her on a plane. What could someone make out of that? The man called Myron knew Graham Connolly. It was pure accident he connected Marva to that city. She happened to know Gray, that was all. She happened to go to Waterfront 90, not out of choice, but for Graham's sake only. Such patterns which people made of these things. Wrongheaded. But not even simple in the first place.

But the interrogation had been an insult. A waste of her time, which she'd spent reading again Gray's notebooks and been surprised at how much he had pieced together. She'd made futile attempts at one of Mrs C's puzzles, the box with the tall ship on the front, but more likely three of them all mixed up in one box: flowers, stately home, sailing ship. She had given up on her sorting of all these irregular shapes. She wouldn't want to any more.

Because her thinking was always about two people called Connolly. And she needed to get started on someone called Marva, away from this family tangle. She couldn't be expected yet to understand her old life with these people. It all takes such time, a stretch of a lifetime, to disentangle.

And the new one has to get started before that process can begin. But here she was, held in temporary custody in this new country, not yet out of Kennedy Airport, delayed in a windowless room.

'You'll be glad to hear that we have everything in place now,' one of the interrogating officers assured her. 'The man we asked you about has been charged with narcotics offences and will be kept in custody. We understand UK wants him extradited for firearms offences last month, including attempted murder.'

When all she wanted was the chance to ask if someone might know her real mother from way back. The person she dreamed of must be out there somewhere. Of course, if she was still alive she wouldn't know to be waiting for her daughter. But she must have left clues.

'You're free to go now. We certainly hope you enjoy your visit with us, ma'am.' At last she was able to start her walk away from that table. With a big too-long-awake yawn that woke her into life again, she piled her cabin bag on to the airport trolley where the rest of her luggage was wedged. She pushed the whole unwieldy bundle out of the dark room with relief, dumping Graham's notebooks and the jigsaw box into a grey bin halfway along one of the long corridors. Her mystery would be hiding from her, somewhere out here. Somewhere past the puzzle of faces meeting planes.